(STING OF)
# THE DRAGON'S TALE

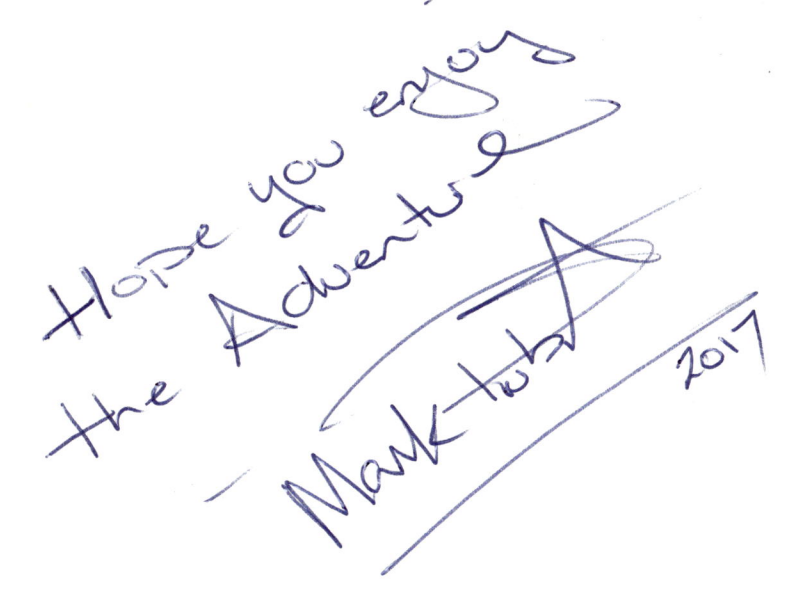

*Hope you enjoy the Adventure*

— Mark tob— 2017

# Mark Probert

(STING OF)
## THE DRAGON'S TALE

Author's Note: During the many seasons I spent in Sri Lanka, avoiding the Welsh winter months, I kept a diary and one day decided to transcribe it into digital format. As I was typing away I thought:
*Hey, perhaps there's a book in here somewhere? ...and there was.*

Text copyright © Mark Probert
2017

The moral right of the author has been asserted

All rights reserved. Without limiting the rights under copyright reserved above, no part of this publication may be reproduced, stored, or transmitted, in any form or by any means (electronic, mechanical, photocopying, recording or otherwise), without the prior written permission of the copyright owner of this book.

Cover design by the author

===============================

To my amazing wife Julia
My two beautiful children: Emily and Carwyn
My brothers: David and Simon
And to my Mum and Dad

•

To my great friends
Steve and Liz Hopkins
on whose front door I never have to knock

•

Paul 'Grandee' Dean
one of the most generous people I knew

•

Rich (The Timekeeper) Murray
who was my unique and most colourful
mountaineering friend

•

===============================

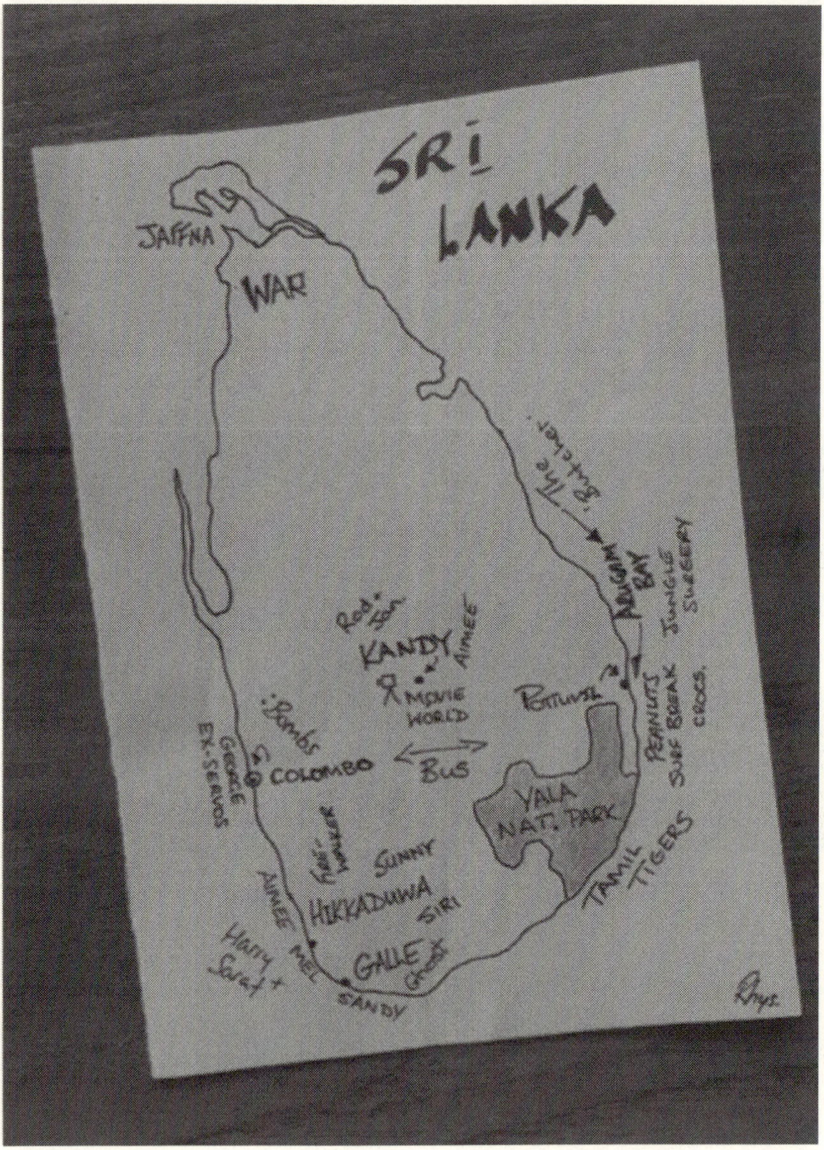
SRI LANKA
JAFFNA
WAR
The Butcher
ARUGAM BAY
JUNGLE SURGERY
KANDY
AIMEE
MOVIE WORLD
POTTUVIL
PEANUTS SURF BREAK
CROCS.
Bombs
COLOMBO
BUS
YALA NAT. PARK
TAMIL TIGERS
SUNNY
AIMEE
HIKKADUWA
SIRI
MEL
GALLE
SANDY
Rhys

FLIGHT

The Air Lanka Tri Star jet smacks down like a thundering bobsleigh on the steamy third world tarmac. Before the seatbelt lights are extinguished hoards of gluttonous passengers abandon their seats. They hunt for their overhead hand luggage transforming the plane into a wild shit fight. What ensues is an apparent fear of confinement, a pandemic urge to escape the stale, residual odour that exists after a long ten hour flight. Me, I just sit and wait quietly, because unlike these fellow travellers, I've really no place to go.

The airport is an open affair. There are no comfortable air-conditioned gantries leading from our plane to the main building. Instead, it looks like a disorganised aviation carpark outside a busy Saturday superstore. Planes cruise by with ear deafening weight, passing only metres away from airport workers. Refuelling trucks swerve dangerously close to spinning turbines, and we, as the most recent arrivals, disembark down aluminium steps to land smack bang amid this tropical mayhem.

At the Immigration Area I am summoned to an old wooden kiosk. Within it stands an official, but he asks me no questions. No *whys* or *whos*, and I feel somewhat deflated by this. Is my life now so questionless? Isn't he meant to probe into my past? Ask me why I'm here? Ask me why I have travelled so far from home? Ask me about my pain? About the hurt? But no, instead he simply stamps Sri Lanka's postcolonial mark onto a vacant page in my British passport, and dismisses me with a curt wave.

I follow other travellers to the Arrivals area where I spot my bag and surfboard. They are lumped with everyone else's luggage and on seeing my sole possessions they extend a comforting tendril to a world I have left eight thousand kilometres behind. I reach, grab, and pull them free, then move off towards the Customs Hall. The high rooved building resembles an oversized town hall, sparse and dusty, and a place where I witness intimate clothing splayed bare on long wooden trestles. On walking past these piles of dishevelled baggage the stare from a customs official triggers in me a wave of emotional spill.

> *Am I walking too slowly - or perhaps too quickly for a man laden with so much guilt? Perhaps it is the remnant blood he can taste? Or perhaps he smells the foul stench of it about me? Perhaps the vulgar reminder of the beating I inflicted that Saturday night is so pungent, so odorous, that my very soul stinks of it? Perhaps he can hear the painful memory of knuckle against flesh, of fist against bone, thumping around inside my head?*

Then perhaps it is none of this? Perhaps it is simply the raw heartache he sees? The seeping of lifeblood he smells? The silent cries he hears? And all because my girlfriend is back in Wales: because she is lost to me. All because I am here, and she is not, and that I am still very much in love with the two-timing bitch.

Outside.

Having passed through the sliding doors, which appear to be the only automated addition to the airport, and having walked free of the airport terminal, I am now standing in front of the Arrivals building. I am alone and unprotected, where the heat of the day rests about me like a cumbersome overcoat, where it slugs me with oppressive waves causing sweat to trickle about my body. My luggage has become slippery in my wet palms, so I set it down for a moment to wipe my hands down the length of my trousers.

I look about and feel as if I am standing on the precipice of an alien world, where droves of dark skinned people carpet every roadside and street corner. I am outnumbered, triggering in me a feeling of uneasiness. I am standing alone among this multitude of unfamiliar faces, all wanting to do their very best for this naive traveller. I am a travelling virgin outside a third world airport with two bags, a Wave Graffiti surfboard and a crotch-full of well-hidden rupees. As I pause at the edge of this strange world, gathering my thoughts, the inhabitants offer up kind words.

'Welcome to Sri Lanka,' they say. 'I hope you are to be enjoying your stay?'

*Their accents so unfamiliar.*

'Can I be helping you with your baggage? Are you to be needing a hotel?' one offers. 'My uncle is to be having a most particular one, and it is being most cheaply for you.'

*All so alien.*

They say these words with friendly nods and open smiling faces, yet I cannot help thinking that all this niceness, hidden efficaciously behind their bright sun-shiny smiles and warmth of character, is just too good to be true. Because whilst everything appears to be so pleasant, so warm and so fuzzy, my foremost thought is that these dark skinned, well-mannered locals are in some way, conniving to rip me off.

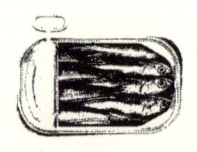

## SARDINE BULLETS

It's all a bit pseudo Casablanca.
No fez.
No Turkish.
Just noisy.
And busy.
And dusty.
And alien.
And everyone wants to help.
And it's chaos en masse.
Cars en masse.
Black 'Morris Thousand' taxis with yellow roofs, en masse.
Buses en masse.
People en masse.
Everything is everywhere.
And everywhere there is everything, from fresh watermelons to clean arak bottles refilled with dirty motor fuel.

I decide to plough through this bevy of a misshapen existence toward the carpark, with one arm around my surfboard and the other hand fending off the Sri Lankan hospitality. I eventually give in, succumbing to the slick tongue of a thirteen year old who has bounced up alongside me, somewhat like Eric Idle as the cured ex-leper in the *Life of Brian*. His name is Diva' D'Silva, but you can call me 'Rocky' he says, as he releases an animated wink.

The boy looks ok and I guess I can trust him as much as any of the other street urchins who look on in eager anticipation should Rocky's prowess falter.

'Welcome to my country,' says this self-assured child. 'What is being the purpose of your visit?'

'Hang on a minute,' I say. 'My feet are boiling over. I've gotta' get these shoes and socks off and put on some flip-flops.'

'Oh, flip-flops!' Rocky laughs. 'You must be English.'

'No bloody way,' I retort. 'I'm Welsh,' and as if to confirm this I point to my small tattooed Welsh flag. 'See. That's the Welsh Dragon.'

'Welsh!' He smiles infectiously. 'Bloody good *Tom Jones*!' and with that he whistles a few bars of, 'It's Not Unusual', causing me to smile at the sheer irony of the moment.

Now this boy's an ace, and appears to know everyone. He struts forward as if commanding Caesar's troops, and oddly enough I feel a strange sense of safety as this urchin meanders through the oceanic throng of vehicles. He nods and waves in a bright and familiar manner to passers-by, as I pursue in his casual teenage wake. When we reach an enclosed island of awaiting vehicles I hand over probably more than sufficient rupees, thank my newfound acquaintance, then clamber aboard a practically empty minibus. After being cooped up in the sky, for what feels like days, a good stretch across the back seat is just what I need. With my back in one corner and my feet across the seat I lounge comfortably, and wait for the bus to start up.

But the bus doesn't start.

It just sits, without a driver.

And as it sits without a driver, time nudges on, allowing my practically empty minibus to systematically swallow homeward bound commuters to the point of bursting frustration. My fellow travellers board with knowing smiles and quiet assumption, and it isn't long before my bags are on my lap, my surfboard is down the aisle, and my fostered seats are taken up by needy Sri Lankan arses. My practically empty minibus is now everyone's minibus, and is jam-packed to the lining.

The bus starts, and once it squeezes itself free of the bus station's traffic it begins its journey like a bat out of hell. I am tinned meatloaf. Stuffed in the back seat of a Toyota Coaster and at the helm is a manic driver who periodically screeches to a grinding halt to take on even more passengers. Amazingly enough these additional passengers are prepared to pay their dues, then hang precariously at the van's open sliding door, adjusting their balance at each teetering bend to prevent us all going arse over breakfast.

Three and a half sweltering hours later the minibus comes to a sudden stop in the small coastal village of Hikkaduwa. I look around the crowded van at the expectant faces and ask if this is my stop?

'Yes. Yes. Go. Go. We will be passing you to your baggage,' insists a passenger, who is already moving in to relieve me of my sweaty seat.

So here I stand, at the side of the road, amongst an unknown Asian culture, with my arse out of the bus but with my board and belongings deep within the confines of the sardine bullet. The engine is being revved and the sense of urgency within the bus is all too apparent. Our agitated driver is practically foaming at the mouth with surging anticipation and I can't help but think,

> *Jesus that driver is practically foaming at the mouth with surging anticipation and is about to take off with all of my stuff!*
> *'Now that he's off!' he's probably saying. 'Let's get going, then we can share out the booty of another dumb-ass tourist that we've just taken for a ride!*

However, less than a minute later, everything is as my fellow passengers had promised. I'm standing at the side of the road with my possessions safely beside me, watching the rear of the bus career off into the shimmering distance, narrowly missing two cyclists and an overladen bullock cart.

*Welcome to Sri Lanka I whisper.*

## HIKKADUWA

The village of Hikkaduwa loosely translates as the 'Sword of Knowledge'. It is scored into two strips by a frantic stretch of tarmac called the Galle Road, which is the island's main four hundred-kilometre highway, running from the capital city Colombo to the southern Portuguese city of Galle. From the side of the road I see the ocean, which must be less than fifty metres away and on looking south I notice an array of small shacks, nestled along the periphery of this busy road. There are no glass windows, instead each is simply open to the road, harbouring groups of women and children busily running out cotton garments, water buffalo luggage and moonstone encrusted jewellery for the rupee-laden tourists. Coconut palms lean out over the road, giving the impression that each racing vehicle is passing through a tunnel of jungle foliage. Between some of these small shacks, there is the occasional brick and windowed guesthouse, I guess belonging to Hikkaduwa's more affluent residents. They have names majestically displayed on ornately hand painted signs at each frontage, signs like the Blue Fox, The Lion's Paradise and The Three Brothers Inn. I decide on the Blue Fox, however fate intervenes as

a slight man,
typically Sri Lankan,
wiry and easy paced, catches my eye.

He is semi-naked and sports a brightly coloured length of cotton wrap, or lungi, which flows from his waist down to his shoeless feet. And he is smiling at me. I smile back. This fine limbed local crosses the road and comes on over. *Sunny*, or Amaray as his Sri Lankan people call him, speaks reasonable English, has a welcoming disposition and, unsurprisingly, a house in which I can stay. I am absolutely knackered from my journey and so I throw caution to the wind and accept the good will of this complete stranger.

'A house. That's great Sunny. Can I have a look?'

I pick up my surfboard, Sunny grabs my bag, then leads me directly away from the beach, down a path, over a railway track and straight into the jungle.

As tired and as desperate as I feel I am becoming a little anxious as we move deeper into the jungle and so I ask the obvious question. Sunny turns, 'My house going,' is the honest reply from this little man, whose wiggle meanders ahead of me on this jungle path.
'Ah…exactly whereabouts *is* your house Sunny?'
This time he stops, turns to me, and is at first a little confused by the question. On realising my confusion Sunny simplifies his answer. He smiles as he opens both of his arms in a wide arc, enveloping all that we see. 'Jungle-side,' he says. 'My house is being Jungle-side'.

Sunny eventually turns into a neatly presented tropical garden that is about a quarter of an acre in size, and bound by a fence of woven sticks and vine twine. It is a garden that houses plants I have only ever seen in botanical gardens, some with leaves the size of hammocks, and flowers that scent like a dutyfree mall. Then amid this wonderland of greenery is a single storey house that beckons us from thirty metres, rectangular in shape with a Tuscan styled clay tiled roof. Its walls are whitewashed and sport a welcoming table-top sized yellow motif of the sun painted above the doorway. To the left of this doorway is a plaque, crafted from coconut wood, spelling out the name of Sunny's jungle establishment, 'The Lucky Sun Inn'.

Sometimes in your life you experience a place that feels good, a place where lines of coincidence converge. A place to take rest, to take stock of all that is *You*. A place to slow down, a place to recollect those memories worth nurturing, and this place, The Lucky Sun Inn, feels like such a place. Somewhere to begin a new life and start again, a place where Feng Shui can give the demons of my past a really good kick in the bollocks!

We enter the large family room to find four bedrooms leading directly off it. All the windows to the house are iron-barred, painted white, with shutters on the outside. This, however, is no reflection on local crime as I find out later that the front door is often left unlocked. The home is as simplistic as it is functional, and as I look around I notice that, in cost cutting style, there are no ceilings to the bedrooms, only walls that stretch partially toward the exposed clay tiled roof. All occupants perhaps then share memories of intimate nights during breakfast, with saucy romps reminisced by all and sundry over a hot cup of coffee and a spicy green chilli omelette.

In the main room there is a worn three-person leather couch and four low wicker chairs. In one corner is a fridge on which stands a well-used electric fruit blender and above this, affixed to the wall, glows a permanent bluish light, illuminating a framed picture of Lord Buddha. Alongside the archaic fridge is a table strewn with homely paraphernalia. A coke bottle dons a partially burnt candle, (a welcome necessity during the irregular power cuts) and alongside this lie a few unpolished glasses and an array of china plates with mismatched cutlery. Also there are three orange drinking coconuts and a handful of bananas on the red plastic tablecloth on which are printed small segments of brightly coloured fruit. Above the table, and somewhat misplaced, is a poster of *The Clash*, the punk rock group of the late seventies and eighties. The poster depicts one of the band members, Simonon, smashing his Fender Precision Bass on the stage floor from the album 'London Calling', with the title font interestingly lifted straight off *Elvis Presley's* 1956 debut album. It is a comforting discovery as during my university years I was manager of a local punk band called *The Urge* and have the memories of *The Clash* tracks entwined about my youth.

This jungle house is home to Sunny, his wife and two children. Home that is, until the tourist season edges its way intrusively into their quiet existence between the months of November and March. This monetary necessity results in the family migrating out to the back of the house to a smaller room, allowing them to rent out their personal living quarters to strangers with folding money. It is mid-July and off-season. So here I am then, their solitary stranger with a wad of rupees, staying in their house, in the jungle, and one that is smack bang alongside an oozing swamp. Sunny hadn't mentioned the swamp, not as a deliberate omission to snare a fair rent as the locals don't care too much for the swamp, they simply live by it. He does however mention the harmless metre long monitor lizards that occasionally slip up in search of a free egg or other such titbit. I need no introduction though, to the ever-present mosquitoes that are somewhat kept in check by the mozzie coils that burn throughout the night and by the larvae eating swamp turtles that cruise majestically through the brackish swamp waters just outside the front door.

Before the door to each of the four bedrooms is a length of material, which hangs from sill to floor, and on which are printed red and orange hot air balloons, which, oddly enough, have been hung upside down. Sunny gestures that the first bedroom is to be mine and after entering I unzip my bag and unpack. The room is basic, comprising of one high backed chair, a double bed on which is slumped a lumpy coconut mattress and a small chest of drawers, into which I stuff my clothes. In doing so I catch a whiff of stale body odour, mine. I stink from here to high heaven. In fact I stink from what now feels like days back and so I grab my toiletries and head off in search of a shower to soap away the last few days of chaos.

In order to get to the shower one has to walk the length of the house, then out through the back door and into a small back garden area where the family's back bedroom is located. Attached to this back bedroom is a small brick kitchen and next to this, the shower, which presents itself as a rectangular concrete cubicle, devoid of a door, but complete with a tropical ecosystem all of its own.
I step in, slide the plastic half-curtain across the opening and turn on the brass valve affixed to the far wall. My shower is comfortingly wet, tropically tepid and welcomely refreshing. Shower time came to be known as 'slime time' as the algae, which manifests in the open rainwater tank above, regularly slipped through the plumbing to deposit its green veins about your body. I soap up and rinse off, washing away my exhaustion, replacing it with excitement and anticipation. Then, once freshly dressed, I leave the Lucky Sun guesthouse and head off along the jungle path, back over the railway line and into the tropical village of Hikkaduwa.

## CHALK AND CHEESE

I walk along the main road, heading south, taking extra care to avoid the racing traffic and reflect on times past when I would take long walks to shake off residual anxiety; before exams, or important rugby games, or when I discovered that my girlfriend Melanie couldn't keep her fucking legs shut.

Do I laugh incredulously?
Or do I hit him?
Or perhaps shed tears for lost love?

It was hitting him that broke the camel's back. It was hitting him that finalised the end of our relationship. It was hitting him that began this journey. It was watching Melanie run to him that had me turning away…flying away, and now I'm here, away from it all, away from all of that shit.

This emotional handbrake, this unsettling thought, has jerked me to a stop. It has pulled me up tight, pulled hard on something deep inside causing a sudden sharp intake of breath. Thoughts of how isolated I have become from those I love bites hard. My heart begins to race and my breath quicken. I look around, seeking any distraction that may help dissipate the onslaught of this repugnant moment.
Anything:
The sight of a boy wrestling coconuts in a tree ten metres high, the barefoot children playing marbles on rough ground, the three colourfully dressed women laden with baskets of fish, the sign saying, 'Dewa Siri Beachside Café'…

*Dewa Siri Beachside Café.*
*A café?*
*Something to eat and drink.*
*Yes.*
*Perhaps that'll help?*

Below the sign is a narrow sandy pathway leading off the road toward the ocean. It is lined with woven fences, forming small grazing areas in which pigs grunt and chickens cluck. Along the path I pass a single roomed guest villa, with a G-string drying out front, before coming to the beachside restaurant. The place is without doors and what glass there is, all salt washed and streaky, divides the kitchen from the remainder of the restaurant. On entering the place I am literally on the doorstep of the island, having one foot in the restaurant, while the other is practically paddling in the Indian Ocean. It is perfect. A liquid gem of turquoise and jade green, of squeaky sand and inviting ripples. The floor is concrete, which peters out to the whitest beach sand I have ever seen. In the restaurant there are about eight tables, crafted from rough coconut, and haphazardly brushed with sea-blue paint. Yet, despite the vibrant black and white check plastic tablecloths the place appears barren, as it is devoid of customers.

Sparse, empty and fatigued.
Descriptors for my love life.
Off season.

There is a slight rustling of clothing, which detaches me from my thoughts, and when I look over it is into the largest and whitest set of graveyard teeth I have ever seen.

This is Harry.
Singhalese Harry.
Part-restaurant owner Harry.
Harry with the tombstone grin.

Harry hands me the food menu. 'My name is being Harry,' says Harry. 'This is being your first trip to Sri Lanka?'
'Yes it is Harry and it's good to meet you. My name's Rhys.' And Harry and I shake hands like new friends.
 The menu reads as if from a king's cookbook and is a welcomed delight as I am as hungry as the sea. After thoughtful consideration I plan to have the lot, from the pineapple fritters to the chilli squid, then from the grilled swordfish all the way down to the bananas and ice cream. However, common sense prevails and instead I only order, (with a degree of restraint I might add), the devilled prawns, a red onion, cucumber and tomato side salad, plus a banana smoothie

to wash it all down. And why not? After all, I am in the Tropics! Good old Harry nods approvingly, smiles broadly, then shuffles off to the kitchen, leaving me to reflect, once again, on past events: On the blood-running. The screaming girl. At my heartfelt loss. And while I'm contemplating whether or not I should have let up with the assault, Harry returns with my smoothie, and his brother Sarat.

Harry and Sarat .
Chalk and Cheese.

Harry is short, with a body that appears to have been stuffed with mashed potato, whereas Sarat is slim, sophisticated, and obviously the brains of the outfit. While Harry runs his large plump hands down the pleats of his sarong, Sarat is the one who stands easy in his faded designer blue jeans. I take an instant liking to the two brothers, and the feeling appears mutual. I eat alone, but am soon joined by the two who are toting half a bottle of complimentary arak, otherwise known as rice-rocket-fuel. It is five thirty according to my watch, but to the locals it is simply sunset.

As I sit at my table the sun's rays and soft sea breeze bathe me in colourful and aromatic delights, and to accompany this moment there is the arak. The distilled coconut arak is honey coloured, however the more potent rice arak, which I'm drinking, presents itself as a clear, heart-burning pick-me-up. The boys aren't partaking in their token gesture, as they have work to finish, and so with smiles all around they leave me to enjoy a quiet drink alone. And I do, I sip at my rocket fuel, while listening to the Indian Ocean lapping gently only a few short steps away.

# WINDOW

The next couple of hours wind their way gently around the evening as the arak softens the burr of being outside my comfort zone.

Softens being here.
Softens sitting here alone.
It softens the loss.

The moonlight ripples across the Indian Ocean in corduroy lines and for the moment I am content, and a little pissed I might add. Here I am then, sitting in the tropics, immersed in a world other people only dream about. And it sounds good, doesn't it? Then why am I thinking that I'm just kidding myself? That perhaps this isn't 'The Dream' after all? That perhaps I'm merely a Dreamer: A Runner trying to escape his demons. That perhaps I am a fool who is trying to bury his heart within this tropical wilderness. It is a weighty barrage of thoughts, and there is no consolation when I remember a friend's words spoken less than a week ago, *'Running away only increases the distance between you and your problems Rhys. It doesn't make them go away.'* And it hurts, does the truth.
I look to the travelling moon, its fullness slipping through the night's woolly sky.
And I feel so lonely.
But worse than that,
I feel so alone.
And I want to share so much.
I want to share my life.
I don't want to be sitting here on my own, half-pissed and feeling depressed.
  Suddenly my moment of self-destruction is shattered. It is said that as one door closes on you your God leaves a window open. And in this moment, it is true. A bolt of energising adrenaline fires directly into my bloodstream saving me from my moment of despair.

A demi-goddess has just walked into the restaurant, and just like me, she is alone.

If the price of looking longingly at her is blindness, then shape me a cane. This woman, she floats catlike, with her auburn hair trailing her aura in an incandescent fashion. She is dressed in sleek vibrant pink cotton pants, barefooted, with an easy white V-neck lacy top flowing loosely about her body. It is a top that inspires one to get up, walk over and fondle her perfectly formed breasts, but that may be construed as ill-mannered, so instead I choose to watch beauty in motion saunter across the sand strewn floor of this illuminated restaurant. Harry appears, breaking the fairy tale spell. 'Hello Aimee. You are to be eating tonight?'

'Bonjour Harry. Non merci, only une bouteille de soda.'

*Rolling Rrr's.*
*French.*
*Shit!*
*Un, deux, trois, (pedwar)!*
*High school French.*
*Shit!*

Her blue-blue eyes, when they look at you, sing at the turn of a lash.

*Shit I should write that down.*

But it's too late for that because she is standing before me. Here.
'Allo, my name is Aimee. May I please join you?'
You dream of this moment.
A beautiful girl.
Comes up to you.
She speaks English in an accent you want to lick.
You act cool.
She's impressed, and wants to kiss you always.
But then there's Reality.
The pregnant pause - the possible Fuck-Up!
She has taken me by surprise.
'Uh? Sure. Ok, if you like?'
'You are sure it is ok? I can go to another table if you wish to be alone.'

*Quick. Shape up!*

'No, no, please, take a seat.'
And so this delightful woman pulls out a chair and she sits.
And she looks…
Gorgeous.
We shake hands.
'I'm Rhys. I'm very pleased to meet you. This is my first trip to Sri Lanka. Is it yours?'

*Idiot!*

She laughs ever so politely. It is a clumsy encounter, fraught with danger, as my awkwardness may well outlive Aimee's friendliness. I recover quickly and continue, 'I have to say your outfit is most complimentary and that jewellery is stunning. Is it Sri Lankan?'
Aimee's face is kind and is blessed with nature's generous gift of natural beauty. Her cheekbones are geometrically high, giving her face that perfect creative lift, borne to those of European blood.
'No, actually it is from India,' she says. 'A place called Goa. You 'ave heard of this place perhaps?'
I hadn't, and so the conversation flows as Aimee explains the delights of the West Indian seaport, with its unique mixture of Indian and Portuguese heritage, embellished with a raving hippie culture. I intermittently pepper the conversation with Welsh humour and sense that Aimee is feeling comfortable and relaxed in my company, so I ask,
'Would you care for some arak Aimee?'
'It is nice of you to ask Rhys, but no thank you.'
The archery of her full-bodied lips part into an inviting smile.
'But I will 'ave une beer.'
Her blue-blue eyes are sincere, they are alight.
Lighting up the world about her.
And presently that is me.

For a while now Sarat and Harry have been hanging off stage like a couple of understudy bats. However, on cue, they cruise into action delivering a tall brown bottle of Three Coins beer and two glasses to our table. Sarat pours the beers with panache while Harry catches my eye and grins. Both restaurateurs are enjoying the moment. They disappear momentarily into the kitchen before returning with a complimentary plateful of nuts, some freshly cut fruit, and some warm bread. Aimee and I enjoy several more beers, the last one of which my newfound friend giggles into as she tries to make a smiley face in the froth with her tongue.

'Where is it that you are staying Rhys?'

'Jungle-side,' I whisper to her. 'Where things go humpidy-bump in the middle of the night.' And she giggles some more. 'I am staying 'ere, at the Dewa Siri,' she says. 'Do you like *Chris Rea*? I have him in my room.'

> *Oh heaven can wait. Just a little bit further past the dashboard light if you please.*

'Yeah. Chris Rea. I'd love to meet him. But won't your room be a little crowded with the three of us?' With that Aimee friskily smacks me on my arm. 'You are too funny, Rhys from Wales.'

Then Aimee, from France, gets up from the table, releases a smile that would halt Wellington, and with a slight tilt of her head, (a playful nuance I might add), I too, am soon to my feet. With Aimee's hand in mine we thank the boys for their kindness and hospitality, and head off to Aimee's room to listen to Mr Rea sing to us about love on the beach.

We make love. It is the type of sex that appears for short bursts in tasteful adult movies, not the kind shown in a musty backstreet Castle cinema. Instead it is a fine length of footage, where you feel the director has been too discreet, too bloody arty, and you'd feel, if you were a voyeur, that you'd been cheated of the cherry pie. But not me, I'm all front and centre. And we enjoy ourselves as if we are lost lovers. Squeezing, teasing, and whispering niceties between the bars of Rea's love songs. All fruit cage and honeybee. All fun and frolics, with the tropical rain smacking itself rhythmically on the tile roof above, as we ride, like wild brumbies, into the small hours of the morning. Eventually we collapse into a slurry of sweat, as a final deluge adds its crescendo to our own steamy finale. We lay within the warmth of mutual satisfaction and gaze into each other's eyes.

We are on par.

As rich as melding souls.

Skin to skin.

Akin.

As pseudo-lovers are.

I stroke my Mel.
And oh how I love to caress her.
Her long soft hair.
Her swan-like neck.

'Mel, are you awake yet?'
She stirs a little, but says nothing. So I caress a little more, to ease her into our waking moment. She moves gently now, releasing the smallest of sounds. But when she speaks I find her difficult to understand. Still half asleep, I guess? Lost within a dream, perhaps? But when she stirs once more things change completely. I tumble, not out of bed, but into another world. For this person who lies next to me is not my Mel, this is somebody else; a comparative stranger. And we are in bed together. And for a moment I cannot fathom where I am.
Then she fully awakens, this girl.
Not *my* Mel, but Aimee.
The French girl from last night.
The girl who drank beer, and laughed with such ease, amid the froth and the bubbles. The girl who told me how her manipulative ex-boyfriend practically ran her life. This girl, she rolls over, looks at me and says,
'This Melanie. You are still in love with her. Yes?'
Aimee laughs with the kindness you find beneath a tender kiss.
'A woman can always tell you know,' she says.
I am fully awake now, fully conscious.
Aimee's words hurt and I can smell the distinct burnt odour of a lover's betrayal, hanging in the air above us. Aimee's words singe my flesh as I struggle with my infidelity. Yet deep down I know that what we have done is no wrongdoing. To have made love to this girl last night deserves no reprimand. So why then do I feel so guilty? And to make matters worse there exists this sense of betrayal toward Aimee too, because the truth of my transparent love for Mel has been so effortlessly exposed. It just doesn't seem fair on either of them. In fact it just doesn't seem fair on anyone.

I look into Aimee's eyes, those soft sapphire dewdrops, and see them smiling. I see no malice hidden there. No judgement. No hurt. Only a depth of understanding, which serves to enrich the remnant warmth felt between us.

'Yes. Perhaps I still do? I don't know Aimee? Everything is such a mess. She has done such a terrible thing.' Then I catch myself before I expose my feelings any further, and apologise.

'I'm sorry Aimee, to talk to you about such things. It's just that my life has been very difficult lately.'

Aimee lifts herself onto one elbow, allowing her nakedness to spill out from beneath the sheets. 'You do not need to apologise to me Rhys. You told me last night. About Melanie. You do not remember?' She laughs, not unkindly, not because I am in need of a kind word, but because she is kind. Then she leans in and kisses me. 'I really like you Rhys. You are a good person. If it were another time, who knows, perhaps we could be more than friends?'

Aimee's words are both uplifting and tragic, as they have momentarily culminated up thoughts of a parallel life, of sliding doors, of a life of 'what if's' and 'maybe's'. And I hear myself whispering from deep within, from where it is secret and quiet. Rhys and Aimee: Aimee and Rhys. Yeah, that does have a nice ring to it. And although we do not deny there exists chemistry between us, we both understand that the road on which we just ventured is a road to nowhere.

Breakfast is delicious, and to spend it in the company of such a beautiful woman further compliments the perfect off-season day. It is blessed with unusually clear blue skies, quiet seas and harmonious winds. Aimee rests her hand on my forearm. 'We 'ave a beautiful day together today Rhys. What shall we do with it?'

I say, 'I've a great idea! Have you ever been scuba diving?'

There's an instant reaction. My words cause Aimee to flinch, all visible and sharp. Her eyes glaze over and to me it appears as if time has stopped for her. She has become trance-like. Her head dips amid the silence and I wait, fearful that any intrusion may adversely affect this strange spell. The moment probably lasts for no more that a handful of heartbeats but to me it feels like forever, and when Aimee finally answers it is in a dreamlike fashion.

'Oh yes, I love to scuba,' she says. 'My father took me diving in the Red Sea only last year. C'est magnifique, to dive with your father you know? To have such special times together. As father and daughter. It is a beautiful thing.'

Aimee's words are no more than a whisper. 'But then the good can go so very wrong,' she says. 'So very bad…in a heartbeat.'

At the last word Aimee clicks her fingers and in doing so breaks the spell. When she lifts her head I see a line of tears rolling down her face. She smiles defensively, gently brushing them away with the heel of both hands.

I hand her a napkin.

'Look at me, I am being so stupid. I am so sorry Rhys, I thought I was ok. I thought I could talk about it, you know? Be ok with it, without crying like this.'

But it is obvious that she is not ok, and she tells me why. She tells me her story through salty tears and with the burden of a heavy heart. Of why she is so hurt. Of why she is so guilt-ridden, and I resonate with the depth of her pain.

'It was the last time I ever saw my father alive,' she says. 'We were diving together, choosing shells for his collection. It is only the two of us, and we are diving buddies. A duo. And we are supposed to be looking out for one another. We had always looked out for each other after my mother's illness.'

The words tear at her and she begins to sob as she endures the pain. I move to her, taking her into my shoulder and I nurture her. I take another napkin from the table and give it to her and she wipes away a mixture of snot and falling tears.

'I was supposed to be looking out for him,' she says, into the short distance between us. 'But we drifted apart, both searching for that one special shell. And my father, he could always stay down longer than me. He would joke about it, saying he had the lungs of a baritone, whereas I was just a sweet lullaby.'

Aimee chokes at her last words, causing her to cry such heartfelt sobs it is as if someone is shaking the very life from her. I draw her in a little closer, and rub her back gently,

'It's ok Aimee. It's ok. You don't have to say anymore.'

But she does. Because she says talking about it helps, and so she says, 'Then when I surfaced I could see that he was already there. I could see my father being pulled into the boat. And the men on board were shouting. And I didn't know it. I didn't know that my father was dying. When I finally got to the boat I tried so hard to save him. I used all my medical skills to try and bring him round. I worked on him for thirty minutes. Mouth to mouth: Pumping on his chest. Pushing down on him so hard I could feel his ribs crack beneath my hands. Still, I couldn't save him. And the irony of it all is that he'd worked twelve hours a day to put me through medical school and I still couldn't save him. Then I felt one of the crew's hands on my shoulders: Firm and halting. And so I stopped pumping because I knew I had lost. When I looked at my father laying there I knew I could do nothing more. It was hopeless, because my father was dead.' Aimee takes a sip of water, and smiles gently as I pass her another napkin. 'At my father's inquest they told me it was his heart that gave out. They said there was nothing I could have done. But this is no help. I have lost my closest friend. Mon père. Toujours et pour toujours. So this is why I have taken some medical work here in Sri Lanka. To help escape the loss.'

And it does escape. The hurt, the blame, the guilt. It loosens from her like caked mud as she begins to shake like a lost child and all I can do is be here for her. So I am. Here for her. I want to kiss her, to soak up all of her hurt. I want to wipe it all away with a soft napkin, but I know I can't. Her hurt is too deep, and I am someone who only floats helplessly at the surface of her misfortune. I speak lightly to her, as gently as I know how.

'We don't have to go diving Aimee. We can do something else. We can take a bus ride to Unawatuna. There is a beautiful swimming beach there. We can eat, and drink coconuts, and laze in the sun.'

But Aimee is resilient and refuses to buckle.

'No, it is ok Rhys. I'm sorry to have cried like this. I really would enjoy to dive with you. You make me feel warm and safe.'

Then she kisses me with her salty lips.

'Thank you.'

I smile back at this remarkable woman, and say,

'You see that small peninsula over there?' I point to an outcrop of rocks a few kilometres away. 'I've been told that's a great spot for a dive. We could go there?'

Aimee nods. 'Perfect,' she says, and we kiss again, cementing the oncoming day.

Aimee and I ride through the village of Hikkaduwa, then on for a further twenty minutes where we come face to face with the large weather worn boulders, humping their way out to sea. They sit in the water, loch-like, with their wide backs smoothed by season-old storms. At the foot of these boulders, nestled on a small curve of beach, is a small shack. It has a sign above it, purporting it to be 'The most best diving in Sri Lanka'. The shack is painted in multicolour hue, having pale blue walls supporting a yellow painted tin roof. The door, which is pink, feels as if we are about to walk into a life-sized doll's house.

Aimee and I park our bicycles against a nearby post and enter the shack, hand in hand.

'Ouah Rhys! It is such a treasure trove, yes?'

She is right, because once inside it feels as if we have entered an ancient mariner's cave. Encased in four long cabinets are row upon row of beautifully polished shells that have instantly delighted Aimee. She picks one out and rolls it around in her hand, then caresses it against her heart ever so delicately as if dropping it could break the day. As I watch her replace it I wonder if her father had one like it in his collection or perhaps that was the very shell they were seeking before he died? Above us, strung from corner to corner is an old fishing net, filling the entire breadth of the ceiling. It is a great expanse of hand-woven twine, displaying all manner of petrified sea life, and on the wooden planked walls around us are dotted other wonders from the sea. On one of these walls are dinner-plate sized starfish, whose white sun-bleached crusted arms stretch out like flattened crowns. Affixed to another are dried tropical fish, each re-painted in gaudy colours, which contrast heavily against the wall's rough sawn timber. But the pièce de résistance is displayed on the third wall. Hanging there like a rich man's trophy, in this third world beachside shack, is a colossal marlin. Its elongated, seven hundred kilo body ends in a spear-like snout, resembling an old mariner's marlinspike. The long rigid dorsal fin extends forward to form a magnificent crest, however, in its deathly state, this glorious animal appears nothing more to me than a wasted life. It is beautiful. Stunning. But in its beauty I see tragedy. In its cold black eye I see Death's stamp of finality. Its majesty is lost within the air we breathe and I sense this in Aimee when she releases a small sigh and looks to me with a question.

'How could someone do that to such a beautiful animal Rhys? How is it that Man can be so wasteful and cruel?'

She says it as soft as a whispered rumour and when I look at her I see such beauty in her. She looks beautiful. But this is not the beauty that rests upon the beholder, this is beauty that flows about a person as a rare gift. An aura. And I agree with her, for who could not. But what's done is done, and neither I, nor Aimee possess a magic spell to make right saddening events of the past.

The shack displays all manner of diving apparel on its shelves, but on close inspection I see that a great deal of it is both worn and dated. The masks, snorkels, and fins are ok, but the dive tanks appear battered and the BCD's and regulators look as if they have been fished from the remnants of a World War II quartermaster store. In light of this Aimee and I decide to hire two sets of snorkelling gear instead.

The walk out to the end of the boulders is a fun experience. We slip and slide while we climb, hand in hand, over these huge lumps of granite, laughing at the sheer delight of it all, and when we arrive at the end of this outcrop we are rewarded with complete isolation. Aimee changes quickly and is first into the water, where she dips her head below the surface to take a peek.

'It is so beautiful Rhys. La clarté, c'est fantastique.'

I slide off the boulder and drop in beside her to be welcomed with a stolen kiss. As we glide across the surface the fish life darts before us in a splay of colour, flashing iridescent light off their armoured sides as they twist and flit before us. The fragile coral below enchants us with its rough coral reds and spongy yellows, and with its soft baby blues and pink tipped fingers. We swim above and amongst this oceanic rainforest for what feels like a million moments, all wrapped into one. Diving and surfacing. Twisting and tumbling. Picking up shells, and exploring caves. And sometimes we bump into each other, just for the fun of it. We take special care of each other, Aimee and I, as we swim together amongst this paradise, and we stay close as we swim, so that we are no further away than an easy touch.

After our swim Aimee and I dry one another. Then we lie on our backs in the sand, naked, where we share a feeling of heightened self-awareness and of daring voyeurism.

'You are my white knight,' she says, as she lies naked beside me with her eyes closed and her face towards the sun.

I turn ever so slightly and take a peek at her.

'You know,' she continues, 'before I came here and after losing both my mother and father I did not think I could find happiness like this again. I feel as if you have saved a part of me Rhys. You have made me smile and laugh, and you have given me the gift to look to life again.'

In the lightness of such a moment, when I answer her, I answer with heartfelt and honest words.

'It is easy for me Aimee. Because of the person you are. And because you make me feel happy too.' I say this with my eyes set upon this beautiful woman, and as my words fall softly upon her I watch as she moves her hands and feet to make a sand angel. And I think to myself, how easy it must be for anyone to fall in love with this girl.

We make love, between the boulders and the lapping shoreline. And it *is* love, this making. It is love filled with joy, with happiness, with cloudless skies, and with the pleasures felt when soft warm sand moves beneath you.

'If only this moment could last forever,' she whispers.

The morning light sheets under the door to find a room filled with an aura of warm satisfaction. I twist over to Aimee's side of the bed to check on her, but she isn't there. Last night we dined late and swam even later. So I'm thinking that she must be in the shower, rinsing the salt and residual sweat from her body. But the shower isn't running. Perhaps she didn't want to wake me and has gone for a swim, after all it is such a beautiful morning. But as I slide my legs over the edge of the bed and take a panoramic sweep of the room I see that it is devoid of all things feminine. There is nothing of Aimee's left. All of her possessions have gone. I race to the bathroom only to find my toothbrush, my glass, and my water bottle. Nothing of Aimee's is here. It is as if she never existed. An empty dream and so I walk back into the room and collapse onto the bed.

There is a knock on the door.
It is Harry.
And with him, Harry's grin.
'Harry, Aimee has gone! Where's she gone?'
It is more of a pleading than a question, and there it is again, that tombstone smile.
'All packed up and having been gone to Colombo on the early train coming.'

Harry waits patiently, as if he has spoken a foreign language and that I require some time to decipher his words. Then, when he has deemed enough time has passed, he continues,
'Would you like to be eating some breakfast Rhys as I have to be cleaning Miss Aimee's room.'
I grunt a reply and fall back onto the pillow feeling lost.

*It's coming Rhys. Be prepared.*

Then an emotional tidal wave hits. It rolls in from the past and batters at my self-esteem, kicking at the core of my self-worth. But what I didn't expect is this shortness of breath, or this level of anxiety, or this emotional purge of tears, endeavouring to cleanse away a soiled past.

*Christ it hurts.*

Something on the table catches my eye.
It's a note.
And the note is from Aimee.
And it reads like this:

---

*Dear Rhys*
*My Gentle Lover*

*Thank you for the past few days.*
*It was so much fun to be with you. I have known great joy being with you because you make me laugh too much. And because of my feelings for you I must go before I am hurt.*
*I must go now to my work and try very hard to forget you. This will not be easy for me. Please do not think bad of me for not saying goodbye. I did not wish to wake you because it would be so much harder for me to go.*
*I wish you a beautiful life and a happy heart Rhys. Perhaps we may meet again in another life?*

*My Love for you*

*Aimee*

*XoXoX*

At breakfast I sit alone, drawn to the same table Aimee and I shared only last night. At the table with no straight-planed edge to be seen, the table that is all bent and twisted and as I run my hands along its misshapen existence I smile at the irony of our similarity. How wrong it feels that the rest of the world is going about its daily business while I sit here immersed in such desolate thoughts. Doesn't anyone care what is going on here? Doesn't the rest of the world know how much I'm hurting: Of how much I've been torn apart? Doesn't anyone around here care about the loss I've endured? They don't, and I know this, but somehow it helps to whisper it into the emptiness around me.

And as if to prove that life stands still for no-one, I see a man heading up the beach toward the front of the restaurant. He has the physique of an Olympian. The beach is this man's gymnasium and the soft sand his machines. He is a strapping local, non-indigenous judging by his skin, all wet coal and black tattoo ink. Straddled across his wide muscular shoulders lies a yolk made from petrified driftwood, from which dangle an array of edible drupes.

This silken 'coconut man' carries both green coconuts, housing the soft white edible fleshy meat, and orange drinking coconuts laden with translucent milk set to quench a tropical thirst. I watch in fascination as he lowers his produce to the sand, untwines an orange coconut from amongst the others, and in one of his huge hands holds it aloft, as if a prize-winning baby. Then from around his waist he removes a small bihar, a Sri Lankan machete, and strikes into the nut. It takes him a series of short masterful blows before the lid of the coconut spins off, leaving a thin airtight membrane. He then carefully pierces it with the tip of his knife, into which he pops a plastic straw, and in doing so, this slave to the rhythm, this Coconut Man, has produced one seriously oversized tropical drinking vessel which he then hands to an off-season tourist.

After my solitary breakfast of egg hoppers (a delicious Sri Lankan open pancake), fruit juice and wood fired toast laden with garlic, I decide to head back to Sunny's house to grab my beach shorts. I need exercise to quell the hurt and to release some endorphins into my body. It is hot, humid, and sticky, and as the misshapen waves are reasonably large I figure a bodysurf in the grunt of a shore break somewhere will do me the power of good.

I stroll back down the Dewa Siri path, up the main road, then over the railway line and into Sunny's majestic garden of botanical hugeness. Sunny is at the front door, with a concerned look on his face.

'You are not to be coming back for the last nights Mr Rhys.'

Sunny's formality catches me unawares, and I detect a note of embarrassment.

'Please Sunny, just call me Rhys. No, I have been spending some time with a girl.'

I smile.

'Oh, you were to be having much sexiness these nights,' and he giggles as he wiggles. 'It is never minding then that I was to be having dinner for you with my family.'

I was both touched, and slightly put out to think that there was an expected dish of obligation at the house in which I am simply a paying guest.

'Hey, I'm sorry Sunny. I didn't know the girl was going to happen,' I say, trying to make amends. 'Tonight would be great though. Is it possible for me to join your family for dinner tonight?'

'Oh yes, tonight is being very possible.'

So it is then.

Made possible.

I thank Sunny for his courteous invite, then grab my beach stuff and head off to the coast for what is to become a life-threatening beach bash.

## FEAR

I decide to check out the southern part of Hikkaduwa called Narigama. In season it is a place frequented by topless Europeans, parading the smallest of G-strings, and that's not just the women. Today, however, I'm hoping it's a place where the swell is pushing up onto the beach.

Walking along the roadside I am sun-soaked by the delights of this small tropical village. Alongside Galle Road is an array of shanty shacks, no bigger than a small kitchen. Each of these small wooden sweatboxes churns out anything from cotton shirts, to black and white striped drawstring bags. You can even buy rough wooden carvings or an array of tanned water buffalo holdalls, if you so choose. Despite there being few travellers around, several of the shacks are open in the hope of squeezing a few rupees from the money belt of a wandering off-season tourist. Stopping at one I am pleasantly surprised to see Sunny's wife, Shanika, spinning out colourful garments as she works away on her antique Singer sewing machine.

I choose and pay for a pair of long black cotton pants, fashioned at the hems and pocket entries with a colourful band of material, and explain that I shall pick them up on my way back from my swim. Shanika is both delightful and visibly delighted with her new sale. I also mention that I will be eating with the family tonight, to which she is again visibly pleased, rewarding me with a fresh white smile.

After a kilometre or so south I reach the beach at Narigama, to find it wild and practically empty. About fifty metres out to sea there is a decent two metre wave, voicing its annoyance as it crashes onto a shallow sandbank. It looks ideal for a body workout so I drop my towel onto the bleached sand and head on in.

The water is superb, as warm as a bath, and I delight in its soothing quality as the small inshore waves break round me. However, on swimming a little further I begin to feel a sense of uneasiness. I am the only one in the water, striving, stroke after stroke, towards the impact zone, and it has become a little eerie. Then, as I swim further out to sea, I realise that this particular section of ocean deserves a weighty measure of respect for it has concealed a sweet, melodic voice that now whispers to me between strokes.

*Take care, it says.*

Swimming on into deeper water I sense a strong undertow below. And adding to this unforeseen danger there is also a tugging sensation present at the ocean's surface. It's pulling against each of my strokes, carrying me perpendicular to the beach. I realise that I have foolishly swum into a rip that is now carrying me to the ocean-side of the reef. It is a dangerous situation, but one I am familiar with, so remind myself that if I remain calm I'll be fine. I reassure myself that I have played this oceanic game many times before and that everything will be ok.

*But you've not played amid such a powerful undertow, whispers a voice.*
*Not in a rip like this.*
*Never here.*
*Nothing about this place is familiar.*

After all I saw no yellow flags on the beach, no lifeguard tower that now watches over me. I have only personal experience to get me out of this mess. As I wrestle against the pull I have this overwhelming urge to be back at the beach, back to where I can stand up. This sudden burst of apprehension has caused me to feel unsafe and I feel my heart rate quicken. I can hear the pounding of blood as it rushes about my head, thumping with a thunderous pulse, and I know that this sudden eruption of doubt is linked to my recent turn of events. I know that the acts of betrayal and deceit have hacked into my self-esteem, and have caused a huge shift in my self-confidence. And I know that this barrage of memories is compounding the danger I now find myself in.

*I know all this, so for Christ's sake do something about it.*

I literally smack my open hand against my head.

Smack!
Smack!
Smack!

*C'mon!*
*Think!*
*You can get yourself out of this.*
*Think!*

*Ok, I must stroke at an angle to the rip, allowing myself to be carried further out to sea.*

*Yes, because trying to swim against this rip is futile.*
*Trying to make a B-line to those breaking waves is foolish.*
*I will become exhausted.*
*I need be able to break out of the rip's grasp.*
*I need to edge my way to its perimeter.*

I know that I need to find its weakest point and ease out of it from there, only then can I swim directly back towards the impact zone and catch a wave back to the beach.

It's a hell of a swim as the chop on the ocean's surface constantly slaps me in the face, forcing me to periodically gag mouthfuls of salty water. At times I even feel myself being dragged backwards, losing such precious ground, it is soul destroying and adds to my uncertainty, and for twenty minutes or more I struggle against this hidden menace.

Eventually I break free of the worst of it and by my reckoning I still have another hard ten minute swim before I reach the line-up. My body aches all over as the lactic acid burns into my muscles, tightening around my resolve. For the next ten minutes I pull more with my arms than kick with my legs. Thankfully my years of surfing have given me good upper body strength and I'm drawing on all of that now. After what seems more like forever, than ten minutes, I arrive to where the swell manifests itself into a wave and from where I must exact my escape. It is here where I must exhibit control, and at precisely the right moment, stroke into the face of an oncoming wave.

And before I attempt this please allow me to explain to those of you unfamiliar with the wilds of the sea. An ocean wave is caused by the action of the winds on the ocean surfaces. When this body of water, or swell, approaches a reef or sand bar, the lower part of the wave slows due to the friction caused between itself and the seabed. But the upper part of the wave is still gaining momentum causing the top section of the wave to fold over the water below in a crashing motion. It is a thundering torrential slab of water and is the most powerful part of the wave. If you're careless it is this thick slab, the Lip, that will take hold of you and drag you to its heights, before smashing you towards the sandy bottom below. Therefore it is the lip of a wave that you must avoid at all costs.

The water around me begins to move seaward. The whole body of water I am floating in is being drawn out to sea, and I am moving within it. This means a set of waves is coming.

Then there it is.
I see it.
The first wave of the oncoming set, looming towards me.

Experience depicts that I allow this first wave to pass by as it can be the most difficult to catch. If I did try, then missed it, I would be left too far inside the break and so out of position for the better shaped and more powerful second wave. I tread water patiently, breathe deeply, and wait for this first wave to collapse under its own weight and pound down on top of me. I time my duck-dive well, stroke hard within a world of fluid green, and allow the tonnage of water to surge past my body. The second wave approaching is far bigger and more menacing. However its power will take me closer to the beach, providing I don't fuck up! It looms, rolls closer, gathers in height, increases in mass and so then does the danger. I turn and wait until it is almost upon me, then stroke for several lengths, waiting to be lifted up into the face of this watery giant. Timing is everything. Too late and I miss it. Too early and I will be driven to the sandy bottom. As I stroke, and pull, and kick hard, I feel myself being drawn up into the face of the wave. I angle my body across it, anticipating the forthcoming free-fall. The wave sucks me upwards but I daren't be drawn too high or else I will become engulfed within the lip, become powerless and will be driven into the seabed. My arms are angled in front of me and now, with one final kick, I propel myself downwards and sidewards, slicing into the face of the wave. My inside hand is flattened, spade-like, and my elbow, inside knee and foot cut into the wave, setting up my bodyline, allowing me to surf across the face of the wave and away from the merciless lip. The ride is exhilarating as my body cuts along the face of the wave, riding hard against this solid mass of water. Then behind me I hear a section of the wave come crashing down with a deafening roar. It is now that I have to 'pull out' and exit else I will be dumped within the wave as it folds over in its final implosion. I wait for the moment when I need to half somersault, when I need to feed my hands forward into a diving position. Then, at the right time, I must forward roll below the surface and allow the wave to pass over me, thereby freeing me from its grip. If all goes well I should be spat out the back of its wall to safety.

*And now it's coming!*
*This critical moment.*

I ready myself.
I tumble and somersault beneath it. My timing is perfect and the wave passes by me, so I kick to the surface and flick out the back of it. I have made it, but on looking landward I see that I am still a fair way from the shore so I take a moment to locate the rip. I kick hard, lifting my body as far out of the water as I can, and spy two differing oceanic surfaces rushing against each other. One calm, the other life threatening. Thankfully I spy that the rip is far enough away. I am safe from it. I've made it. Not only that, but now I have regained a sense of calm. My muscles feel good and the exhilaration from that last wave has me turning, duck-diving under successive waves, and swimming back to the line-up for some more action. Exhaustion has given way to an adrenaline spike and so I figure with the imminent danger passed I may as well enjoy the thrill of a few more rides. After the fourth wave I feel a twinge of cramp in my right calf, highlighting my body's limitations, so I decide to call it a day and head on in head to the nearest restaurant.

# X

MAP

The café is called The Casalanka and boasts a wood fire stove out the back, laminated menu cards, cane chairs and a poster of a young Mick Jagger on the wall.

Mel loves Jagger and even though I find discomfort in looking at those puckering lips I cannot help but think of how much she would love the euphoric atmosphere this world has on offer. How much she would love the way in which the locals skim along their path of friendliness, and saunter within their relaxed way of life. How much she would love their easy pace and the way in which they meander through the day, living hand to mouth, while resting on the laurels of their religious beliefs for common comfort. But Mel isn't here and as I wait for my lunch to arrive the music track, 'Miss You', fills the open-faced restaurant with its Ooh-baby lyrics, Wyman bass and unwelcomed mockery.

My prawn salad and waiter arrives, cutting into my thoughts and breaking off my simmering stupor. The waiter, your stereotypical barefooted, sarong clad, friendly brown face, is standing by, awaiting my approval.

'Mmm,' I say, and compliment this with a curt nod exacting the correct degree of confirmation to please my expectant onlooker.

'You surf, yes?' says his brown face.

I have difficulty deciding whether this is a question or statement. I also have difficulty in replying as I have just taken in a face full of seafood.

I chew, swallow, and finally dredge up a reply.

'Yep, I sure do.'

'You go *arugambay*?' says his brown face.

Now I'm not sure if Brown Face is having me on? Perhaps *arugambay*, when translated, is Singhalese for 'you kiss me mister'? Could the scrawny little mite be making a pass at me? Is he perhaps the mastermind behind the running of some illicit sex market, where unsuspecting foreigners are eased into a life of 'sleazery'? Am I

victim to a drug-laced crustacean salad and to become Frank Zappa's *Mary*? Brown Face is looking at me in an odd and questioning manner. He tilts his head from one side to the other, reminding me of my Nana Bess' budgie when it appraised its food. I feel his beady little eyes undressing me as he repeats in perfect cockatoo fashion,
'You go surf aru-gam-bay mister?'
'Aru-gam-bay? What is 'arugambay?' I ask.
Brown Face wiggles his head to aid in the clarification of the following disjointed statement.
'Oh long way going,' he says. 'Many hours sitting in the red buses. It is being down east side of Sri Lanka. Aru-gam-bay. My friend Mick. He is being in Aru-gam-bay. Mick from Sydney. 'Stralia Mick. Very good surfer. Very good friend is my friend 'Stralia Mick. You will be knowing him, Yes?'

Brown Face's enthusiasm should warrant a more elated reply and from the look on his face he expects it, he waits for it, beadily tilting his bony cranium from side to side. But I have no such reply to offer him and so his enthusiasm falters when he hears,
'Uh? No. Sorry. I haven't been to Australia yet so I have never met your friend 'Stralia Mick.'

Brown Face's face noticeably drops in light of my limited international social network, and so with a friendly and acceptant nod he takes off to fetch the rest of my lunch, leaving me to reflect on his curious words.
What is this arugumbay? And if it exists, where is it? Is there really a secret surf spot hidden somewhere in the jungle? And who is 'Stralia Mick? Or is it all simply free talk, of tall tales between a bored waiter and a sole patron?

After finishing the remainder of my lunch I pay, and on receiving the change from my enigmatic waiter, he smiles, wiggles his head and repeats,
'You go surf Aru-gam-bay mister. Good waves. You say G'day to 'Stralia Mick. Mick from Sydney. From me, Mashalla. My name is being Mashalla. Ok?'

And so I make my promise to Mashalla that I shall indeed give 'Stralia Mick, Mick from Sydney, his good wishes should I ever meet him. Then I turn and exit the restaurant, leaving him to glide off into the depths of the kitchen, noticeably displaying a lightness of pace.

Heading back towards Sunny's the word *arugambay* niggles like the forgotten name of an old friend. Mashalla has indeed sewn an adventurous seed. In fact it has become a foremost thought, a possessive need to discover the mystery surrounding this elusive location. At each pace I feel my excitement heighten at the thought of an anticipated adventure. It is decided then. That I shall accept this conjured mission, this quest to discover this mysterious place, to seek out this *arugambay* and boldly head out into the tropical boondocks.

When I reach the house I throw my newly tailored trousers onto one of the wicker chairs then cross over to the southern wall of the lounge. On the peeling wall, set between an old wardrobe and a similarly worn map of The World, sits a dilapidated map of the Island. The map is an old classic, a schoolboy's dream of stained tea and burnt edges, of illustrations of rock-torn wrecks and mythical fish. The map looks as if it may well have come straight out of Barti Dhu's treasure chest if the 17$^{th}$ century Welsh pirate had ever ventured into these parts. In faded tones it clings to the wall and on studying it I see that the rail system only runs halfway across the map, terminating in Badulla, one of Sri Lanka's oldest black marketeer towns. This means that a trans-island train journey is therefore out of the question. However, the map does depict a clear and detailed road system, spreading its winding and pothole-ridden tentacles all over the island. I run my finger past the hill country town of Badulla, where the terrain flattens out to become the gateway to the East coast. From there I trace my finger along a road that runs the length of this plain and down to the beaches of the East coast. I tap my finger on the map, because there it is! Located slightly below the town of Pududuiyiruppu, printed in small black lettering, I find the small town of Pottuvil, and immediately south of this appear the words *Arugam Bay*. On closer inspection though I soon realise that the break is set precariously close to the northern part of the Yala National Park. In fact it's only forty kilometres away from the semi-arid nine hundred and seventy nine square kilometre park, which is an exciting, yet daunting discovery. Exciting, because to seek out a little known surf break is a childhood dream borne from 70's surf movies like Endless Summer, and daunting, because I'm frighteningly aware that harboured within the depths of this park is the Indian terrorist faction called the Tamil Tigers: And you can bet your last rupee that they're not hanging around there to sightsee the largest leopards in the world.

Having recently read Sri Lanka's national newspaper, 'The Island', I know that it is a time of war between Sri Lanka and India and that these militant Indian freedom fighters are using this unguarded area as a place to conduct their covert military operations. Their demands for the establishment of a Free Indian State in the northern province of Sri Lanka, called Jaffna, are being met with an offensive from the Singhalese government. The overriding problem arising from these demands troubles the local Tamil Indian families whose ancestors have been living on the island for generations. They consider themselves Sri Lankan Tamils and so do not advocate this war for independence. And to further complicate matters, intercultural marriages between the Singhalese and the Tamils have been celebrated for centuries. But this local cultural acceptance does little to stop the bullets flying about their heads, or the bombs exploding about their feet, or the lives of frightened children being destroyed by senseless bloodshed.

In studying the roads of this teardrop shaped country more closely I see that the thick red line depicting the A4 ColomboRatnapura-Wellawaya-Batticalo Highway spans the island from the capital, Colombo, across to the small town of Pottuvil. Even though the road journey will take longer, I figure that it will be less taxing to catch a single bus across the breadth of the island, rather than mess about catching the train halfway then picking up the bus for the rest of the journey. And so I begin visually plotting my route with eager anticipation, taking great interest in all of the small towns and villages I will soon pass through. Names like Avissawella, Rambukpota and Obbegoda, all of which fascinate me like ancient mystic spells.

Now though I am spending the evening with Sunny's family, trying to appear enthusiastic every time my plate is laden with taste bud shattering runner beans and cabbage. I thought I could handle a reasonably hot curry, being a veteran of the after-pub-curry-brigade, but this is an explosive, tastebud-numbing minefield. Chilli warfare with seeds. The meat is grey and unfamiliar, and it sits unmoving in an overcast sauce. Yet I find it surprisingly appetising once I have taken the plunge and have hoed on in. Here then is the proof that there is a culinary art in preparing the egg stealing swamp monitor lizard to please a hungry guest. Dining with the family is a remarkable moment and an honoured insight into these gentle people's beliefs and their simplistic way of life. Sunny and Shanika have three children who are a trio of joy, a boy aged eight, a girl aged three and the bouncing baby. The boy, Pasindu, is neatly dressed each morning in a school uniform of grey cotton shorts, white socks, black shoes and a starched white shirt. It is only the middle and upper classes that have the fortune of sending their children into the educational system and Pasindu wears the cost and proficiency of the family's laundry capabilities like a badge of honour. Sure, the educational system is available to all those who live deeper in the jungle, but unfortunately every able-bodied family member, with their calloused hands and tired eyes, are needed to work below the jungle canopy in order to bring in a square meal. The children then, these miscarriages of jungle justice, miss out, and as there is no truant officer circulating the jungle tracks to enforce the impracticality of lifting these future generations above the breadfruit line, the trend is unstoppable.

Their little girl, Noni, spends most of her time at her mother's feet in their small roadside shop. At other times I see her around the house, barely dressed, helping to prepare food, washing clothes, or sweeping the house out with a broom made from flattened twigs. Every now and then I buy her sweets, so her pet name for me becomes 'Bonbon', which I love, and which fosters an even deeper bond with my Sri Lankan family.

Shanika, Sunny's wife, is twenty six and is a roundly blessed woman, having more girth than her height should carry. Her eyes are large and brown, lending beauty to her soft oval face of smooth skin and coloured warmth. Her teeth are a blaze of white, cleaned daily using a small twig and powdered charcoal and her limbs are strong and purposeful. Shanika has not spoken a word to me whilst we sit here on the cool concrete floor amid modern plates, wooden bowls and placemats of coconut leaves. It is months before we eventually strike up an easy conversation and laugh freely within each other's company. Both she and Sunny are happy with her outward appearance, as it is one that depicts proof of healthy living and of plump prosperity.

A happy family.
Of quiet joy and of loving spirit.

And I envy their simple ways.

After dinner, Shanika clears the plates and bowls, discards the coconut placemats, then tends to the children. Meanwhile Sunny and I embark on a game of carom, a 'strike and pocket' game similar to billiards and table shuffleboard and vastly popular in both Sri Lanka and India. Sunny, my skilful opponent, is thrashing me. He is a man of fundamental values and a wicked finger flick. He is thirty four and has previously worked two jobs, night and day, to save enough money to build The Lucky Sun Inn. Sunny is a man of quiet conviction and of rewarding results. And you can learn a great deal when sitting down with a man in the jungle, reflecting on those who live in the Developed World. On those who would be mistaken, indeed ignorant, into thinking that Sunny is a naive jungle native. A man appearing to sadly lack all of those materialistic wants that the modern world presents as its prize. We reflect together, on these modern world cynics who traverse busy concrete corridors, discarding sorrow-strewn dailies at the day's end but doing nothing to aid those they read about. These people, who seek, with some desperation, to rid themselves of their bewildering lifestyle, one that has somehow manifested itself into a perpetual and dysfunctional merry-go-round. (Perhaps it happened while they were out shopping for things they didn't need?) Whereas Sunny lives his life in a holistic way and therefore truly understands how *life* is to be enjoyed. And as he explains this in his ordinary way, I realise that it is Sunny and Shanika who have attained true happiness here in their jungle, while others out there remain stuck in peak hour traffic.

As my learned friend and I flick these small disc like pieces into the wee hours of the night we talk about the different facets of life, just as I might with a friend down at the pub. We talk about sport, religion, beer, friendship, past lovers like Aimee, and my smouldering feelings for Melanie.

## THE DHARMA SYNDROME

I ooze myself off my coconut mattress after a particularly sticky night, don my sarong, grab the necessary toiletries and make my way to the slime room for a 'freshen up' - if you can call it that?

I'm excited. A sucker for spontaneity, and today is the day I head north to the island's capital, Colombo. My plan is to turn inland toward the East coast and head for the elusive Arugam Bay. I imagine myself as Sir Henry Morton Stanley in search of my own David Livingstone, heading off into an unfamiliar world with prime times ahead and presumably not a cannibal in sight.

The 'Express' train leaves at 0718hrs and the shortest way to Hikkaduwa train station from Sunny's is to walk right through the jungle on the train tracks. So on this morning I find myself walking, railway sleeper by railway sleeper, placing one foot in front of the other to quickly discover that the distance between these sleepers is a Sri Lankan step and not one designed for a six foot white fella. At first it is a clod-hopping, mistimed, foot-faulting lurch of a journey, however on adopting a more suitable gait mimicked from the Monty Python Ministry of Funny Walks, I soon begin making good ground. Forty minutes later I am peeling around a bend to be greeted by the kaleidoscopic view of Hikkaduwa train station.

The platform itself is built in the weightiest of colonial style having granite boulder after boulder crushed and compacted into place, then cemented over to form its level surface. Colonial cast iron pillars, shaped in turn style fashion, support gables of heavily pitted steel which in turn support the red tinned roof arcing above us in historic parasol fashion.

We sit on wooden planked benches, myself and these ladies next to me, clad in their coloured splendour with their overspilling woven baskets of market ripe bananas, enormous prickly jackfruit and the skunk smelling 'purportedly aphrodisiac' durian fruit.

We smile politely at one another, periodically turning our gaze down the two illusionary converging train tracks that lead back into the jungle. Then between these smiles and unspoken words it isn't long before we are blessed with an onomatopoeic rumble. The distant shrill of the train's horn blasts through the overgrowth forewarning wayward pedestrians to race to the safety of the sideline before the train growls on by.

Before the locomotive comes around the bend and into view we are audible witnesses to the guttural sound of a thrusting, well-oiled machine, of hot metal fired with coal. We are also visual witnesses to the soiled grey and white plume of power, as its volcanic rise punches up beyond the jungle greenery, challenging all those who would be foolish enough to stand in her way.

The platform is readied into instant upheaval. Small children, pigs, hens, cockerels, market produce and surfboard are gathered in and clutched closely to breast as we all wait for the inevitable break-neck assault into the closest carriage doorway.

There is something magically wonderful in seeing the grandeur of a working steam train peeling through the jungle. It lights up memories from a Famous Five Enid Blyton novel as it makes its way up the tracks towards us. She is an Iron Maiden, with her securely bolted muffin top and dull matted bellybutton protruding out front. It is almost sexy in the way in which the train puffs and whistles, bellowing mutton grey clouds of phallic message into the pure blue sky. With her oven, being stoked to fury level, and his funnel being blown off with rhythmic exultation, it is a magnificent hermaphrodite of steel and sweat.

An awesome sight: If Casey Jones were here now I swear he'd be a-steaming and a-rolling.

We all stand at the ready. Ready to board this monstrosity of seduction. There are grown men teetering alongside women and children, all hankering for a prime position. No prisoners are to be taken here. It's every man, woman, child, basket of fruit and pair of chicken legs for themselves. No 'please' and 'thank you' in this arena. It's simply 'game on', no rules…and it's all about to happen!

What I witness is practically a social war zone. As this androgynous bursting beast of steel and coal begins to slow in its journey the crowd form a human maul, worthy of an international rugby team heaving a mad drive toward the try line.

It is of some concern that these experienced train hopping children, these mini-mites, these waist high warriors are at nether region level and could easily fell a Welshman with a cleverly shielded and well-aimed elbow to the goolies! So with one hand guarding the pillar and stones I engage in this war of pushing and shoving, squeezing past metre high weasels and innocent old ladies, past baskets of mangoes and buckets of mangosteens. Past old men, young men, hands of bananas, two bicycles and a hand pushed cart. And all is not in vain for eventually I reach my goal line, a glassless window through which I toss my bag and through which I ram my surfboard. Then with a skip and a leap, finding purchase with one foot on the side of the carriage, I manage to fling myself through the opening to land nicely inside the carriage and onto one of the unoccupied wooden benches.

*Nice one Boyo!*

My excitement is difficult to contain, as it is time to head north to the Big Smoke and on to Adventure. Colombo here I come! My wait in beginning this exhilarating journey is short lived as the platform guard suddenly fires two frantic blasts from his meticulously polished brass whistle. The wheels begin to spin on the forged steel rails below and momentarily we thud forward with a loud metallic clank and a ceremonious jerk.

We're off!
The sense of excitement is electrifying!

I hold in my hands a red cardboard ticket that is as cheap as a pot of noodles and good for the hundred arse numbing kilometres to the Colombo Fort train station.

I am in 2nd Class.
Interestingly enough, there is no 1st Class.
There is, however, 3rd Class. This is the first carriage, which is shunted to the coal truck directly behind the coal-coughing engine.

For those with little money, or for those of you who wish to be percolated in smoke and carbon ash from the boiler's funnel, then this is the place for you. There is no difference in amenities between $2^{nd}$ and $3^{rd}$ class only the fact that the $3^{rd}$ class passengers disembark with complexions resembling that of panda eyed coal miners.

From the onset I realise this journey is no business class junket, as the train's suspension unit must still be lying around in broken pieces at the Sri Lanka Railways workshop. It's real hard arse stuff. As the train rattles past villages displaying jovial locals playing impressive backstreet cricket down narrow alleyways, I squirm to find a bit of cheek that I haven't yet used, abused, bruised and flattened.

Staring out of the window I become *mesmerised* as if having been transported into a scene from Jungle Book. I am Mowgli, transfixed by the rhythm of the journey, swinging from one jungle scene to another. Suddenly I am hit for six. Emotionally bowled out by a torrent of heartfelt goose bumps that explode about my body. It is a piercing of my soul and it sparks a smoulder of inner shame as I make eye contact with a small naked boy squatting precariously from a disused metal 44 gallon drum laying on its side. His business is to add to the quagmire of human filth festering below him and he appears to me to be quite emotionless in his execution. His sullen eyes find my white face in the passing window and I feel laden with guilt. I feel defiled by my own health and disgusted at the idleness of whichever God is supposed to be looking after these people. Is it that God has forgotten this poor child's life even though it is more fragile than the substance of a soul? Who knows, and within seconds he's gone. A few more lines read, a small sigh beneath one's breath, as he slides by to be replaced with luscious green paddocks and tranquil acres of coconut plantations. Replaced with yet another of God's rich masterpieces splayed onto a fresh canvas and within this miraculous Eden the least fortunate individual I have seen so far has, in all likelihood, slipped off his cylindrical seat to live through a day I will never know, nor ever understand.

Gone.

The thin slivers of life, printed between the covers of someone else's destiny. All so easily forgotten within the pages of an unfinished book.

Gone.

A man comes to squeeze onto my already crowded two plank seat. He sits.
'Ah English. Yes?'

*Bloody English!*

'No. From Wales,' I counterpunch.
'Ah New South Wales, Australia. Very good place.'
'No. Not New South Wales. Wales, Wales.'
I really need to make an educational point here, a patriotic stand, an unfurling of the Red Dragon's flag.
'Wales - near England,' I confirm.
'Oh England. Very good. Liverpool Football Club. Kenny Dalglish. PFA Player of the Year 1982 - 83,' he rebuffs.
Possibly, in his infinite wisdom of football this newcomer may in fact know that 'King Kenny' is in point of fact Scottish, but I see no gain in complicating matters. Furthermore I soon discover that during my adventures in this country it is far easier to adopt an English shroud, thereby avoiding the ensuing confusion when attempting to explain the status of a loyal Welshman. A Welshman who is constantly lined up in the face of geographical ignorance then shot in the patriotic cockles. It is a bitter pill to swallow and I figure that the white lie is only skin deep if your heart stills sings out 'Cmyru am Byth!' (Wales for Ever!).

He introduces himself as Dharma, which he tells me means 'path of life' in Sanskrit and is a lively addition to my journey. Dharma is sporting a dark blue corduroy jacket across wide shoulders, thicker black trousers than you would think customary in this heat and a blazing white ruffled shirt. This, coupled with his dark complexion, hooked nose, and strong facial features, gives him the appearance of Captain Hook. I lower my gaze to the floor curiously checking for crocodile shoes but disappointingly find only leather sandals. This deceptive appearance masks a gently spoken man who spouts on about soccer and cricket with infectious enthusiasm and for the next twenty minutes I nod and smile at the appropriate time, enjoying his singsong accent and his astute sporting knowledge.

The train, without warning, stutters to an irregular stop, straddling a tarmac road that leads up a rise and off into the shimmering distance. As we wait patiently for the next twenty minutes in the glistening heat our carriage begins to ferment, along with the fruit within it.

The whole place begins to stink.

From the moment the train stopped Dharma has become noticeably agitated and begins looking nervously up and down our carriage. Then the door to our carriage is flung wide open and we watch as two soldiers step up onto the plate before moving in. It is a menacing sight watching these two battle fatigued soldiers stride down the isle armed with their AK47 rifles.

They turn on Dharma.

Is this a surreal movie scene being played out for the benefit of a bewildered tourist? Where the invisible Director barks,

Action!
Now!
Turn!
Yes!
That's it!
That's him!
The gun!
Yes!
Poke the gun barrel into his cheek!
Do it violently!
Yes! Like that!
Good.
Good.
Yes. Make him squirm!
Now force him roughly from his seat.
Roughly!
Yes.
That's good.
Yes. Like that!
Now yank him across the seat.
Yes.
Yes.
Excellent!

Dharma is hauled from our communal seat on the end of a menacing barrel. He is prodded into submission by the length of cold steel and forced to lie over the back of one of the seats in front of me.

*Holy shit!*

They search Dharma turning out each of his pockets to reveal mere trivialities; a bus ticket, a white handkerchief, an identity card, a small notebook and pencil, and a handful of rupee notes, which are surreptitiously pocketed by one of the soldiers. Then Dharma is yanked back to his feet and firmly marched down the length of the corridor to the exit door. I follow his expedient departure wide eyed, but with my arse firmly glued to my coconut seat. I am scared and scarcely breathing. I am in a state of physical shock. I'm terrified even further when I see the soldiers conversing with one another at the doorway to the carriage whilst pointing back at me. I am trying my utmost to remain calm but the worst of scenarios are racing through my brain.

I feel their cold eyes prying me from my seat and so I turn and look out the window. I figure that if I concentrate on anything outside, anything but the confines of this carriage then I'll be ok. In doing so I see Dharma down at track level. He looks so small and insignificant as he cowers away from the soldiers' well-aimed kicks and heavy handed slaps. As I watch the events at hand, as the plot unfolds, I feel as if I am watching a theatre play from an unsafe circle seat.

When I dare to look back up the carriage I notice that the soldiers have gone and so breathe a deep sigh of relief. Out of the window Dharma turns his bloodied head slightly, stealing a glance up towards me, locking onto my wide-eyed gaze. I smile. A stupid act as it is meaningless and bears no comfort, nor credence. My hands are visibly shaking and it is with a sense of shame that I realise my narcissistic self-centredness. My shame at my cold weakness of character and the warm gratitude I feel when someone else's misfortune does not include me.

Dharma is lost now amid the khaki uniforms. I'm desperate to witness one more glimpse. A small glimmer of hope for my newfound friend. But it is not to be. The train begins screeching its annoyance at being delayed by this unscheduled stop and so lurches back into motion. The train, its drivers, the carriages of onlookers, and myself all exit stage left leaving Dharma and his 'path of life' in the hands of his unrelenting captors.

The sense of loss, sweetened with the sickening euphoria I feel at being left untouched, is almost making me puke. As if the jerk of the train moving forward is a cue for the rekindling of mid-sentence conversation, the carriage of onlookers, once again, erupt into a cacophony of spasmodic dialogue. I look across at two passengers sitting opposite and interrupt their conversation to ask,
'Why did they take him, this man?'
'They are being Tamil Tigers,' says one. 'They are to be just taking Government peoples like that.'
His friend nods and smiles in acknowledgement before their conversation re-ignites back into its day-to-day banter.

And that's it.
That's all the explanation there is.
Dharma has disappeared, just like that little boy.

I never found out what happened to Dharma, if that indeed was his name. But the whole event has put me on the back foot and has left me somewhat edgy. Moments ago I was happy. I was smiling and laughing at Dharma's jocular sporting deliveries.
I felt safe.
Simply rolling along the tracks of life, without a care in the world, when up it comes out of nowhere. The cold solemn facial slap of reality.

SLAP!

And perhaps it is these very same Tamil Tigers, these same heavily armed Freedom Fighters, who will smash down the wooden door to my flimsy hut on one forthcoming night at Arugam Bay? And it will be face to face. And toe to toe. With piss-stained trousers and loaded up to the hilt with their battle hardened intrusion, lethal weapons and itchy trigger fingers.

## THE ISCHIOPAGUS TWINS

As I disembark the train at Colombo Fort train station I am offered all types of food from deep fried potatoes to the ever popular roti – a small rectangular surprise package wrapped in a wrinkly skin of rubber dough then shallow fried on a hot smoking skillet. I buy one, as anything that hot has to have killed all known forms of bacteria lurking beneath its yellow epidermis. As it turns out I find it to be a mixture of potato and other vegetables, those of which I cannot yet identify, and it is delicious! So much so that I eat another one before surging out onto the streets, rubbing the excess oil into my hands as an effective skin moisturiser. And now I decide it is time for a mid-morning cigarette, just the 'one' before giving up!

Giving up smoking is easy in Sri Lanka because the cigarettes can be bought in *singles* from the most intriguing roadside carts, thereby making it both economical and convenient. These cigarette carts are built using simplistic ingenuity, a folding wooden flat-top-surface, two bicycle wheels and a handful of rusty nuts and bolts. Then with a knock here and a twist there, *hey presto!*, a cart is created which can be easily manoeuvred to the vendor's designated post. From dawn until late into the night this vendor will exchange his wares for well-thumbed rupees notes or smooth paise coins, ultimately handing most of it over to the local extortionist who runs the overall street vending racket.

I buy a brand of cigarette called Bristol, a 'single', and light it from a smouldering piece of hemp rope conveniently hanging from one end of the cart. Down goes my first long drag of the morning and it feels good as it caresses my alveoli with its bittersweet toxic scent. I look to my side and notice that two locals have sidled up beside me. They smile within my personal space with semi toothless grins and gums all bright red and demonic looking. And believe me when I say that I'm concerned, it is an understatement, as I have no desire to be impregnated by this unknown rubicund disease, and so retreat a step. 'A'llo,' says one head.

'A'llo,' says the other.

'Hello,' I reply, fascinated by these new arrivals, whose charisma is powerfully intoxicating and it takes no great length of deduction to quickly work out that they are in fact identical twins. But this is only one half of the truth as they are indeed so much more than this, for these blood-red, mirror faced duo, are not only identical in mannerism and expensive white starched collars but have been joined at the hip since birth.

Unlike any other customers and I guess with a pre-requisite agreement from the vendor, the twins take it upon themselves to manufacture their own concoction from the cart. The vendor happily step asides to accommodate them and it crosses my mind that perhaps these two are really the heads honchos of the entire street operation and are quietly making their rounds, looking in on their lucrative empire?

I am intrigued by the flurry of action that now takes place. Before me the twins move with such synchronicity that I am witness to theatre art in motion. On the cart are many different forms of the areca nut, or *puwak*, displayed in various small containers, ranging from the soft immature nut to the more hardened mature drupe. In other containers there is cardamom, sugar, shredded coconut, cloves, fennel, lime and tobacco, all of which add to the palatable array of colour.

One twin selects a suitably sized betel leaf from a pile sitting atop of the cart. He then lays it out flat as the other twin begins to select all manner of strange items from the rows of shelved jars and recesses located about the cart's headboard and base. These fascinating ingredients are carefully spread across one end of the leaf, allowing the first twin to take his cue and spring back in action, rolling up and folding the leaf into a neat package. This twin then arches his back, leaning as far back as creation will allow and with expert airborne precision fires the package directly into his brother's mouth. The gargoyles grin with grand satisfaction and the small crowd around the cart voice their pleasure, applauding the incredulous double act before them. A quick flurry and another concoction is in the making, only this time there is a role reversal where a different combination of seeds and powders are chosen. Then in mirror form, the second twin propels the small leaf package into the first twin's mouth with similar theatrics. Again there is the applause from the crowd and I am clapping and laughing with the rest of them. Then with a duo of slaps to my back and a knowing nod to their patron the twins leave one of their daily ports of call and move away, with four arms, two legs, two heads and a couple of intoxicating parcels. My fascination is obviously apparent as a third package is made by the vendor and handed over to me with good intent. Laughing nervously I stub out my cigarette and slide the secretive package past my lips and chew. It is nutty, tough and bitter and if I'm honest, rather disgusting. I laugh to cover up my embarrassment, chew then gag, chew and gag again allowing a dark red trickle of spittle to escape from the corner of my mouth and run down my chin. The crowd love it. No doubt they've seen it many times before with other unsuspecting tourists and they share my moment of discomfort amid their laughter and frivolity.

I attempt to hand over what I believe to be an appropriate coin for the experience, only to be greeted with a look of distaste from the vendor. A broad vampiric betel juice smile appears across the operator's face and everyone around the cart voices their agreement.
'No, no, my friend. This is being only a present to you, for you to be enjoying it,' he says. And again these wonderful people have shown me that even when you have little in the way of monetary wealth you can still be rich in kindness and hospitality.

Later I learn that in ancient times it was even customary for royalty to chew the Areca nut and betel leaf for their effects. As a mild stimulant, the chewing of the nut causes a mild, hot sensation in the body and a slight heightening in alertness. The Kings employed the services of special betel nut attendants as members of their royal procession, then at the nod of a royal head, the servant would roll one up for their King, Queen or accompanying mistress. There is also a sexy symbolism attached to the chewing of these aphrodisiac nuts as the areca nut represents the male yang and the betel leaf the female ying. Lovers would once entwine, chewing the concoction to freshen their breath whilst enjoying the mild relaxing properties the mix induced. Then after all that masticating and spitting of blood-red slaver, the lovers would no doubt polish off their session with some subtle and intoxicated lovemaking. The flip side to all of this stimulation though, is the scientific opinion that this daily tradition may indeed have a carcinogenic effect. So whilst the King is enjoying getting it off with a nice bit of royal fluff in the bushes, his lustful experiences may well have sparked a backlash of dire medical consequence.

However, for me the experience is all too much and so at a respectful distance I spit out the mass of blood-red muck and immediately head for an orange juice cart to quash the rancid taste that has layered my burgundy coloured taste buds.

## DEMONS AT THE CBS

There is no train station on the east coast town of Arugam Bay because there is no train to take you there. There is however, an elongated red apparition of bones, namely the bus, sporting six semi-bald tyres and a dead man's rattle to bounce you there if you have a spare ten hours in the pleats of your sarong.

In any country The 'Central Bus Stand' is a landmark – a focal point where lifelines cross. But as I stand here, at Colombo's Pettah Bus Stand, it is the last grimy place I want to be. I feel uncomfortable, unsafe and distinctly out of place. And having wandered around the Capital, killing time until my bus is due, it is now close to midnight: A time when the Colombo Central Bus Stand begins its metamorphosis into one of the most dangerous places in the city. A time when it transforms into an open house of thieves, perverts, drug addicts and hungry prostitutes.

I feel as if I have been stripped naked of any social defences and am exposed to any weasel-faced local who is apt enough to spot my vulnerability. To compensate then, I draw on my alter ego and square up, bracing my shoulders and puffing out my chest, tensing my muscles and punching out the stereotypical male macho image. However, despite such Neanderthal animation, deep down I still feel as if I am standing naked within a glass shell, with my particulars hanging out for all to see. I am all soft cock, smoke and mirrors, and I hope to hell no-one notices.

But I have spoken too soon, as there is one such individual currently heading my way. Her form is that of a lame filly who probably fell at the last fence, or became twisted in one of the water filled potholes commuters jump over with hiked up trousers or hitched up saris. You could say she would be prettily dressed in her colourful attire if it weren't for the muck about her demeanour.

From dawn to dusk the surrounding pavements at the CBS are crowded with sweep ticket sellers, peanut sellers, picture post card sellers. Sellers of plastic giraffes, plastic Santa Claus' and succulent fruit, but in the depths of the night all this changes. In the depth of the night the Central Bus Stand transforms into a sinister underworld of sordid vice.

She is closer now, closing the gap between our worlds.
And she smiles.
It is a beautiful smile.
A smile that could light up the dark.
And it does.
Light it up.
So without thinking I lightly smile back.

> *Shit!*
> *I just smiled!*

Her body language becomes even more suggestive and her bright smile widens. She is so close now that I am able to hear her foreign tongue, sung with such soft resonance. It is both sweet and lulling.

So I smile…again.
It is an ignorant smile, one of misinterpretation. A smile that masks my human trait of nervousness. I need to think quickly. To think of something to free me from this impending dilemma.

She is almost upon me.

> *Think.*
> *Think.*
> *For God's sake,*
> *Think!*

My thoughts are so muddled they jump from one idea to another, each as ridiculous as the last.

Run away.
Scream out loud.
All nonsensical.

Then without knowing where, or what, or how, an inspirational thought bursts on through, I upturn my hands and say,
'HIV. HIV positive.'
I say this in a mocked disappointed manner, but this is a huge mistake. Her response is both unexpected and alarming. Instantly she

becomes aggressive and her siren voice turns to that of a spurned vixen. She begins shouting harsh words at me and I need no interpreter to decipher her poisonous message.

I am nothing to her now, no more than a soiled meal ticket.

She begins flailing her arms madly from side to side, causing her deportment to become even more demonic. Then she is with me. In front of me. Standing before me, with eyes the colour of a needy junkie; all yellow and sunken socketed. She is standing so close she could easily put a dagger into my heart, but instead she hacks with guttural intent and spits thickly at my feet. She looks me directly in the eye and I can smell the stench of last night's tricks about her. Her feverous animal eyes burrow into me. Then she turns with a broken twist and walks away, leaving a feeling that she has somehow soiled my cleanliness. She has left me distraught and to add to this dilemma the surrounding street people have now stopped moving. They are looking over at me, as if noticing for the first time that there is a lone white man amongst them.

Quarry amongst predators.
It is as if I'm on the set of Michael Jackson's 1982 Thriller video clip and...

*Oh Fuck! Here comes another one.*

And sure enough, as if I am some freak magnet attracting opposite souls, I see another one of their kind heading my way.
It is no sassy whore this time.
This time it is a man.

A man in rags.
Without shoes.
And with most of his head missing.

We all know of the common expression, 'to be saved by the bell', and at this point in my story, it is suitably apt. For, as this zombie faced individual sets his approach he is caught, rabbit-like, in the beam of my oncoming bus. He is momentarily frozen in its jaundice light before being exorcised out of the road by the blast of the bus's horn. Thankfully he has been discharged to the dark side of the road, and as the bus pulls up beside me I bask in its luminosity. The bus stops, the doors open, and with ticket in hand I board the Pottuvil/Panama bus, expelling a sigh of welcomed relief.

Although it is nighttime the ambient heat has radiated throughout the bus's inner skeleton, warming up the pipework and torn padding on the rickety old fireman-red seats. After boarding I notice that the bus has swallowed only half of its seating capacity and so I am able to settle nicely on the entire length of an empty seat. I relax, enjoying my newfound sanctuary. The death rattle of the idling engine kicks into a rhythmic grunt and with a crunching of gears the wheels roll forward, forcing the bus out into the unruliness of the nighttime traffic. The demonic stage, that is the Pettah Bus Stand, is behind me now, no doubt awaiting the lifeblood of yet another potential victim. But not me, not anymore – I've been saved by the bell and am heading on East.

I have my Walkman in hand and fiddle about with the headphones so that each piece is plugged into the correct ear. After the bus stand debacle I really need some reassuring comfort and music is my Linus blanket. I feel the need to chill out for a bit and to exercise some degree of control and normality in what has become my bizarre and unpredictable world.

I look for something soulful and so decide on playing *Jimmy Cliff*. From the side pocket of my buffalo holdall, designed to my specifications to hold fifteen cassettes at each zipped end, five abreast and three rows deep, I select my favourite album. It is the perfect choice. I slip the cassette into the Walkman, rest my head against the window, close my eyes and depress the play button. The sound of the tape whirring through the machine carries with it the sound of soothing mechanics and seconds later I am listening to Track 1, 'You Can Get It If You Really Want', with its inspirational lyrics and meditative Jamaican rhythm.

The bus meanders its way through countless small towns and villages before pulling over at a local chai stop. The killing of the engine has awoken me, causing me to instinctively impulse feel for the existence of my bag. About five hours have passed so we are about half way to our destination. One side of the cassette tape has played right through but I cannot remember any of the tracks except for the first. I guess my body needed to shut down for a while, however, even after hours of sleep I still feel a little groggy and unsettled.

I grab my bag and alight the bus with the rest of my fellow passengers. Our 'stop' is typical of any wayward outpost in any Asian country. We are greeted by the bare essentials, consisting of bare tables, bare wooden chairs and a Perspex cabinet, barely standing, in which are housed the evening's pre-cooked offerings. Surprisingly, at this time of night they look rather appetising, however I choose the safer option and order a freshly made roti from a sizzling skillet. Then after receiving my snack I decide to join a table of fellow voyagers. They welcome me as if family and for the hundredth time I am asked what is the purpose of my visit, and so explain my quest for the elusive wave. It's fun, and once the small segment of my life story has been dissected, one of the group begins to tell me of the rape of a twenty two year old girl at the Pettah Bus Stand only two nights ago.

'The victim is being a garment factory worker,' begins the narrator of the story, 'who is to be catching the bus to attend a family ceremony and is to be waiting at the stopping place. She has been waiting many a few hours, having to expect to meet with similar friends. But sadly these friends are not showing. Instead, a kindly conductor is to be telling her that the next bus to Matara would be leaving in a shortly time and to get in and to be sitting down nicely. The girl is to be trusting of this man and gets into the bus. The bus is then being driven to a place having no peoples, saying that the bus is in needing of extra fuel. The men, one who is being the driver, and the first conductor man is to be having terrible sexy business with this girl.

'So are they are to be catching these people?' I ask in my best pidgin English.
'Oh Yes. They are to be catching all these fellows and are to be putting them into the police station. They will be having quite a breaking of bones from the policemens for doing such a terrible thing.'
'Then they will be going to jail?'
'Oh Yes. They will be going to Welikada prison. A most terrible place and will be having most terrible times from the other fellows. They will not be living a happy or very good life.'

Our narrator is about to continue, however the bus's horn breaks the flow of the chronicler and so we return to our lukewarm seats. I still wish to sit alone so I position my bag on the seat next to me and pretend to look for something within it. As I am delving in I can't help but think how young and damaged that poor girl will be and how justifiable it would be to painfully castrate these sick bastards then permanently remove them from our planet.

The bus travels on for another hour or so before it rolls out of the dark and into a shadowy dawn. Shards of light pierce the horizon long before the sun appears, pushing up from the earth with the loving grace of an indigenous mother. It is all colours of yellows and reds, splashed and splayed into a birth of blazing light. I am listening to the flip side of the *Jimmy Cliff* cassette and am bathed in a state of contentment, when, without any forewarning I find myself sharing my solitary moment with a recurring demon.

Melanie is back.
She is whispering through the lyrics of Track 6,
'I can't live without you.'
She is whispering the same line.
Again and again.
Echoing each word.
She is here, running around in my head.
Prancing.
Dancing.

*And God she dances so well.*

Leaning in and whispering,
'I can't live without you Rhys.'

My glasshouse has shattered, disintegrating into shards of yesterday's memories. I didn't even sense it coming. There was no clue given. No warning bell heard. No fire alarm rung to prevent this burning sensation from disrupting my world.

Now I see her face. I bathe in her nakedness. So sweet is this vision of her that she has become my imaginative pleasure. But then, all too quickly, I sense 'him', with his intruding ways and familiarity. Then he is with her, clouding my dreams, and overpowering my thoughts. Touching her. They haunt my mind and I can't get them out.

I hear their laughter.
I watch them kissing.
I see them both so clearly…fucking each other!

Suddenly I am roused from this bitter vision. The driver has thumped on the brakes, bringing the bus to a grinding halt and in the process has sent me lurching forward to hit my lip on the metallic seat rail in front. It is a momentary bandaid to the trauma as my earphones are dislodged and the haunting track is cast onto my lap.

    I look to see why we have stopped, and it is not the familiar sweetness of blood oozing from my lip that has unexpectedly stimulated a primordial instinct, it is because outside the bus I see hoards of khaki uniforms, masses of them. My blood runs cold, despite the tropical heat, because I see that the soldiers are back and are surrounding our bus.

# TWEAKING

The reason for the stop is not a welcomed one.

Again I watch as soldiers surge around the bus, creating an undercurrent of dread within it, and again there are the guns. Once again here is another reminder of the differences between my world of coca cola and this one of white rice. Smack bang in my face, only this time it isn't only one unfortunate bastard being plucked from within our midst, this time it is all of us who are torn from the security of our seats and forced off the bus.

*The Dharma Syndrome…shit!*

I reflect on my previous kidnapping experience, which is now cupping my balls, giving them an unpleasant squeeze. I still remember Dharma's face looking up at me from the train tracks. Still wishing he could have finished his untold story of Kenny Daglish missing an open goal against Manchester United in 1980. Still wishing his bony arse was seated on a well-worn wooden train slat heading to anyplace else instead of being bloodied and manhandled into a Tamil Tiger jeep.

The soldiers are suited in khaki battle dress, yet the uniform is different in colour and style to Dharma's abductors. These too are heavily armed; however there appears to be no definitive menace cutting through the air.

There are no curled lips.
No barrel stabbing snarls.

However in saying that I *am* witness to many testosterone fuelled, acne riddled teenagers, these warring hunters, these battle hardened defenders of their land, who would readily put a bullet into an enemy at the bark of an order. They are at war after all and this fact is not a comforting thought.

We are ushered out of the bus with our luggage and huddle together, merino style. Then our human bait ball is dispersed by the soldiers and formed into an orderly single file. We are commanded to move forward to a group of soldiers who check through our bags with expert precision. Once searched the soldiers direct me away from the make shift trestles and usher me beyond a raised boom gate of milled coconut palm to mix with the rest of the flock.

It's a Checkpoint.
'Checkpoint Chapatti', I muse.

But I take little comfort in the fact that this humourous thought hasn't dampened my lingering feelings of uncertainty: Dharma's fate still lies fresh in my memory. We are instructed to walk one hundred metres along the road, in single file. It is an exposed hundred metre stretch of open road, a no-man's land, a length of keenly guarded tarmac by heavily armed combatants. It is where the West is separated from the East. Government forces from Terrorists. But there is no prefabricated concrete wall fixed with cold towers here.

No division of States.
No Cold War.
This is the steamy Tropics.
With live ammunition.
Hot to the touch.

This is where there are live rounds in the breach of semi-automatic rifles and all the while I am praying that the weapons' safety catches are on and that there aren't any itchy fingers nervously toying with them.

I mingle with the other fodder and figure that we have walked about twenty metres along the road. I look to my left and am shocked at the sight of a machinegun muzzle poking out from within a pillbox. It is pointing directly at my head and as I walk past the gun nest I watch with trepidation as the barrel slowly glides with fluid precision.

Matching my pace.
Step for step.
Heartbeat for heartbeat.
I listen to each of my footfalls and question myself.

> *What the hell am I doing here?*
> *All this for fresh fruit and foreign places.*
> *All this for the dream of the remote wave.*
> *All this to escape from that cold-hearted woman.*
> *I must be out of my tiny fucking mind?*

As these thoughts mock my reason for being here our bus trundles alongside us. I concentrate on the revolution of its wheels as it shambles on by, because anything that'll take my mind off that trailing muzzle is a welcomed distraction. I watch as the bus pulls up at another boom gate some fifty metres away and lists, panting in the heat like a spent beast. I wish to quicken my pace toward it as if that would help outdistance the imaginary bullets, but instead, I am hampered by the footfall of the man in front. With each short step the bus draws closer and closer, but with each pace it also feels as if I'm walking on eggshells, strewn on thin ice. I look heavenward for some solace, only to see an oceanic frigatebird passing overhead, silent in flight, and about as much out of place as I am on this alien landmass. The bus is now twenty metres away and I take some comfort in the fact that the sight of the pillbox is, at last, beyond the tail of my eye.

Finally the aluminium steps to the bus appear and I climb my stairway to heaven, move up the isle and glue myself into my seat, savouring its remnant warmth and hard familiarity. Then one by one the seats are reoccupied and the bus pulls away, allowing me to further reflect on how fragile and exposed my existence is in this strange land; especially when heightened by the image of a fifty millimetre barrel of Chinese gunmetal aimed directly at my head.

Again I question myself. What the hell am I doing in Sri Lanka when it is in the throes of civil war? And why, only moments ago, did I allow myself to pass through a safe checkpoint and into a dangerous war zone? It would be laughable if it didn't feel so bloody unnerving.

## WILD DOGS OF ARUGAM BAY

On arriving at the town of Pottuvil, some three hundred and fourteen kilometres east of Colombo, I peel myself from my seat and step off the bus.

With my surfboard, handmade water buffalo holdall, half a packet of Bristol cigarettes and a flat-slap-arse, I stand in the main square. The bus sweats nearby, awaiting its next hoard of human morsels. I, on the other hand, am wondering what to do next? The place is devoid of touts trying to prise precious rupees from the folds of my clothing. There is no-one staring hungrily at my bag. There aren't even any whores wanting to get into my middle pocket. Then leaping between these thoughts comes a nasal injection,

'G'day mate,' it says.

A wiry, suntanned, half dressed, staff carrying, lungi clad individual, Australian by the sounds of it, passes me by. He offers this greeting while crossing the dusty square, then furthers his short acknowledgement of me with, 'Gonna' need a dogstick mate.'

*Dogstick?*
*What the hell is a dogstick?*

But before I could ask him, the strolling Aussie has entered a tired façade of a building covered in torn posters displaying past political events.

Looking around I cannot help but be impressed with the main feature of the square. A massive umbrella of a tree, large in green leaf, rough of trunk and wide in girth. It stands as a gigantic and proud guardian of this rural village. Around the base of this living monster lies a metre high and three metre wide circular platform made from hard packed dirt, secured with a retaining wall of large quarry cut stone. This raised platform has enough width to accommodate a handful of men whom I see lounging on makeshift hessian beds beneath the tree's cooling canopy, all sporting wide smiles and (unbeknown to me) suppressed laughter.

The reason?
The tourist has no dogstick!

Then at attack speed the mangiest dog I have ever seen belts out from nowhere kicking up a trail of dust as it does and attaches itself to the lower part of my trousers. Puny, hairless and practically half dead it terrifies me with its gnashing of teeth.

*Jesus Christ, I'm being eaten by half a dog!*

It has struck from nowhere and I begin shaking, kicking, hopping, screaming, spinning, leaping and bashing this mad fiend with my other leg.

Bang!
Bang!
Bang!

On its head!

Bang!
Bang!
Bang!

On it's head again!

I am practically stomping the shit out of the other half of its life and after a couple more smacks to its head it lets go. But it's not over yet. It has retreated a safe distance and is now growling will full intention, probably wondering how my other leg might taste?

From under the tree a sharp shout and a well-aimed stone from one of the 'loungers' sends the crazy brute scurrying for cover. I'm saved and amazingly only have a few minor scratches to show for the mutt's troubles. The bottom of my trousers however, is in bits. The onlooker's laughter has subsided but the amusement provided by the ignorant 'dogstick-less' tourist is written across their tanned leathery faces. The boys are amused. This probably hasn't happened to a tourist since the last bus and the boys have a well-chosen vantage point from which to enjoy each performance.

I wander over to the tree and ask my saviour directions to the surf break.

'You can be coming with me,' he says, as he slides from his resting place and points over to his transport. It is a tuk-tuk, a three wheeled motorbike come car, come death trap, which is parked across the street. 'Be coming this way my lucky friend,' he says. However before heading over to the bone shaker, I head into the shade, drop my luggage to the dust and to keep the blood sucking flies at bay attend to my wounds with a medi-swab, antiseptic cream and some bandaids. Thankfully there is no rabies in this area.

As I leave with my tuk-tuk driver I acknowledge the remaining men with a short-armed wave and head across the street to the awaiting vehicle. My driver, Asanka, speaks pidjin English, and after a short exchange of broken dialogue, I learn that he has transported other adventurous surfers on their dream run out to 'The Point'.

It is a bit of a squeeze in the back of Asanka's pocket rocket as my bag is on the floor and my feet are resting atop of that. My surfboard is resting across my folded lap and although part of it is sticking out into the street on both sides my driver assures me that this presents no problem. After Asanka's words of encouragement we set off at break neck speed to find the secluded surf break at Arugam Bay.

'Surf good today mister. Many wave. You come good time,' Asanka shouts over his shoulder as we career along the dusty track. We race as if Roman charioteers, all blur and Ben Hur, thrilling the passenger in the back. It is likely we are the envy of all onlookers, whose only machine could be a dual wheeled can opener dating back to its invention in 1925. It is a heart stopping ride as we belt along this narrow jungle path. The plants at the side of the track whip at either end of my board as we race on through, and I am relieved when we finally come to a speedy stop at the southern end of Arugam Bay to find my surfboard still intact.

With Asanka's help I am prised from the rear cockpit and once free I find myself gazing upon one of the most fantastic beaches I have ever seen. I can see the 'point break' half a kilometre ahead with waves peeling off for perhaps fifty metres, maybe more? I am ecstatic and on looking closer notice that there are only a couple of surfers in the water.

*No crowds and a Tropical Dreamland.*
*I must be in Heaven.*

Arugam Bay consists of three small villages, where fishing and farming are the main occupations. The farmers grow rice and keep cattle for meat production and also for the wholesome yogurt dish called curd, while the fishermen take to the depths of the sea for their staple diet of all things oceanic.

Ullae, one of the small fishing villages, is set in the corner of the Bay where the sea is quiet and the land curls to form a natural fishing harbour. It is also where Asanka, my Mad Max of Middle Earth, has dropped me off.

Fishing season is nearly all year round at the Bay so I am privy to a colourful array of locals busily working up and down the beach. Ahead of me I see a small fishing boat being hauled up from the edge of the ocean. It has been handcrafted from a tree trunk and stabilised with a couple of coconut pole outriggers. Nearby I see a glistening catch of fresh prawns and small fish being unloaded into small buckets from another botanical lump of wood that has also arrived from the deep. As I pass by one of the fishermen he scoops up a handful of these translucent prawns, gesturing toward me with generous hands and a fresh, salty smile. I decline his offer and am met with a 'that's ok' wiggle of the head but the sight of the prawns has triggered an unwelcome memory of garlic, white wine and fresh bread; of the last meal Mel and I shared, as a loving couple, at our favourite restaurant.

Prawns are her favourite seafood and we would laugh as I attempted to stop her from stealing the peeled ones from my sizzling plate. It was like that with the laughter. There was always plenty of it to go around.

Laughter a-la-carte.
Laughter between courses.
Laughter between the sheets.
Laughter between lovers, and
Laughter between friends.

But all that has gone now. However the memory still burns, as does the hot loose sand running between my toes as I hike along the beach.

At Arugam Bay a whole community of Singhalese fishing families migrate annually from the west coast to settle down in temporary palm huts smack bang on the beach. In the village of Ullae I came to understand that both Tamil and Singhalese families live here as one community, sometimes unifying ethnic differences through marriage. I was to learn that the gentle practises of Christianity, Buddhism, and Hinduism exist side by side, all cushioned within a harmonious community of cultural acceptance. But for now, as I cruise through this montage of village life, only one word springs to mind: *Perfect*. And it brings with it the widest of grins.

Before me is a tropical scene you see nestled within the waxy lift-outs of the Sunday papers. The place where you imagine living out your dream.

This *is* my dream.
A dream of great surf.
A place of peace,
A place where tranquillity appears to seep from everything I see.

However at such a moment how was I to know it was also a place where the Tamil Tigers were to become menacingly close. I am aware of none of this and it is probably just as well, for if I knew, I may well have turned back at the checkpoint.

I arrive at The Point.

When I look back I see the beach swooning like a maiden fair, holding her tranquil jade green ocean at bay with one long sweeping alabaster arm. The crispy white sand is home to scattered palm huts and dugout canoes, which, for now, lie dotted along the beach before embarking on their daily dusk crusade out to the deep. Farming and fishing is their lifeline. It is their primitive existence in a primitive world. A far cry from the sanctuary that is Hikkaduwa, where the village bathes in electric light and has the luxury of running water. Arugam Bay has none of these amenities, but it does have surf and it does have accommodation, and my accommodation for the next few months is owned by a local father named Chandana who has seven daughters.

Chandana's daughters' ages range from babies to legal. But these daughters are off limits, unless you want your nuts cut off with a ragged shellfish in the middle of the night. Off limits, that is, unless you were to marry them, which two of my newly befriended mates have indeed done.

My, 'You're gonna' need a dogstick mate!' mate, 'S'tralia Mick', who was at the square when I first arrived, is married to one of the daughters, and his mate, Gus, is married to another of the lovely ladies. Lovely in nature, but to look at, well, they are a little tricky on the eyes. However, it is only Mick and Gus who are getting their leg over, whereas the rest of us have to make do with a sweet and ongoing affair with Mrs Palmer and her five willing daughters.

The elementary mud and coconut frond huts, in which we live, have been masterfully created by the local handymen, and are in close proximity to the surf. So close in fact, that I could cast a throw net into the ocean from my front door and catch dinner. It is true caveman stuff and I love it!

I am living alongside the boys. We have one hut per person or couple, with each hut having either two single beds or a double. Mine has two singles, with the second bed acting as an open wardrobe, having all of my stuff strewn across it: clothes, medicine, books, and music tapes. At each end of my headboard is a small portable speaker which is connected to my Walkman. I slot in one of my thirty cassette tapes and its magnetic sound conjures up another memorable occasion. A ska group called *The Specials* begin pumping out their infectious energy in the form of the track 'Too Much Too Young', from their 1979 self-titled debut album produced by *Elvis Costello*. I can see them now, the home crew at the Crab Island Hotel, playing pool, talking about the day's surf and drinking translucent pints of Stella Artois.

My surfboard rests in one corner. The Welsh flag, which I had made in Hikkaduwa from a table-top sized piece of batik, forms the patriotic feature wall. Photos of family and close friends are taped to another wall and a mozzie coil whispers its toxic scent beneath my bed. It is a good place. A safe place: Or so I thought?

## THE G.D.B.

It is months after my arrival at the Point and is a little past sunrise. The surf is about five foot and is the perfect recipe for a fine start before breakfast. There are five of us in the water; S'tralia Mick, his brother-in-law Gus, Sooty, a local surfer, nicknamed as such due to his harelip and subsequent speech impediment, myself, and Butch, a tough looking Dinky-Di, Sydney-ite from Cronulla. We are all having fun paddling around, splashing, laughing and enjoying an ideal morning's entertainment fresh from the Gods.

The point doesn't deliver the very best waves in the world. There are no second-after-second barrels, no double decker bus 'drops' or concrete slab lips, but it has length and enough power to allow one a few self satisfying moves. After our three and a half hours of aqueous play, and feeling as hungry as a pack of Mongolian steppe ponies, we head on into the restaurant where we slide our boards into the roof rafters and sit down to contemplate the world in general. They're a good bunch, this motley crew of adventurers; all mates from Australia who have been surfing these secret woods since the late seventies. As we tuck into breakfast Mick asks,
'So whaddaya reckon on the Tigers then Rhys?'
I explain that I had recently read in *The Island* newspaper that the conflict is heating up in the northern province of Jaffna.
'Look, since the Singhalese government have reduced the Tamil's available placements in universities and in years past have declared Buddhism as the State's primary religion, the Tamils, who, as you know are mostly Hindu, have been festering since the early seventies. It's a recipe for disaster whichever way you look at it.'
'Well let's hope they don't start thinking about taking any foreign hostages or we could all end up in deep shit,' Mick adds with concern. And Mick may have every right to be concerned. After all, he *is* married to one of the local ladies and plans to be on the island for the foreseeable future.

'Listen me old Spinach,' replies Butch, 'they're not going to start messing with any foreigners or then the dirt will really hit the fan and none of us, or them, need any of that bullshit around here. The last thing they need is to have their arses kicked in the international papers. They know we're here and we know they're training in Yala Park. It's all dinkum. We just leave each other to it. Simple.'
But I, for one, am not convinced that the situation with the Tigers is 'dinkum' and is something to be dismissed lightly.
'Mick could have a point you know?' Mick looks up. 'I'm just thinking it would be too easy for those guys to waltz up here and take any one of us on a joy ride to nowhere. I've already seen it happen once, remember?' I remind them of Dharma and his execution from the train.
'Hey you know your problem Welshie?' says Butch. 'You think too much, coz you're heart's fucked and your cock's soft.'
I laugh freely at Butch's comical dig, then turn toward the kitchen as I'm awaiting my sardines on toast to arrive. I'm so hungry my stomach feels like someone has pinched my throat. I laugh at this too, remembering that it was something my grandmother used to say when I was a child. I think of the ninety eight years that she lived on the planet. Blessed with her singsong sense of humour, spoken in the historic Welsh language, with its absence of k's, q's, v's, x's or z's.

All guttural and sweet.
A soothing oxymoron.

My brothers and I would feel blessed each time we were wrapped within her infectious presence. When she lost the sight of one eye, she laughed it off, saying that she still had one good one with which to keep an eye on us. What spirit. And when, as kids, if we'd ask if she knew where a misplaced toy might be, she would say it was upstairs, in the jug, behind the wallpaper. What joy these loving memories hold. And we called her Nan. And others that loved her called her Bessie. And she was 98 when she passed away. She was Welsh speaking and she was all loving and lovely…and I still miss her.

The food arrives and is a welcome addition to our breakfast table. Down come the banana smoothies, sardines on toast, pineapple fritters, coffee, omelettes and fried rice. It is an Islander's smorgasbord and we destroy it with gusto, and once finished we each sign in 'The Book'. But this is no ordinary book. It is more of a Gastronomic Doomsday Book, a GDB, listing everyone's eating idiosyncrasies from the time they first arrive at the point. This Gastronomic Doomsday Book, this GDB exists because all of the local banks are dead. They were shot up and robbed blind by the Tamil Tigers, issuing their own version of a withdrawal slip in the form of a loaded AK47. So for the islanders to save money at any local bank became a fruitless exercise and a bank having no security, you could say, is as useless as a banana padlock in a monkey forest. So 'The Book' was borne of necessity. A book in which your every edible transaction is listed, meal by meal, drink by drink, then totalled, rupee by rupee, until it teeters and breaks through the cash barrier. Once this occurs, once your obligation finally equals any currency note in your possession, it is duly handed over to your anxious creditor. So your debt is paid and your slate wiped clean. This, of course, is sweet music to the ears of the restaurateur, who allegro-like, would pass its wrinkled existence further up the food chain to 'Uncle', the Head of the village, who, for a small commission, kept it well hidden in the depths of the jungle. And so is the way of the point: A place having little change.

# PANIC

The noise of an engine has awoken me. It isn't a dream and it shouldn't be here. It is out of place. Alien to the point. But it *is* here. And it *is* coming from outside. And what's more it's becoming louder.

There were always things that went bump in the night when I was a child. Scared to a shade of deathly white by Peter Cushing movies and pillow hugging as Christopher Lee stole in for another vampiric bite. Not a glass of Chianti or a serving of fava beans to be had during this era of adolescence, but still enough suspense and horror to silence many a lamb of the seventies.

Now I hear voices outside my hut. They sound angry. And I can hear one of these voices, barking! There is a loud thump, more of a crash really, that has scared the hell out of me. However this time it is neither a zombie's knock against a glass window, nor a coconut submitting to the gravitational pull of the jungle. No. This time the intruding noise is that of a rifle butt smashing into the poor excuse of a door which once hung precariously at the entrance to my hut. Then following this rifle butt is an aggressive arsehole who quickly reverses his weapon to point the significantly more dangerous end at my stomach.

I feel the rise of sour bile at the back of my throat and gag, as I'm about to be sick.

'Up! You get up!'

His icy voice has me jumping out of my bed. And although his command of the English language, like his face, is pockmarked with imperfection, it is nevertheless extremely effective and has me grabbing my sarong and heading out the door. This time, unlike the soldiers at the checkpoint, the lips are curled and the trigger fingers itchy.

Once outside my hut it is apparent that we have all suffered the same ill fate, for standing in front of their own huts are Mick, Gus and their respective wives. Butch is there too, as are a few other frightened locals. I glance over at the boys and read their worried faces,

> *Why have these soldiers come?*
> *They must be the Tamil Tigers?*
> *And if so, what do they want?*

I think back to my earlier conversation with the boys.

> *Are we all to be like Tom Petty's refugee? To be kidnapped, tied up, taken away and held for ransom?*

I begin to move over to the boys but as I do one of the soldiers moves in on me and kicks me into a kneeling position. The others are forced to do likewise, then it is animated that we should place clasped hands on our heads. Images of POW's executed by samurai sword come to mind as we so vulnerable out here in the middle of the jungle, at the lawless mercy of these freedom fighters.

We watch one of the soldiers drag Chandana, the owner of the place and father to the seven girls, to the middle and force him to kneel before us in his own patch of dirt. The same soldier then rams the end of his AK47 in-between Chandana's pearly whites and while he is literally pissing himself, I feel like I am manfacturing bricks. These mongrels have come barking right up to our front door and there isn't a dogstick in sight!

Chandana's wife and five of the seven daughters are nowhere to be seen. The hut they sleep in is around the back, near the drinking well, and a terrible thought comes to mind: The worst thought.

> *Bastards!*

But these thoughts are interrupted by a string of obscenities that ring around the encampment. In Sinhalese, or perhaps Tamil, I don't know? But they are surely angry words, loaded with deadly consequences. Ugly words spat out to induce terror. We all watch as Chandana pleads before them, with both hands prayer-like, and drooling frightened words through a gargled mouthful of battle forged steel. Something about 'Uncle'?

The confrontation appears to have hit a stalemate as the soldiers have taken a few steps back, marginally reducing their menace. Then the nightmare begins to dissipate as their commander orders the soldiers back to the jeeps and the noose in which we have all been hanging loosens.

*They're leaving.*
*They're fucking leaving!*

As quickly as they had coasted their jeeps and battle paraphernalia down the sandy track to our huts, they are gone. We all bleat a second sigh of relief as we see Chandana's wife and daughters emerge from around the back of the compound, frightened but unharmed. Unnerved but untouched. And the crazy thing about the whole drama is the only violation to this idyllic piece of our world is the theft of Chandana's small 12 volt black and white TV, a car battery and our interrupted sleep.

With the danger now apparently passed and a change of personal attire, we replace fear with laughter, and pangs of anxiety with a sense of calm. I share with the boys that I was purely bricking myself back there and reckoned I could have built a double brick toilet.
'Dunnie mate? I thought we were all cactus. Reckon I could have built a whole fucking shower block the way I was feeling,' adds Mick.
'Yeah those guys sure as hell meant business,' agrees Gus. ' All I could think about was that you might have been right Rhys, about being kidnapped and all!'
'Yeah, well I was just about to leap into action you know,' says Butch. 'Had my hand on my trusty Swiss army cobber. It was only a matter of choosing the right moment to let them have it.' And with that Butch stands up and amuses us with a Crocodile Dundee excerpt.
'Yeah, well that figures,' chides Gus, as Butch resumes his seat, 'coz being single around here you've more often than not got your hand on your weapon of mass flaccid distraction.'
Then between the ensuing laughter Butch decides to add, 'Grouse laugh though.'
'Oh yeah. A right fucking laugh,' says I. 'If you enjoy being woken up in the middle of the night, and being held at gunpoint by a bunch of terrorists.' With that we break into further posttraumatic mirth, masking the real concern we harbour beneath, namely: When are these terrorists likely to come back?

The following day it comes to light that the soldiers were seeking the whereabouts of only one man and had stormed several places in each of the three villages. They were chasing Uncle, the local moneyman, as it is common knowledge that since all of the local banks have closed, Uncle has become the 'Bureau de Change'. And so, we hoped for Uncle's sake he had heard the warnings of the jungle drums, borrowed a dugout canoe, and buggered off into the inland waterways where you only hear the crocs' fart.

## MIA AND DOCTOR STARCH

As daylight breaks at the Bay we all wander down to our vantage point to check out the surf. It's picked up. We had half expected this from the increase in the sound of the waves breaking throughout the night but what we didn't know was how good it was going shape up to be...or that a girl is about to arrive at the Point.

Her name is Mia.
Spanish.
And she surfs.
A couple of hours into our session and she is spotted paddling out, creating havoc. You just have to love the Europeans.

Their sense of style.
Their music.
Their clothes.
Their minimal choice of bikini.
Pequeño.

Mia is all bum, breasts and beautiful. Weeks without so much as a sniff, and lo and behold here is a scantily clad woman stroking toward us.
'Buenos dias you boys,' she calls out.

Sun bleached blonde hair to her shoulders, a tan to tantalise and mosaic Moorish eyes to tumble into. She's greeted with adoration and respect. After all, she surfs. Not that we aren't thinking of how her salty kisses would taste, but we lads uphold a decent moral code and we are expellers of friendly virtues. In that respect then, Mia is more than safe; she is protected.

'G'day,' Butch calls over.
'Morning,' laments Mick.
'Hello to you too,' I smile, 'and welcome to The Point.'
'Thank you boys. I am called Mia. And you boys?'

'Well the ugly one over there with the beard is Mick. That's Butch. Would you believe he's a nurse? But when he grows up he wants to become a plastic surgeon so he can work on his own face. And the guy paddling back out is Gus. Gus thinks he's gay coz he keeps touching his penis, but don't mention it as he's a bit sensitive about the homosexual thing.'

We all laugh.

'By the way, my name is Rhys. And may I say that I was just thinking my day was perfect, but now it is a little more beautiful because you are here.'
'Grazioso,' Mia says with a tumbling wave smile.
'Would you like to join us for some breakfast after the surf?'
'Sure,' she laughs.' After we surf, yes.'
'After we surf then,' says I.
And with this she turns her board, strokes into a wave and takes off. She comes off the bottom of the wave with flowing ease then pushes her board vertically, to flick it off the lip with a well-defined and fluid snap.
Just like that! With froth, and spray and bubbles, and a body to die for.

*Man, I feel like I'm in love again.*
*What a Re-entry!*

I have this frustrating habit when surfing. When I wipe out and am trying to reach the ocean's surface I kick out with my right leg. It is a subconscious move and an annoying one as it results in me striking the reef and cutting my foot. This inherent stupidity produces a constant battle with sores, which manifest themselves into weeping ulcers, then becoming small volcanic pus-oozers. So this time, when I kick out from below the surface, true to my word, I strike the seabed with the instep of my right foot.

It is believed there are several practical ways to treat such a wound. First, you can use a citric remedy and watch the cut turn black as you squeeze lemon juice over the wound, which purportedly dissolves the coral. Or you can pour a mixture of hot water and antiseptic lotion on it, but this keeps the wound wet and prone to continued ulceration. Or thirdly, you can use the old age remedy and piss on it. This may be of some benefit but can result in a few raised eyebrows when performed in public. Or you can take a pharmaceutical approach and use Betadine, but you must make sure that all coral is removed first as Betadine is made from shellfish, which actually feeds the coral, and will inevitably make the situation worse.

Whichever you choose it is imperative that the wound is kept dry, which in itself presents its own set of problems in the perspiring tropics. And when carrying a wound such as this there are also the disease-depositing flies to contend with. Those that insert their needle-like proboscis into your body to forage for the sweetness of decay. Not good.

So now I'm lying on my bed with a wounded leg and I am depressed. I have constructed a crude form of triage with a surfboard leash and have suspended my miserable pulsating leg from the rafters.

And I have been like this for a week.

A whole week of lying up, drying up and putting up with gibes from the boys. I can only just manage to walk the short distance to the back of the hut to take a piss. It is a shitty existence and I'm going mad staring at the walls like Shirley bloody Valentine. Staring at my leg. Staring at its unnatural form, because it's huge.

Mia visits each day and I'm so grateful for her company, for without her feminine kindness my days would be abysmal. She brings with her fresh fruit, the 'Island' newspaper, a kind word, and an enjoyable environmental change to my bleak hut-bound existence.

My foot has now ballooned to the size of a small soccer ball and is hot to the touch. It even wobbles, as if having a mind of its own. The infection from the accident has become a real problem and has me worried. Even the word amputation raised its ugly head in the small hours of last night's delirium. So, if the truth be told, I am more than worried, I'm really scared. It is even agonising when Mia bathes my foot with cool water and to even move my leg slightly has become excruciatingly painful. On seeing me in so much pain today, Mia has decided to go and fetch the boys.

Mick, Gus and Mia turn up a short while later, followed by Butch, who is in full medical swing. After all he is a highly qualified nurse, although to look at him you'd think he was a full blown bricklayer. It is obvious by the look on their faces that Mia has made her concerns known to the crew. Butch moves closer to my leg, lowers his nose to the bandages and sniffs like a bloodhound. He doesn't need to say anything as his face tells the story, but nevertheless he tries to lighten the situation.

'Dunno why you don't just let me have a little play with it Rhys?'

He says it light heartedly, but we all know that Butch is deadly serious. Even I know that this wound is now well past the 'put-a-clean-bandage-on-it-every-day' stage.

'It'll just be a little bit of muck stuck up inside your foot mate. But it's become badly infected and is not looking good. Look, a couple of nicks here and a few slices there, I'll clean you up and you'll be as dandy as a champagne cork and back in the water in no time. Whaddaya say?'

Butch might be all heart and I'm sure his intentions are sincere, however seeing a nurse with a double six pack and hands the size of boxing gloves, has me doubting his medical capabilities. Besides, as I said earlier, I'm scared, and the thought of someone outside a hospital cutting into my leg is just too much to accept. After all, it is Butch we're talking about here, and he isn't exactly the sanest person on the planet. So I look to Mia, attempting to camouflage my fear with a humourous retort.

'Yeah, as if I'm gonna' let Mr Hyde, Igor and Dr. Frankenstein here hack away at my foot you crazy bastards! Just help me get to my feet so I can go to the bloody hospital will you.'

'Bloody hospital! Yeah, nice one Rhys. Like the pun,' says Gus, causing me to groan at my own inattention.

'Right. Enough of the arsing about Gus. Give Butch a hand and get me to my feet.'

I have decided then to forgo the blade of the Butch'er. Instead I am going to take my chances at a third world hospital on the remote east coast of an island out in the middle of the Indian Ocean. Either way the prognosis isn't looking good, but in my mind the trip to the hospital is the lesser of two evils.

Using two dogsticks as crutches, Mia and I begin trucking up the road to the bus stop. The boys did offer to carry me but I said no, as the aftermath of ridicule would have been life long. Each step is hot and as painful as the last and on looking down I see my whole foot wobble with each move. We try to stay in the shade as much as possible, as even the sunshine stings the over sensitive swollen pink skin. The walk is hell.

The bus trip is a welcome rest after the pounding I have just taken along the uneven village tracks, however Mia is witness to me wincing in agony as my leg is at the mercy of each bump and pothole.
'How far to this hospital?' Mia asks, resting her head on my shoulder. And I find such comfort in this, as it would be so much harder to cope if she weren't here.
'I don't know exactly, but surely it can't be more than an hour away? At least that's what Chandana said.'

Two hours later we arrive at the hospital. Or what can otherwise be described as a dairy milking shed, only a dairy milking shed would have doors. There are no windows to the building either and not a bloody cow in sight. Well, that's not strictly true, there are windows, albeit minus the glass, and there are doorways, only without any doors. The cows may be chewing the cud out the back for all I know and again the reality of being in the third world strikes home like a well-aimed goal. I should have known better, and have expected less. There's a whisper in my ear, but it's only me talking: To myself.

*Christ Rhys, what were you expecting to find on this island...Paradise?*

'Jesus Christ Mia, would you look at this place,' I pant between the beads of sweat and the pangs of hopeless desperation. 'It's a bloody barnyard!'
Mia displays a concerning smile. She is trying to comfort me I know. But it's hopeless. The evidence around us is all too conclusive. We move in through one of the doorways, past children with runny noses and expressionless eyes. From around a corner an old woman appears, sporting what looks like 'suspended golf balls' hanging from within her neck. As she shuffles down the corridor each step causes these growths to lollop to and fro under folds of aged skin. They remind me of those perpetual metal balls which are suspended from string and which clack back and forth against each other. The lady

smiles with a warm, near toothless grin and shuffles on past. We step over men swaddled in soiled blankets, too infirm to move, their only comfort is being here at this godforsaken hospital. The fact that they have made it this far is a triumph, but they have received no winning line trophy for their cross country ordeal, no medals to be pinned on their emaciated chests. It is a sickening sight, this corridor of human hopelessness and is such a far cry from the readily accepted crisp white sheets and medicines of the Western World. What lies before us is a stark and honest reminder that this is not our home, we're welcome, sure, but I was never prepared for this.

A doctor appears from a doorway. He is wearing a remarkably clean white coat, reminding me of a 'Daz' washing powder advertisement and speaks good English. Doctor Starch walks over to us.

'Hello my good fellow and lady,' he says politely. 'How can I be helping you?'

'It's my leg Doctor. Can you take a look? It's pretty bad. I really need some help.'

As the words tumble from my lips they leave a bitter taste. My plea burns with narcissism, causing me to blush, however the good doctor smiles past my embarrassment, displaying only warmth and compassion.

'I am being very sorry but I cannot be helping you,' he says. 'All medicine is nowhere to be seen. The Tamil Tigers, they are to be taking it all. And he says this without malice, conveying it instead as a matter of fact, delivering it in the same manner a 6 o'clock newsreader might relay a story of an unforseen traffic jam. Something these war torn people have come to accept I guess? It becomes obvious to both of us then, that the hospital is quite simply a place where these people come to lay down and rest. There is only one hospital within walking distance for these poor people, and some have walked for days. Perhaps they have come to share a last glass of loneliness with other kindred spirits, before travelling onward within the folds of their belief.

Reality bites.

*Shit.*
*No medicine.*
*No help.*
*No good.*

Butch's words resonate around the confines of this dank and squalid corridor – *fortissimo* – bouncing off the walls with repetitive sureness.

*'Dunno why you don't just…'*

Echo.
Echo.
Echo.

*'Just a nick here and a prod there…'*

Echo.
Echo.
Echo.

Bouncing around and around in my head.

*'…I'll have you fixed up in no time.'*
*'Just a nick here and a prod there…'*

Nick!
Nick!
Nick!

Butch by nature and nurse by profession.

> *The Butch-er.*
> *Jesus wept.*
> *Please don't tell me that it has come down to this?*

## HISS OF THE DRAGON

By the time Mia and I had caught a bus back to the Square and a tuk-tuk to the bay and had taken a blazing stroll down the beach to the restaurant I am shagged, hot, and sweating profusely.

My foot is fiercely red.
Bullfighting mad.
In volcanic pain.
Where Pamplona meets Pompeii.

On entering the restaurant Mia relays our journey. I can't help but notice an excited, clinically insane matador, sitting at one of the tables, grinning from ear to ear. The look of anticipation on his face is one so full of glee it's sickening.
'You're one sick bastard, you know that Butch?'
'Look at it this way me old spinach. I'll have a little prod around and have you fixed you up in no time. Besides, what's the alternative, a hell journey back to Colombo?'
Butch is as keen as Colonel Mustard to get in and have a dig around, especially when he can show off his alleged expertise in Mia's company.
'And I'm cheap too!' he adds.
'Yeah, that goes without saying. Anyway you're not going anywhere near my foot tonight. Not by candlelight.'
'So it's a 'Yes' then, me old spinach?'
'Yes, it's a 'Yes'. Now slide me over that bottle of arak will you. Tonight I need to get horrendously pissed and not think about you or the hell ride I'm in for tomorrow.'

The early morning light finds me waking here on the restaurant floor, feeling extremely sorry for myself. Not only does my leg feel worse, but I am also covered in mosquito bites that have polluted my body and left me with lumps the size of small hives on all my exposed skin. The little bastards were particularly fierce throughout the night and I am cursing myself for not climbing under one of the nearby mozzie nets in the restaurant or making it back to my hut. So much for the myth that arak fuelled blood will keep the sucky little bastards away.

I doctor my hangover with a tumbler of coconut juice, and await Nurse Butcher to front up, donning his sickle and cape. And I don't have to wait long. The surf is flat and the word that the hospital was a failed attempt has spread quickly. So much so that there is an entourage presently making its way toward the restaurant within a cloud of self important merriment. After all, it isn't every day that jungle surgery is performed at the point.

Before long Butch and company are within the low walls of the restaurant where he does his best to mimic the English gentry, bowing like Sir Walter Bloody Raleigh.

'Fine morning we have here young man,' he says in a clipped English accent. 'And as you can see I'm here as promised. Can't keep the patient waiting. What! What!' Butch straightens up from a full theatrical bow, and sweeps his arm in true Shakespearean style, acknowledging the rest of the clan. 'My medical support team as you might call them,' he says. Butch has a gleeful smile on his face. Mick is grinning like the proverbial cat and Gus is practically drooling with so much anticipation you'd swear he was on heat. I focus on – No, actually, I fixate on a foot long scroll of green canvas that has magically appeared in Butch's left hand.

'What the hell is that?'

'Tools of the trade young man. Tools of the trade. But before the skulduggery begins, a surgeon must first feast on a hearty breakfast.'

He clicks his fingers above his head, and calls out, 'Waiter! Waiter! Bring me your finest! Your finest I tell you, and pray do not disappoint me else the scalpel may slip!'

Butch is served no faster than the next budding surgeon, but once served, he proceeds to gorge his way through his breakfast. This is no pleasant sight, neither are the devilish smiles he casts my way between hungry mouthfuls.

Once breakfast is over, he stands up and delivers a command.

*Christ now he thinks he's Bligh on the HMS Bounty!*

'Clear that table there lads! And throw a boardbag or two on top of it! Poor bastard should at least have some form of creature comfort.'

Gus grabs a couple of boardbags down from the rafters and lays them across the table.

'Right. Up ya get cobber and let's get you started.'

With my heart in my mouth and a pulsating leg at the extreme I climb up onto the makeshift theatre table and lay down.

'Remember that's my fucking leg down there you crazy bastard, so you go easy with the steel. This is no dress rehearsal. OK!'

At times like this I wish I had taken up some form of meditation. Where I wish I had delved into a world of effective escapism instead of spending long hours down the pub mastering how to pot the black ball off three cushions. I could have been a black belt Buddhist by now and would be able to whisk my way off to some sweet floral paradise, or wander off lonely as a cloud. Our eyes meet and I am witness to a strange grin seeping from the Butcher's mouth. Mick lays out a heap of cloths and bandages, while Butch unfurls the 'green scroll' on an adjacent table, exposing the tools of his trade.

I turn to look at them. They're shiny. No, they are more than shiny, they're positively glistening as they reflect sunlight from each razor edged blade. In their pristine condition they even smell sharp, and as if to prove this I get a whiff of surgical spirit fresh from the tempered steel.

*They look so useable, so efficient. Jesus, they look so fucking sharp.*

If you were to come across them in a pawnshop you would buy them, even if you didn't need them. They look that enticing. They look that fucking dangerous. One scroll of very very sharp surgical tools with which to perform surgery.

On a friend perhaps?
At a remote beach.
In a restaurant.
On a wooden table.
In the middle of a fucking jungle.
And 'Oh, what a poor sad sod your friend would be'.

Dogstick Mick is the designated theatre nurse for the forthcoming ordeal. He is given the title of *Swabber*, and is barking orders to another member of the medical team, namely Gus. Gus is the self appointed anaesthetist. He sings, I am *The Gasman, (I am the Walrus goo goo g'joob)*, as he dances around the restaurant enjoying his newly found status. And, as any anaesthetists worth their pound of salt, it is their job to prepare a suitable sedative to deaden the ensuing pain, and so Mick grabs the bottle of arak and some fresh orange juice. I down the heavily laden cocktail but the effect on me does little to alleviate the concern welling up inside. The fact that my foot is splayed on an improvised operating table, in the middle of the jungle, and is about to be operated on by Butch, is like having an enormous crocodile in the room: It's all consuming. I knock back another couple of neat shots from the bottle, but it doesn't work. All I can do then, is to ready myself on a makeshift pillow of beach towels and prepare for the inevitable: The ensuing first slice.

Butch finishes washing his hands in a bowl of hot water procured from the kitchen. Mick the Swabber cleans around the infected area with Betadine. Gus looks at Mia and Mia looks on as Butch selects a surgical tool from his array of 'steeley' knives.

I take a peek at my foot, lying there at the end of the table, and see that the Swabber's job is done. Then the Surgeon's voice segues between my thoughts.
'Here we go then Rhys. Just lie still for me cobber and it'll all be over before your Aunty climbs off your fat Uncle Albert.'
He says it so matter-of-fact. Even the joke is delivered as a statement, and a small part of me hopes that he's not actually going to go through with it, but on the contrary, Butch takes up the scalpel and makes a clean incision deep into my foot.

And it hurts.
A lot.
In fact it hurts like a bitch!!

I let out an agonising, but controlled series of muted grunts, as *The Stranglers* pump out their 1977 debut single, 'Get a Grip On Yourself', from the nearby stereo. Somebody in the entourage obviously thought this would be amusing, and perhaps it is, but it's lost on me as Butch wiggles the steel around inside my foot, searching for the cause of the infection.

The pain is unbearable.

Mia sees that I am in sheer agony and am not coping well. She tries to comfort me with a smile and an affectionate cool cloth to my forehead. A small amount of saliva dribbles from the side of my mouth, which is deftly wiped away by Swabber Mick. I look up into the rafters of the restaurant and begin to count the twisted beams, to at least try and take my mind off the fact that Butch has begun cutting even deeper into my foot.

He is still searching.
Still probing.
Still slicing.

I don't want to be here. Lying on this table. In the middle of a jungle. Undergoing surgery. This is not how a tropical holiday is meant to be, laced with pangs of nauseating pain and an open festering wound.

It hurts.
A lot.
Have I said that already?
If I did, then please excuse me.
It's because I'm in so much fucking pain.

The surgeon slips the scalpel in a little deeper, circumnavigating the freshly man-made hole. The arak is finally taking effect but is only serving to slightly dull my senses. It is not taking away the pain.

*Surely, after having had a couple of hefty shots, there shouldn't be so much…*
*…AAAAAHHHHH!…Fucking…Pain!*

It floods.
Torrents of tiny red hot needles pierce my nervous system causing me to cry out in full blown agony.
I rasp between teeth, 'Jesus fucking Christ Butch! What the fuck's going on? I'm really fucking hurting here mate.'
The sweat drips.
Gasman Gus, looks at the Swabber.
Swabber Mick, looks at the Surgeon.
Surgeon Butch looks at them both.
Then all the lads look at Mia, but Mia has turned away…because there's so much blood.

The Swabber grabs a cloth and passes it to the surgeon. The surgeon attempts to stem the bleeding.

'Streuth mate is there meant to be so much blood?' the Gasman asks, and from the worry lines on his face I can tell he's concerned. Even from my position I can see a pool of green tinged blood running onto the boardbags. My level of anxiety has moved up a batch of notches.

'The blood Butch. What's with all the fucking blood?'

It stinks. I can smell it. We can all smell it.

Butch looks me straight in the eyes. All blue steel and knowing.

'The blood's normal Rhys. The bleeding is good mate. It's pushing all of the infection out of your body. It's a good thing, ok. A good thing. Besides, there isn't that much. It looks like a lot because it's mixed with all of the shit and pus that has been stored in the swelling. We're almost done now. Hang in there cobber. Just hang on and you'll be back in the surf before you know it.'

Butch then removes the pressure bandage and true to his word the blood flow has been stemmed but the level of pain I'm experiencing is accelerating at a rate of knots. Butch moves up from my foot and looks me dead to straights.

'Rhys. Listen to me now cobber. I am going to have to stitch you up ok. This is gonna' hurt like a bitch. Hang in there mate. We're nearly done.'

But when Butch attempts the first suture into the raw wound it is all too much. A tsunami of pain rolls up from my foot and through the inside of my thigh, hitting my groin with a hefty double thwack. My ego has packed up and left the building, leaving the animal in me to let loose a guttural roar.

Gasman Gus is worried so he puts forward the following suggestion.

'Look mate I know it goes against the grain, but I reckon you should *Chase the Dragon*.'

'Yeah. Dragon!' I hiss. 'Get me the fucking Dragon.'

So, with the intensity of pain beyond endurance, my anaesthetist runs off to Chandana's medical store.

To fetch the heroin.

Gus places a small mound of the brown powder onto a piece of tin foil, then holds a lighter underneath. This causes the heroin to form a bubbling ball, which then rolls across the foil, vapourising as it moves. I lean over the foil and eagerly suck up this dragon's breath with a shortened straw.
In long, deep breaths.

Down.
Down.
Down.

It takes only a few moments for the vapour to enter my body and take control. Soon I find myself thinking about Hunter S Thompson and the studying of electric snakes. Then I'm off, riding in a boat full of Chi, gently gliding down serene rapids made from folds of fluid silk. I am no longer on the table in the restaurant, but have been released into the World of Opiates, where panpipes play familiar tunes from my childhood, all soft and pillow nestling.
Opiates.
Another first in a chain of overseas experiences.
So pleasantly soporific.

*Then from the rapids I sail back in time, to the Sixteenth Century. Into the Great Dark Wood (Coed-y-Dugoed Mawr) in Merionethshire, and fly with the Tylwyth Teg, the Welsh 'fairy folk', who live in dens in the ground. They are blessed with fiery red hair and long strong arms, and we steal sheep and cattle by night together. And still I float with them and we have just bagged our last steer and neither are we entirely good nor are we completely bad.*
*We just are.*

My foot is still throbbing as Butch tucks in a truss of stitches to hold his handiwork together, but now there is only a dull ache instead of the searing pain and blood tears. My body is aware of the tugging and trussing, but my mind is on shores afar. The heroin has worked its magic. It takes me a while to work out that Butch is staring down at me and is holding a pair of tweezers to my face.
'There's the little beauty me old spinach. See it? Black sea urchin spine. It had worked itself all the way into your foot, but there's nothing left in there now. The wound's all cleaned up.

*The Surgeon.*

He's been promoted from Butch-*er*, and he rightly deserves it. After all, the guy's a middle-of-the-jungle operating legend!

'You'll have to keep it dry for seven days though cobber,' he says. 'A week for the piss weak,' he laughs. And as the others laugh with him I twist over the table's edge, and vomit; spewing out the Dragon's filthy bile.

## PEANUTS

It is Day 7 after the surgery and the length of time out of the water has been an eternity. At least this time I'm not confined to my bed with a painfully swollen appendage, swotting mozzies and flicking through The Lonely Planet Guide, looking for that remote unridden wave. Instead, I am sitting up at the restaurant with leg and eyebrows raised, as Mia lies close by with a G-string dividing her shapely European form.

The surf is good today, a couple of metres, fluid, and beckoning me with its mocking furls and cumulus curls. And today is the day on which Butch extracted my sutures, which he did sometime between dawn and freedom. Although closed, the wound on my foot still looks a little angry and so I have decided to spend one more day out of the water, just to be on the safe side, as I sure as hell don't want to go through all of that shit again.

'Got a surprise for ya cobber,' says Butch, as he walks up from the beach, salty from his three hour surf session. 'Me and the boys were talking out in the water and figure a trip to Peanuts is in order. Been a while since we've been there and checked out the break.'
'Yeah thought we'd fire up the old jeep and head off tomorrow morning,' says Dogstick Mick, following up behind. 'Whaddayya reckon?'

The only Peanuts I knew of was the infamous nightclub in the heart of Kuta, Bali, however the place the boys are talking about is a secret surf spot located further down the coast.
'Sounds awesome. Gus in on it?'
'Naw,' grins Mick. 'It's his turn to go to Colombo with Chandana for supplies, but you can be sure we'll give him all the goss' when he gets back.'

The following morning the game is afoot and so here we are, eyeing up Mick's ex military open-top jeep, complete with collapsible windscreen and aging camouflage. It is a beast to be reckoned with and sure as hell has adventure written all over it. It looks like something straight out of the TV series, MASH. We tie the boards onto the roof rack, load up the back with the day's necessities then clamber into the rear of this war machine. It is a bit of a push here and a polite shove there as Mick's in-laws and wife have also tumbled in for the ride. All up there are six of us: Mick, Mick's wife, Mick's in-laws, Butch and myself. It's a bit of a squeeze, but worth it for this 4 x 4 fun-packed adventure.

Unlike the west coast of Sri Lanka, populated with its abundance of tropical flora, the east coast resembles more of a mix of tropical plant life and the Australian bush. As we bounce along the terrain there's fire in our blood and a song in our heart. I delight my fellow passengers with a rendition of a famous Welsh hymn, called *Calon Lan*, Welsh for '*A Pure Heart*'. As I finish the hymn and the clapping and hooting subsides, a tyre bursts and the jeep lurches to the right, putting us straight into a large pothole. In doing so this sends Arjuna, Mick's father in-law, tumbling out of the jeep and onto the track. Mick hits the brakes but in the soft dirt the jeep skids for ten metres or more, careering out of control. Mick twists the steering wheel this way and that, fighting to bring the machine under control and with a little help from the Gods, eventually manages to bring us to a dead stop, directly in front of a large jeep-crushing tree. The five of us breathe a sigh of relief at our near miss and pile out. As Arjuna joins us, with a smile, we see that his pride is intact, unlike the war machine, which has picked up a few extra scrapes during the ordeal. It's time to change the busted tyre, however we soon discover that the jeep is minus a lifting jack.

'This is being no problem,' says Arjuna who signals that we should follow him into the bush to hunt for a 'bush-jack'. As we traipse closely behind, Arjuna turns and in his local dialect speaks the words, *naja naja*, wiggling his hand theatrically as he does so.

'Hey Dog-Stick. What's he saying?' I ask our resident translator.

'Aw, nothing mate, just keep your mince pies peeled for any cobras that's all.'

'Cobras! Whaddaya mean cobras?'

'Joe-Blakes mate. Keep a lookout for any snakes.' Mick has said it so matter-of-factly, and I guess coming from Australia snakes are an accepted way of life for him, but for someone who comes from an Isle where snakes are practically non-existent this is not happy news. I am now looking and listening for the slightest movement or sound of any reptilian wildlife. I am a David Attenborough clone on safari, with eyes darting about like Marty Feldman.

'Snake! Snake!' shouts Butch a minute later.

I panic and am racing my knees up and down faster than Mrs Brown, before quickly hopping up onto to a nearby log. The boys are in stitches and the laughter, being so loud, could no doubt be heard by the two ladies back at the jeep.

'Ha! 'Gotcha' that time me old spinach. Snake! Snake!' laughs Butch.

We travel another twenty metres or so before Arjuna stops at a suitably long and well-girthed limb. Soon we are trailing back to the jeep, with him sporting our very own bush-jack across his capable shoulders.

Back at the vehicle I grab a large rock to use as a fulcrum and place it under the limb. Meanwhile Mick chocks the wheels with a couple of stones to stop it from rolling forwards then grabs the spare wheel and brace from the back of the jeep. Butch loosens the wheel-nuts then Arjuna, Mick and myself lean down heavily on the limb, lifting the jeep easily. Butch quickly springs into action and has the old wheel off and the new wheel on in pit-stop time. We jump back in, Mick fires up the old girl and once again we are off on our adventure.

When we arrive at the coast we park right on the beach, where there's not an Inspector in sight. In fact there's not a soul in sight, only the soothing Indian Ocean and a short stretch of beach on which are strewn large ocean-worn, metamorphic boulders. They are partially buried in the sand and resemble beached humpbacked whales, similar to the ones Aimee and I snorkelled around in Hikkaduwa. Further up the beach, other lumps of granite help to form a natural groyne, which stretches out to sea and where a decent right-hander is breaking. It looks as if it could be fun, yet as I am walking along the beach I can't help but notice these strange marks in the sand.

Sliding marks.
Dragging marks.
Unnerving marks.

'Hey Dog-Stick, you're not going to tell me these are sodding croc' tracks are you?' I yell after him.

'Nah. Wouldn't do that to a mate, mate!' he shouts back. 'Just keep an eye out is all!'

Eye out! Jesus Christ my arse couldn't be any tighter if it was playing a bugle at an Arctic nudist camp. First snakes, and now bloody crocodiles. I can't say I'm fond of sharks but at least they only eat when they're hungry, unlike a croc' which will larder you like a granny stockpiling after the war.

We stop a short while later at the foot of the groyne. Mick's in-laws begin building a triangular makeshift shelter from coconut fronds to protect them from the searing sun. Meanwhile we break out our boards and begin waxing up in readiness for our jaunt into the tepid unknown.

I am enjoying the sensation of the ocean running over my body. It feels so pleasurable as it washes away the last fifteen days of trauma. The idea of a prehistoric amphibian lurking out to sea weren't far from my thoughts, however after a few fun-filled waves the fear of predators has now dissipated. I'm almost at the line-up when I look to my right and see Mick picking off a nice right-hander. He snaps at the lip, pushes hard with his back foot, bringing the board around in an arc and grins as he sends a spray of white water straight into my face, before shooting off down the line.

I guess we have been surfing for about two hours now, enjoying each other's company, and the fact that it is just us with no crowds. Suddenly I spot something further out to sea…and to me it looks like a croc'! Or is it a croc'? The sun is bouncing off the ocean's surface, making it impossible to tell for sure, especially having never seen one in the ocean before. It looks like a coconut log trailing in the water, but I'm unable to convince myself that the waterlog fronds aren't the tail of a hungry beast. I keep watching this imaginary monster moving in the current, desperately trying to prove that there's nothing to worry about, but I can't shake the tendrils of paranoia that are wrapped firmly around my imagination.

*It is only a coconut trunk, right? Not a croc'? Surely it can't be a croc'?*

But as I continue to watch this figment of reptilian mass I realise that something's wrong. The object is actually moving 'against' the current. It shouldn't be where it is. I see that it is making a B-line for us all. This waterlogged spiny coconut tree trunk has metamorphosed into a real predator and has me bricking myself...again! Christ, if I had a robe and a pair of sandals I swear I could jump up and run to the beach. Now having taken on its true form, it's that close, perhaps less than eighty metres away, without waiting for a wave I turn my board and begin paddling towards the beach. In my haste though I have lain too far up my board and in doing so have caused the front of my board to dip into the water. It is called 'pearling' in surfing jargon and consequently I am upended into the ocean, and now find myself thrashing about in the water, with appetising legs below. I quickly grab my board and clamber back on, however panic has rolled into the station and all I can think about is steam-rolling out of the water as quickly as possible.

*Feet.*
*Cuts.*
*Ulcers.*
*Pain.*
*Jungle surgery.*

I have dismissed any thoughts of self-preservation. I've locked into 'escape-mode'.

*Cuts.*
*Pain.*
*Jungle surgery.*
*Fuck the consequences!*

Without a care I paddle straight over to the rocky groyne, throw my board away and begin to clamber up the barnacle encrusted rocks. However, a new set of waves arrives and I am lifted upward by the swell and dragged back over the rocks by the receding white water of the broken wave. My scarred feet have again become sliced with further lacerations, but I don't care. All I can think about is how fast can a croc' swim? I have to get back onto my board, as the groyne is a spent option. My board is close but when I look I see that it is being held up vertically, half-in and half-out of the water. My leash is stretched taught between my ankle and my board, and not shifting. My board is being held in the same spot and is called 'tomb-stoning' in surfing terms, *but for Christ's sake, enough of the terminology, let's get the fuck out of here!* The turbulence then subsides without warning,

allowing the leash to do its work and ping the board back toward me. I pull it under my body and belly board like crazy toward the beach, passing Mick and Butch as they are paddling back out.
'Croc' boys! It's a fuckin' croc!'
'Yeah. Yeah. Sure Rhys. Snake! Snake!' the boys call out, practically in unison at my supposed joke.
'No! No! Really!' I shout back. 'There's a fucking croc' out there. Get out now!' Then I'm past and into the shallows, and safe. But the boys are still paddling out, straight into the beast's path.

I stand up, look seawards and see the solitary mass moving even closer to Mick and Butch. Now it's Arjuna who shouts out the words of warning, 'Crocodile Mick! Crocodile!' The warning, now having come from Mick's father-in-law, has the boys realising that it's no revengeful prank. From my position on the beach I see that the croc' is practically upon them. It's only metres away, perhaps twenty, before it dips and disappears beneath the ocean's surface. We are all shouting from the shore in mass panic. Arjuna is waving his arms frantically. I'm shouting as loud as I can for them to paddle harder and faster and the two girls have quite literally burst into tears. The boys turn quickly, paddling for their lives and pick up the white water of a broken wave. The croc' is still nowhere to be seen and I wonder as I watch them belly-boarding to the beach, 'How fast *can* a croc' swim?' Although the crocodile is nowhere to be seen, we know where it is. It's somewhere under the boys, perhaps trailing them to shallower water? Arjuna and I are still shouting, willing the boys on. And they are close now. I am praying that we'll not witness a flash of grey, nor a twisting of prehistoric mass as it latches onto one of my friends. We wait and I feel that my heart is just about to burst. Christ, where the hell is that croc'? But there's no flash of grey, no mixing of blood with salt water, no gore. The boys have made it. They have escaped and are now running toward us through ankle deep water.

As they leave the shallows they both look shaken. The croc' could have only been metres away from their legs before they caught the whitewater to shore. Mick takes his sobbing wife into his arms whilst Arjuna is shaking Butch's hand vigorously.
'Bad croc' today Butch. Very bad croc', he says. 'You lucky boys today Butch. Very lucky boys.'

When Butch looks at me I give him a surgeon's grin, then flick my tongue in and out and sound out a revengeful reptilian *hiss*, much to my amusement.

We all turn to watch the ocean's surface and before long see the reptilian local surface in the shallows, right where the boys were, then cut its own silent course parallel to the beach. It must have been that close, but nobody says a word. Instead we decide that the day's surfing is done and dusted, so we pack up our belongings and head back to the jeep. It's a nervous walk, as we know that the croc' is still around and has more than likely left the ocean. We load the gear and boards quickly and when safely in the jeep agree that there was a clear and distinct message from our newfound acquaintance.

*I eat people.*

The following day I pack up my belongings having told the crew that I am heading back to the west coast with my freshly acquired wounds to use the medical amenities of Hikkaduwa. Besides, the season on the east coast is coming to an end. The onshore winds will soon be prevalent whilst the west coast winds will soon begin to blow offshore, plus Hikkaduwa should be picking up some decent swell round about now.

At the point I have met such good people, and as we have become like family it is all the more difficult saying goodbye. I bid a fond farewell to the lads, we exchange addresses, hugs, and a couple of friendly punches here and there and talk about catching up in Bali. With Mia it's a warm sibling's embrace and a vow to stay in touch forever. It's been both fun and trying at times at The Bay. I've laughed, surfed and screamed for the dragon and know that because of this I will always carry a small piece of the Point with me wherever I go: Probably in my feet.

I head to Pottuvil to catch the bus back west, knowing that I'm in for a long hot ride, but what I couldn't know of is the existence of a pile of letters sitting at Hikkaduwa Post Office:
And one of them is *pink*.

## HOBBIT

Months at The Bay have passed. It is now November and Hikkaduwa welcomes me with its flavoursome aroma of coconut oil and culinary treats. As I glance up the street I feel its vibrant soul meandering from one structure to the next, ducking in and out of each shanty shack, connecting the whole village in communal unison. I trek off jungle-side, over the railway line and past the swamps to Sunny's house. I feel like I'm coming home.

Sunny happens to be outside and greets me with bright white teeth and a brotherly wiggle of the head.

I wiggle back.
My first wiggle.

As we enter the house I feel a strange emotional pull as I realise two of the other three rooms in the house now have tenants. I am delighted for Sunny as it means more money for his family, but also a little jaded as I am no longer the family jewel. In the room adjacent to mine is another Welsh lad going by the name of Tyrone, which is about the only thing going for him as he has about as much money as a pensioner at a slot machine. He hails from the Valleys, where the accent is thick, the rugby serious and the beer fluid. Tyrone has sold most of his possessions so that he can prolong his stay on the island, but has retained two; namely his navy blue G-string, which is partially camouflaged by his other possession, an orange-coloured lungi. His frame, a hungry mutt couldn't even nibble on, is topped with a balding head and when he speaks he whistles all of his 'esses'. When you listen to Tyrone talk it's like listening to an antique kettle speak.

Tyrone makes a little money on the street touting the virgin tourists for local shops, tour guides and restaurants and wonders why the gays in the village choose to follow him around, wanting to fondle his arse. Tyrone's effeminate, not gay, but choosing to bounce his tackle around like some fishing lure is bound to draw in a flurry of gropers. He seems more queer than 'Queen'. Denies it of course. But who truly knows in which wardrobe a gay lion slumbers?

In one of the other rooms is his travelling mate, Tony. Tony's a five foot ten, square shouldered Scouser, hailing from the borough of Wirral. He has a broad smile and a subtle sense of humour that slips between your ribs while you're still laughing at his last pun. They're both great guys and an act to watch, as Tony often delivers slicing blows to Tyrone's self-esteem, piercing him under the weight of his northern genetically-borne humour. We make friends instantly and ease into a few arak cocktails. Blurry eyed and giggling like a schoolie, Tyrone begins to tell us how to fuck a cow…in the correct manner of course!

'Look it'z like thiz. In Indo, 'that'z Indonezia right, they avz theze cowz whatz beautiful right. I mean absolutely gorgeouss.'

Tony casts an eye in my direction. There's no sense of shock in his eyes, only a knowing look. He's probably heard it all before and is enjoying watching Tyrone reel me in like a nice piece of haddock.

'They're brown, right *mun*, (he uses the familiar Welsh pronoun), lookz like Bambi with big beautiful brown eyez and eyelashez az long az your arm. Well I'm staying with this farmer right and he showz me doesn't he. We're pissed on arak and he showz me. Tailz to the side he sayz. Tailz to the side. So this iz what you duz right. If you wantz to fuck a cow, first you cleanz its arse, coz thatz hygienic, right. Then you pull itz tail to the side to tighten her up. Corss you've got to find something to stand on, like a bucket to fuck-it.' And with that Tyrone laughs fantastically before continuing. 'Brilliant init? And no kidding mind you, they really lovez it!'

There's a moment of stunned silence.
Visual horror.

It is Tony who breaks into this frozen moment. He whispers across to Tyrone, 'Bugger off Ty. You couldn't get laid if you were a Persian carpet in a bare room.' Laughing with us, the authenticity of his fictitious tale questionable, Tyrone says this, 'Fuck, I've got the munchies after all of that sexy talk. Whatz in the fridge mun?'
'Coconuts, bread and jam,' says I. 'But I can do better than that. C'mon. All aboard the Skylarks.' I lead the way outside to our pushbikes and we clamber on, pedals at the ready.

'Where're we off to lad?' asks an excited Tone.
'Mystery trip Boyos! We're going right into the boondocks. Jungle style! Oh and lover boy, no vaulting into the paddocks on the way alright.'
Ty giggles like a one-liner, lending a fraction of credibility to his bovine yarn.

At night it's reasonably dark on the main drag of Hikkaduwa, but we don't turn right out of Sunny's driveway towards the main road, instead we venture left which takes us even deeper into the dark jungle. Into the deep-deep, where the bananas curl and night creatures lurk on limbs above.

It's practically pitch black. I am riding up front, holding the only torch we have, with the boys riding just behind. The weak yellow beam from this poor excuse for a torch is giving us little warning of any impending potholes and exposed rocks. Suddenly there's a rattle and thump from behind. Tyrone has taken a hit. He has bounced off his precarious seat collecting his nuts on the bike's crossbar with gusto.
'Orrrr! Fuckin' hell mun. How much further iz it? My bollocks and arsse can't take much more of thiz.'
'Sssh Ty,' chides Tony. 'Be careful about mentioning your rear end around here lad. Remember we're deep-deep in jungle land and this is quite possibly arse-bandit country.'
'Fuck-coff mun,' replies Ty.
'Haven't gotta cough lad! What are you now, a doctor?' Tony counters.

After a further series of potholes, rocks, ditches and precarious ill lit twists and turns we finally arrive at our destination.
'This is it boys. We have arrived. Behold before you, Bun-house bliss!'
And sure enough we have arrived at a well-guarded jungle secret, for nestled amid the tropical lushness lies a small, hand-built, one-roomed, stone-age bakery, fresh from the past. A sense of magic emanates from its wholesomeness, where at any moment I expect to see a hobbit run out to park our bikes, charging us a silver penny for its trouble. Instead, we set them gently against a nearby wall. The doorway to the bakery is ajar and from within, a soft spiritual light beckons we three wise men to the birth of countless buns.

Inside the oven roars as if belonging in the great hall of Valhalla: Where row upon row of doughy buns are laid out neatly, awaiting their rise to be claimed. As one tray comes out, another tray goes in. It's archaic, but works a treat, like a well-oiled timepiece. It is as if we are in the den of the Warlocks, only in this time warp it is we who are to do the feasting.

I open the door just wide enough for us to squeeze through, causing the three lungi-clad inhabitants to become momentarily transfixed. They take check of our presence, then, seconds later, at the slide of a baker's tray, fall back into their timeless rhythm, reminding me of *Genesis'* carpet-crawlers on backstreet Broadway. In a mix of pidjin English and schoolboy mime we, the 'munchie-prowlers', present our order to these men of the past.

The aroma is all-powerful and enticing. There are hundreds of buns. Sweet buns, meat buns, fig buns, big buns, tall buns, small buns, and banana buns. Basically they've got the lot. Looking around, it has to be said: These guys have bags full of buns! Our hosts bundle up our order in last week's newspaper with nods and smiles and the back-handed money we pay is a welcomed bonus, as the extra cash will find its way to buying a book or some clothing for the little ones at home. And now that we've been served we become overtly aware that a sense of urgency has arisen about our bakers. Because for these men there is the pre-daybreak deadline to make and somewhere out there is a Boss-man, wielding a stick in one hand, and the threat of a jungle UB40 in the other.

The freshness of the early morning is brought on with a shower of slime and while in here I once again check the leg wounds collected during my recent croc' encounter. I clean them up, the worst being around the ankles. Thankfully they were relatively superficial and are manageable enough without the local quack's assistance. A lucky escape, plus Tony has given me a course of precious antibiotics which should have the wounds cleared up in five days or so. I grab some electrical tape and a plastic bag to protect the most damaged foot should I decide on a quick swim, then head off for an island breakfast at a beachside café called Buddes Restaurant.

I order toast, laden with garlic, a cheese omelette and a filthy local coffee that tastes delicious if you hold your nose tightly and think of Colombia. I order it from Darcy, the local waiter.

Darcy is an elderly waiter who has probably outlived many of the dilapidated structures dotted around this beachside haven. Even in this heat his shirt is buttoned up to the top-notch and his white lungi, both starched to the height of perfection, belay a character of virtuous pride. He glides around the tables more than he appears to walk. It's like being served by the nun from the movie, The Blues Brothers. If it weren't for the fact that you can see his shoeless feet, you'd swear he was on roller skates. He is a fine and noble man is our Darcy. Darcy's welcoming grin is a tonic and behind his eyes there is always an expectant twinkle. Regardless of the number of patrons in the restaurant I always get gold class service, as every now and then I slip him a few extra rupees. It is a game we play, like a couple of budding 007's.

A sleight of hand.
An acceptant nod.
And breakfast as quick as you like.

So with the deal done and breakfast finished I decide it is time for a quick dip in the ocean to massage the aches and loosen up the muscles. Buddes Restaurant, like many others, finishes on the shifting sand and as I glide down the short sand bank to the waters edge I can't help but think how perfect this all feels, despite having a plastic bag taped over one of my feet. The ocean gently laps between my five exposed toes as I move in to take my dip. I spin onto my back and marvel at the sights before me. Looking south, the beach stretches away to Hikkaduwa's main break and at intervals there are several small restaurants gently poking their noses out onto the sand. From my vantage point I can see the Dewa Siri where I met Aimee, *ah mon amie*, while further down the coast is the Casalanka restaurant and the memories of my body surfing fracas.

Then, having concluded my morning's salty bath, I decide to cycle to the post office to check if I've any mail. By the time I have walked back through Buddes, said a fond farewell to Darcy, and am astride my two-wheeled trusty steed, I am practically dry.

## PINKY

My bicycle is a law unto its self. Not that they make it go any faster, but my pushbike is strewn with an assortment of coloured streamers that flap wildly from the handlebars. The bike belongs to my local friend, Siri, it is new, and in paying him mate's rates, it is mine for the duration of my stay. The other poor excuses for pushbikes that rattle along the tracks and tarmac, are left quivering from its magnificence. As I saunter along Galle Road toward the main town of Hikkaduwa, with my cheap paraphernalia fluttering in the wind, I think how such trivial extravagance can bring on a smile. And you can witness the same sense of nonsensical satisfaction in the faces of Indian truck drivers, whose thundering machines are mobile shrines, all decked out in true Bollywood brilliance. All flare, glare, bold, gold, and the fucking bollocks.

Having been in Arugam Bay these past few months I'm excited, as the chance of getting friends' and family letters is better than good. But I don't rush it, because I choose to enjoy the moment. I ride past the Cool Spot Restaurant, where you can buy the most excellent red banana curry. Then past Rangith's Ice-Cream Parlour, who will delight you with his limited selection of vanilla, strawberry or chocolate ice cream, served in tubs, and eaten while enjoying a friendly game of backgammon. Past the Coral Seas which serves up the tastiest crab soup, then past the Blue Ocean with its colourful array of arak cocktails. All such wonderful places, each harbouring their own hidden gems.

It's a casual twenty-minute ride to Hikkaduwa's main town, where a conglomeration of dusty shops sell just about anything. I see well-branded paints, mozzie coils, tin pots, tin pans, Lanka Gas bottles, rice sacks, open bags of spices, bicycle parts and fistfuls of bananas strewn up on metal hooks. Basically, you can get absolutely anything you need in the town of Hikkaduwa: That is, if you have chosen to live out a meagre existence.

Halfway through the town I veer right, taking a back road to the main post office. I park my bike and go in.

It is dark.

It is always dark inside the building, regardless of the weather. The post office has that heavy bees wax smell, customary of colonial furniture. It is usually calming, but today it does little to stem my excitement.

I queue.
I wait patiently.
I wait for a little longer than I care to, but when it is my turn to collect the clerk turns to me and hands over no less than fourteen letters.

Fourteen! A real treasure trove.

There are four from my mother, two from my father, one from each of my two brothers, five from close friends and one that is pink. The pink one, the fourteenth, sits beneath the pile.

Almost hidden.
And it is pink.
And it is perfumed.
Flipping it over, I read the sender's address.
Mel's.

Callous Mel.
Hell Mel.
My ex-Mel.

I hold the letter up to the light, turning it over and over, looking for a safe way in.

> *Oh, how a moment like this must be nurtured.*
> *Oh, how a moment like this must be gently caressed.*

As I twirl Mel's letter between my fingers I realise that I have said this out loud.

To everyone.
Within my daydream.
But out loud.

It is an embarrassing moment and I smile at those watching, then leave quickly. In fact I practically skip out of the post office. Moments later I'm back on my bike, pushing off to find a quiet space to read the letter, the Pink One. And I know just the spot.

Beachside, there's an old fishing boat washed up on a vacant lot. She lies there within her own abandonment, quietly and without fuss. Her name is Thora and she lies there as seven metres of silent sea tales. She has no cabin now, but several pieces of loose petrified planks about her deck and a wooden box, mid-ship, which once covered her engine. She lists on the sand in such a way that she provides me perfect cover for my covert operation. I sit down and rest against her welcoming bow, facing the ocean. It is just the three of us.

Just Thora,
Pinkie,
and Me.

In front of where we sit is a local surf break called Bennys. There is a small swell gently rolling in, licking the reef beneath, trying its best to muster up a clean right-hander. I stare at the letter in my left hand.
There are two ways to open a letter. You can choose to carefully slice down the full length of it, or you can simply tear the hell out of it. Those letters that are to be ripped ragged, scanned quickly, then discarded, are the junk mail of life. They hold no importance. But a letter from a soulless woman does: Because such a letter will have impact. Therefore a letter such as this must be grasped firmly and sliced open in a deliberate manner. A letter such as this must be opened with the utmost caution, so that your emotional well-being remains steadfast. And, as you know, if there's one thing you need when opening a 'bitch-letter', it's a solid dose of emotional stability.
And fortitude.
You need fortitude too - just in case.
And so with the envelope held firmly in one hand I slide my elongated thumbnail into the envelope's crevice and slice in a slow and deliberate manner. The envelope opens and lays its contents bare like a prised oyster. I remove the single page of perfumed paper and a solitary sigh escapes my lips. And that stab of momentary dread that preceded the sigh - well, I hadn't expected that.
The letter sits on my lap.

Folded.
Safe.
I think of Zeus and of Pandora's Box and of all the evil that spilled from it; once opened.

Because if I don't unfold it. If I don't open it I'll remain safe. If I don't unfold it and I don't read it, then the status quo stands fast. Life will go on as before, with me gliding from one day to the next. If I don't read this pink letter of Mel's, then I'll remain untouched.

Unburdened.
Protected.
If I don't read it, I'll be ok.

But I do.
I go ahead and unfold it.
Then I go ahead and read it.
And this is what it says…or at least the gist of it.

*My Darling Rhys.*

*I am missing you so much. I realise now how much you mean to me and how I know that we are meant to be together.*

My mouth becomes dry.

*I have told Dad that I am leaving the firm for a while and coming out to be with you.*

WHOOSH!

My head reels.

Boom!
Boom!
Boom!

*I have bought my air ticket and will be arriving on April 1st.*

Sudden shortness of breath.
Finding it difficult to breathe.
Heart racing and head spinning.

*Mel's coming.*
*April 1ˢᵗ.*
*April Fools Day*

The irony of it draws a wry smile, only to be wiped clean by the memory of a dirty betrayal.

*My Mel.*
*Naked.*
*With him.*
*Fucking.*
*Coming together.*
*Both of them.*
*Coming together.*
*Being together.*
*Both of us.*
*Mel and me.*
*Together.*
*In Sri Lanka.*

…and I can almost hear Le Carré's Little Drummer Girl drumming.

I read the letter again and again and my cold heart begins to warm, cracking the icy foundation of my resolution. Each heartfelt word has caused my defences to melt.

My castle stormed.
My keep so easily breached.
I fold the letter, lay it on my lap, close my eyes, and whisper to myself,

*God, the Devil drives a hard bargain…*

And to share with you the gravity of this letter. To share with you the enormity of its impact I should mention that how could I know that this letter, full of its whispery words and idyllic promises, is nothing more than a poisonous catalyst. That this pink letter laying lightly on my lap will set off a chain reaction taking us both into a place of heavily armed police, Class-A drugs and a world of pain.

In the light of my recent and confusing discovery, and the fact that the beach is only a stone's throw away, a swim is needed. I jump up, touch Thora for good luck, and head down to the ocean.

*To hell with the wounds, I'll tend to them later.*

The ocean is perfect and although bodily soothing, does little to dispel my underlying anxiety. As I look back toward the shoreline, with its serene tropical beauty, I imagine my Mel walking down to the water.

Her head held high.
The subtle swing of her arms.
Her shoulders square.
The sway of those model hips.
The parade of a perfect 10 body.
All sex and confidence.
All fiercely charismatic.
All so uncontrollably consuming *is* love.

April 1$^{st}$ is two months away, but it can't come soon enough, as my sense of longing stings for her sensual embrace.

The five minute ride back to the house is all spinning rims and wide-mouth grins. I am so happy I feel like a divine being, and if I didn't have my bike with me I swear I could flap my arms and fly back to Sunny's. I park my bike and walk into the house to find Tony and Tyrone there.
'Fuckin' Hell mun. You just got your end away or what boyo? Look at him Tone. Have you ever seen such a happy chappy. Come by here mun and spill the beanz to your old matez. Gives us all the goss like.'

Tyrone, Tony and I have spent many late nights bearing our souls, trying to wash away the dirt tainting our past. We are kindred spirits and so I give the boys the bare bones of the letter and in doing so the enormity of what has just happened hits home. I feel overwhelmed with the fact that my world has just been turned upside down.

And just like that. It's done.
My life sliced wide open.
With only pen to paper.
I need a diversion, something to take my mind off this dilemma. Something else to do instead of hanging around in this house.

'Bollocks to this! The surf's pretty well flat. What say we blow this taco-stand for a couple of days and head up to Colombo for the Navam Perahera Festival.'

'Pera what?' says Tone.

'Navam Perahera Festival, you heathen.'

I had recently read about this festival in a tourist pamphlet at Rangith's Ice-cream Parlour so I lay on the 'smart-arse spin'.

'I believe it's to commemorate the day the Buddha made two of his greatest followers his disciples, some two and a half thousand years ago. It's where they dress up about one hundred elephants in lights and shrines, then parade them through the streets. There're firecrackers, all different types of bands playing, there's acrobats and whip dancers. I reckon it'll be a blast!'

'Whoo…hoo! Listen to Mr Holiday Snaps here,' says Tony. 'Whaddaya do? Swallow the Lonely Planet Guide?'

'Whip danserz ey?' whistles an excited Ty, whose eyes have glazed over. 'Can't remember the last time I was whipped.'

I look over at Tone with an, 'I don't even want to go there' look.

And he reciprocates. Neither of us wants to visit another one of Ty's tales. Not now at least, 'coz we're off to meet the pachyderms.

## FRIENDLY GEORGE

I stuff the bare essentials into a backpack, namely: Passport, money, toiletries, water, music tapes and spare clothes. Then I take a fresh slimy shower, wait until the boys have done likewise, before we all embark on another funny-walk along the train tracks bound for Hikkaduwa train station.

Arriving at the platform we find we have enough time to devour some filthy string hoppers, which is a soft circular noodle cake, dipped in curry sauce. They taste great, but are a dead set recipe for mass indigestion and fierce heartburn, with further consequential bowel movements if you're not accustom to their toll. As we finish our final dips into the gravy-like sauce, the old steam locomotive is heard in the distance and the platform busies itself for the ensuing attack. We push, squeeze, and shove with the rest of the clan, finally clambering aboard to find a bit of arse-space on a wooden slat, and subsequently zone out for the ride.

Three plus hours later we pull into the main train station at Colombo and head straight for the Ex-Serviceman's Hotel on Bristol Street. It isn't much to look at but it's 'clean-ish' and cheap, and has obviously been made from truckloads of concrete. It is not pretty, but it's functional and dominates the street with its wide five story high façade, full of wrought iron rectangular windows and sweeping stone steps. At the top of the steps and set into this wall of concrete is a pair of large double wooden doors. We pass through these and find ourselves within a foyer, which is also testament to further truckloads of solidified concrete. Yet for all the cement about us the place has a degree of warmth, which emanates from the soothing wall panels of ebony, cinnamon, teak and calamander that grace the walls around us.

At practically any time of day you can sit down with one of the old boys over a nice cup of tea or a tall glass of beer. These Sri Lankan remnants, these men who have served with the British forces during WWII, can spin a yarn that'll make your hair stand on end.

Unlike their overseas counterparts they are more than willing to share the horrors of their war experience. If the walls of the Ex-Serviceman's could talk, then they would be positively encyclopaedic.

We take room 33, which looks out onto the street and is a haven from the grime of Sri Lanka's capital city. The room is basic, having three single beds, but we are privileged in having our own ensuite in the form of a small wet-room. The ensuite is grimy, wet and smelly, but at least we don't have to share it with squirters and loose dumpers. There is no shower, instead we are to use the 'mandy'. This comprises of a bucket of water and a ladle with which to pour the water over oneself, using a specific technique. First, you douse yourself with two ladles of clean water from the bucket. This is usually enough wetness to enable you to lather up, then using a few more scoops of the ladle you rinse yourself off. It is an art form, soaping up your body, then rinsing it off with a plastic kitchen utensil and using as little water as it takes to make a decent soup. The porcelain drop-toilet is in there too. No flushing, just a well-positioned squat to take care of business. Then using the same 'mandy bucket' you pour an adequate amount of water down the hole until your ablutions are swilled away. Challenging, but necessary, before we change into a fresh set of clothes in readiness for the thriving streets below.

Spit, cleansed and polished we descend the concrete steps of the hotel to the ground floor and leave through the beaming front doors. On heading down to the street, George, from George's Travel Agency, calls over to us.

'You boys. You must be coming and having a beer. We must celebrate the full moon before you are to be going to the festival. I can be giving you all of the most advantageous of places to be watching from. Come! Come!'

George is standing in his doorway and above his door is a purposeful orange sign on which is written, 'George's Travel, Tickets and Information', in fancy yellow writing. The window of George's Travel Agency is plastered in posters, enticingly describing faraway places. There are posters depicting 'Bargain Britain', 'Oslo for Christmas', 'Ski in Italy', and it is ironic to think that in all of these places the inhabitants go to their local travel agents to buy an air ticket to the idyllic isle on which we stand.

He is an easy talker, is George. His manner is that of a friendly uncle, with a warm smile and an enriching presence.

'You boys must be having at least one beer with old George,' he says. And we do. We sit with George for the better part of an hour. As we drink his beer we listen to his local knowledge about the festival, delivered with his own brand of explosive enthusiasm. And George, when he laughs, which he does readily, draws you into his honest and friendly world. George, it appears, has his thumbs hooked into many pies on the Island, and also the ability to put together any travel itinerary you care to challenge him with. And as we sit and listen to him, I cannot imagine that George has ever let anyone down.

George shares with us that he originated from a small village high up on the west coast. Here he lost his family and all his possessions in a violent storm. This raging storm, he explains, ripped up the coconut trees around his home causing them to fall onto his family hut, killing both his wife and infant son. 'I am coming back from working in the plantation when the storm hit. And I am to be breaking down into many pools of tears,' he tells us. 'But now I am saying to you boys that life is a wonderful thing, because now I am having a new family, and am being blessed with three beautiful children. And look,' he says, 'also I am to be having a fine business that I have been building up from the dust of the streets. Long ago I was working these streets, handing out leaflets and now as you can see I am to be having this fine office.'

George lifts both his hands to the sky, palms upwards, closes his eyes for a moment and whispers a short prayer to his God. When he opens his eyes they are crystal clear, refreshed. Then George places his hand on me, over my heart, and looks right at me. I mean he *really* looks at me. I feel as if he is looking deep inside, as if he is putting something there. Something strong. Something permanent. His hand begins to feel hot to the touch. It is a strange and slightly unnerving sensation, a powerful moment where intimacy has its place. Then George muses in his quiet way, 'What could I say to you that would be of value,' he says. 'Except that perhaps you seek too much. That as a result of your longing you will never find what you are looking for. Be patient my friend and all will come to you.'

Then George breaks away, taking his hand from my heart and laughs so fantastically that it startles the three of us. 'Go now you boys and be enjoying yourselves.' George claps his hands rhythmically before opening them in a wide arc. 'Go now my young friends. You are to be free spirits. Free spirits in this world we share! You must be going now and enjoying all of the wonderful things that life is to be offering you. Do not seek too much as good things will come to you. You'll see. Go now. Go.'

We rise to our feet and on leaving George it strikes me that he is one of those people you think you have met before. Mr Déjà vu. A kindred soul you could say. But this is impossible. This is the first time I've met George, with his wide smile and generous ways. But it was not to be the last. Throughout the ensuing months George was to become a good friend of mine, and I of his, although unbeknown to me I was to become a friend in desperate need of his help.

The capital is buzzing with excitement. There are children running crazily along streets and men dancing wildly in the alleys. The crowds are enormous and it feels as if we are part of a major uprising, but instead we are all engaged in a fusion of religious and cultural delight. The three of us manage to squeeze our way to the front of the thronging crowd and await the procession. And when it comes, it comes with gusto.

First to be seen are a dozen men clad in white, swinging long broomsticks to and fro, attached to which are large silver pots with fragrant incense wafting from them. Behind them are the percussionists in red and white garb thumping out a beat at each end of their cylindrical drums, while dancing rhythmically to the sway of their tempo. There are cymbal players, stick players, ladies in rainbow coloured dresses, all dancing wildly to the music. There are conch shell blowers, flag bearers, motorised floats, laden with brightly lit shrines and adorned in garlands of flowers. There are whip crackers and fire-dancers holding life-size catherine wheels, spinning and ablaze in flame. We see men perched on stilts, so tall that a playground seat, suspended by ropes beneath, supports a thrilled child swinging pendulum-like between the walker's legs. There are the Buddhist monks in their plumb coloured robes, bobbing like corks, lending an air of spirituality to the parade as they pass close by.

Then there are the elephants, full of long memories and deep calling, followed closely by the poo-boys whose job it is to shovel up the dolloped steaming business after it has been evacuated onto the road. In all their glory these pachyderms troop past, clad in sequin studded cloth, vibrant in colour and fully adorned from tusk to toenail. Some fabrics are bright red, some shimmering pink, some jade green and some are encased in a blaze of golden weave. These gargantuan silk tarpaulins cover the heads and bulk of each beast, spilling down to their lumbering feet. It is as if we are witness to a prehistoric hippy migration. On top of these beasts I see shrines and lanterns alight, powered by diesel generators being carried behind the elephants on flatbed Toyotas. It is a fantastic melding of Eastern and Western worlds.

The festivities will go well into the wee hours of the night, however we have decided to retreat to Bristol Street. We sit in quiet seclusion on the steps of the Ex-Serviceman's Hotel where we can still hear the humming of the ongoing festivities in the distance. Each of us is smoking a 'single', bought from a kerbside cigarette cart and drinking a tall bottle of crisp, dust-dispersing Lion Lager.

'Way-man that was some parade,' says Tony. 'Absolutely awesome. Did you see those cute little elephant tails Ty? And those whips. Pure joy, wouldn't you say?'
'Listen you moronic ignoramus', counters Tyrone, in his thick Welsh accent. 'You probably wouldn't knowz joy if she sat naked on your lap and rocked on your cock like a porn star.'
At this Tony instantly howls out into the depths of the night, 'Aaahhhh…Moooooover Daisy, I'm coming on in!' and I laugh tremendously, sharing in the wonderful bond that exists between my two fun-packed friends.

## TINSLETOWN

Today the boys have decided to take off for a cultural experience and visit some ancient temples on the island. I would have gone but have the shits after eating some roadside junk food during the festival and figure that I couldn't cope with any pothole persuasion.

So here I am sitting in the bar, which is actually a large concrete vault of a place attached to the bowels of the Ex-serviceman's Hotel. I'm drinking with Lal, one of the old boys, as he spins a few gut wrenching yarns about World War ll. He's in the midst of a naval battle where his vessel is attempting to outwit a German U-boat, when some dude interrupts us. I am calling him a dude because he looks like a free-lover whose teleported in from a Californian sixties commune; all mop hair and psychedelic garb. Then Cool Sixties Dude states the obvious.

'Hey Man, I'm not interrupting you am I?'

'No, actually *man*, we were expecting you. You see Lal here?'

I point to Lal.

'Well Lal and I are actually clairvoyants and we're in Colombo to have our crystal balls de-cracked and polished. Apparently there's a small fissure in each of our orbs which is playing havoc with our Nostradamuses.'

In point of fact I only imagine saying this, as good manners prevail, and so my sarcastic whip is replaced with a fair and just reply. The conversation, therefore, goes something like this,

'No, not at all. Lal here was just spinning me a yarn about World War II. He was in the British Navy you know.'

Lal relishes the recognition, his expanded head wiggles and he beams the width of a frigate.

'Cool man. Cool.'

Then Cool Sixties Dude looks directly at me.

'Hey man, you interested in being in a movie?'

I laugh coz it's kinda' funny. Who the hell sits in a bar where some guy comes up to you and asks if you want to come play in Tinsletown? It's gotta be a con. Stuff like this just doesn't happen in the real world, but what the hell, I decide to play along with it anyway.

So I say, 'Who me? Sure man, I'd love to be a movie star. When do we start?'

Cool Sixties Dude then goes on to explain that there actually *is* a movie being shot in the hill capital Kandy, and that they're looking for 'extras' to play American GI's. He goes on to say that although the movie is filmed in Sri Lanka, it is in fact about two opposing soldiers in Vietnam who touch base on an interpersonal level, and that it's all based on a true account from a serving Vietcong's diary.

'Hey, sounds great,' I say, with less reservation than moments ago. But it still all sounds a bit surreal, so I dig deeper.

'Do we get any weapons?'

'Hell man! You'll be loaded up to the hilt. They've got AK 47's, M16's, grenades, mortars, rocket launchers, jeeps, and helicopters. Shit dude, they've got the fucking lot. You could seriously rock the world with what they've got up there! It'll be lock and load man, lock and load! It'll be such a gas. Whaddaya say?'

I mull it over in my mind for about a nanosecond, then answer with a resounding 'Yes'. Cool Sixties Dude goes on to tell me the extras will be billeted in a hotel and that food is supplied. We even get paid in cash, and when I work out the total it amounts to the equivalent of about ten beers a day with some small change to spare. Not bad for a kid who loved to play 'cowboys and Indians' with his schoolmates in the local caravan park on Mumbles Hill.

Cool Sixties Dude leaves me with the hotel name in Kandy and instructions that I have to be up there tomorrow to secure a place in the Hall of Fame. My scepticism has given way to Cool Sixties Dude's honest ways and I am so rapped that I buy Lal and myself several bottles of Three Coins beer to celebrate. I can't believe that Tony and Tyrone have missed out on such a great adventure, and unfortunately there is no way of getting hold of them. We could have been Brothers in Arms.

The three-hour journey along the Matale Line to Kandy is a scene of majestic beauty: *All harmonious, all in perfect taste are the colours and costumes of this land'*, as Mark Twain once described The Island of Ceylon during his visit in 1896. And how right he was: It is the original paradise. It is seductive and tantalizing and easy to imagine Adam giving Eve one up against any one of the luscious coconut palm tree trunks, which stand phallus-like alongside the edge of moistened paddy fields.

The journey takes me from the lowland plains up to the highlands, where the train tracks meander past roads sharing their limited space with cars, carts, bikes, bullocks, and even the occasional elephant. The roadside is vibrant with life and the lush landscape presents a palette of colour overspill, worthy of a Rousseau masterpiece. We pass wayside merchants selling everything from ink to incense. There are small quarries where artisans nap at lumps of stone, shaping statues to adorn their shrines and temples. Further on there are open-air batik factories, where the cloth is washed and waxed in large open tubs, then dyed in earth colours and indigo blues. I see open mines, just pits in the ground, no bigger than a small sea container from which blue sapphires, moonstones and star rubies are prised free. I see tea leaves plucked from fertile trackside plantations and elephants being scrubbed lovingly by their mahouts at the base of sun-sparkling waterfalls. Eventually, the train branches off the main line near the world famous Peradeniya Botanical Gardens, before pulling into the train station at Kandy, home to the relic of The Lord Buddha's Sacred Tooth.

When the train comes to a lumpy stop, it is one mad dash and grab for all that is yours. On leaving my carriage I am touted by a young tuk-tuk driver, named Winston, who presently whisks me off to my hotel. At reception I am greeted by an immaculately dressed and softly spoken lady who hands me a key and the instructions that I am to be in the lobby for a meeting at seven, to meet with the rest of the murderous movie crew.

## AT WAR WITH OLD FRIENDS

The room's a beauty. Fresh bed, starched hotel linen, a small table complimented with two chairs and a balcony looking out onto undulating plantations of rice and tea. I take a soothing shower, wrap on a lungi, make an arak cocktail to celebrate my safe arrival, and grab my Hermann Hesse novel; Siddhartha.

It's all free and easy, and why not? As I lay on the bed I hear a conversation between a couple next door and they are Welsh accents.
My ears prick up in disbelief.

*No it couldn't be?*

With glass in hand I saunter out onto the balcony, not really believing what I am overhearing. I'm in a time warp, a whiplash back to the seaside city of Swansea, the graveyard of ambition, as Welsh poet Dylan Thomas once called it. The room next door shares the adjoining balcony and so it is easy for me to walk around from one open door to the next. I am standing outside, looking into the room, but they can't see me as the lady is facing the other way and the man's too busy imitating a crustacean.
Their conversation goes something like this,
'Rod, time to stop with the yoga my love. It's coming up to six thirty and time to get ready.'
Rod has somehow managed to get his legs over his shoulders and is swinging back and forward on his hands with legs dangling in the air, humming along to Frank Zappa's, Tinseltown Rebellion, playing from a nearby Walkman and speakers. It is a sight for sore eyes.
I say,
'Christ Jan, the things you see when you haven't got a crab-hook.'

They both stop dead.

What happens next is as if the scene is played out in an old pre-talkies movie. It is animated and in slow motion. The next few seconds drag themselves into the present as if someone has sped up the projector, and we all find ourselves back in real-time.

'Bloody hell Rhys,' says Rod as he unfolds himself.
And Jan follows him in monosyllables, 'Oh... My... God!'

It is a religious experience.

Jan is the sister I never had and with arms outstretched I make a beeline for her and we hug, a double hug, as close family do. Then it is Rod and myself hugging, and laughing. Then it's the three of us hugging, hooting and laughing, and marvelling at the hand that fate has dealt us. Rod and Jan had both planned to travel straight to India from Wales, but as it turned out it was cheaper to fly via Sri Lanka. They go on to explain that it was the very same Cool Sixties Dude that had offered them the same movie deal at their hotel in Bentota.

We move out onto the balcony and talk about their intended trip to India, then it isn't long before it's close to seven and time for the pep talk downstairs. Jan and I decide to take off as we've already showered so we leave Rod to spruce up.
'I'll sithee,' calls out Rod in his Welsh-Geordie accent as we depart, leaving him with his genetically mixed-up roots.

The meeting area is in the lounge. We know this because there is a small sandwich board in the foyer with the words, *The Iron Triangle*, written on it and an arrow pointing the way. In the lounge a gaggle of chairs have been arranged in a loose semicircle and filling them is an array of honking travellers. We meander past a couple of people, say 'Hi' to a few, and park ourselves on a couple of seats, saving one on the end for Rod, who soon joins us all spruced up and grinning like a basket of chips. An Irish guy, named Turbo, then hushes the excitement within the room, silencing the twenty or so of we Extras. Turbo goes on to explain, to we naive war-virgins, the details of our employment before leaving us within the buzzing oxymoronic atmosphere of thrilled peace-loving warmongers.

## MELONS AND WAR MANGLED MANGOES

After breakfasting at the hotel, all we Extras are bussed to the 'set'. It's only a twenty-minute ride and when we pull up to our stop the scene before us blows us away. The backdrop for the movie is incredible. Whoever found this place either stumbled on it by chance or owes some hillside local a buffalo cart full of greenbacks. The sky is faultless, blue and shimmering. In the distance is the mountain, Adam's Peak, (or Sri Pada), where Gautama Buddha's rock footprint is guarded by local priests, while closer are folding hills, each landscaped into tiers of edible greenery. These row upon row of perfectly manicured steps finish at a wide plateau below where a mocked-up village has been created.

'Wow!' comments one of our fellow Extras. 'This is no longer Sri Lanka baby. This is wham-bam-thankyou-Nam!'

From our vantage point, in the village we can see a wooden humpback bridge spanning some ten metres over a shallow river. The river is quietly navigating its way around large boulders, run smooth over the course of time, and strewn at its banks are smaller river stones nestled in soft riverbank sand. The bridge has been crafted from poles of giant bamboo, cut from the surrounding jungle, allowing a makeshift road to roll up and over the river and into the mocked-up village.

The village itself is a display of temporary huts, made from walls of bamboo and mud, then topped with coolie roofs crafted from rice thatch. There are ox carts and bicycles, stalls laden with tropical fruit and other stalls spread with an array of multi-coloured wooden bowls, harvesting turmeric, cloves, chilli, cardamom and other exotic spices. It is visually delightful, and in essence a perfect place to bomb the hell out of, thereby thrilling Joe-Blow back home as he sucks on a beer and stuffs another wedge of 'El Supremo' down his neck.

The special-effects lads are all cockneys who recently finished working their magic on a caped crusader movie. They have implanted doors, walls, roofs, melons, mangoes, pineapples, and durian fruit with incendiary devices, all designed to explode on cue.

When we got off the bus we were told to wait in the shade of a nearby building for further instructions, and within the hour were fitted out with combat attire and killing machines. For us, the GI's, there are the American M16 rifles, and for the Singhalese, playing the Vietcong, they are armed with the Chinese built AK47 gas operated combat assault rifles. Added to this there are knives, bayonets, pistols, revolvers, machine guns, grenades, rocket launchers, and flame-throwers. Cool Sixties Dude may have been wearing some sleeveless cow jacket when I met him, but he was no bullshit artist when he said we'd be fully armed. Because we are. We're armed to the fucking teeth! And it only took Rod and myself one day at the shoot to establish a scam that was to make the adventure even more exciting.

The scam has everything to do with the arrival of the gun-truck and the handing out of our weapons for the day. The gun-truck is a simple van, similar to those used to transport white goods, whose back door rolls up to expose all manner of standard and replica weaponry. Each morning this gun truck rolls onto the set and parks. We collect one M16 rifle, two packs of 45mm ammo, four grenades and our 'kit'; which comprises of black boots, khaki shirt, matching pants, flak-jacket, a black cotton combat belt and one G.I. helmet. But the thing we look out for is a small green circular sticker found on the underside of some, (and only some), of the M16s. This is of paramount importance as this sticker signifies that these rifles are fully automatic and therefore loads more fun when let loose on set! Also, if you slipped the local truck attendant a fist full of rupees you walked away with six magazines of ammo instead of the instructed two. With our kit in hand, bulk ammo and our green-stickered, fully automatic weapons, it was time for Rod and myself to undergo metamorphosis and become American killing machines.

The first scene of the day is to catcall a female South Vietnamese Officer who is being driven through our Base Camp. The Base Camp comprises of tents, huts, speakers from which appropriate 'Nam music is being blasted, chewing gum packets, pizza stacks and 44-gallon drums in which some Vietcong are tortured during one of the scenes. None of us would likely pass a RADA audition, but it isn't difficult for most of us to play this part effectively. After all, she is a single woman.

The lady officer is driven up in a jeep and we boys set off, cat-calling like young guns on heat. The take is performed successfully and I thought with a good deal of respect. I saw no one grabbing their dicks or masturbating their cheeks with tongues to simulate a blowjob, but then I wasn't watching the lads, I was too busy cheering the hot babe in the jeep. 'It's a rap!' calls the director and that was that.

The next scene we are asked to undergo is for Rod and I to carry stone-laden ammunition boxes, about the size of elongated treasure chests, back and forth behind two of the main actors. The scene is ballsed up that many times due to the lisp of one of the actors that our shoulders are on fire and our knuckles are practically dragging in the dirt like an orang-utan with a bad stoop. The actor's line, after he has raced across the dusty compound and slid to a stop in front of the leading actor, is, 'Excuse me Sir. You gotta' come quick Sir. I think they're gonna' dust him Sir!'

(The line was written for impact as this soldier has seen a captain of the AVRN torturing a Vietcong soldier in one of the afore mentioned 44-gallon drums of water. In the scene the racing soldier figures that his American Captain will be able to prevent the atrocity.)

Unfortunately, instead of saying, 'I think they're gonna' dust him Sir', the actor keeps saying, 'I think they're gonna' *duthst* him Sir', on account of his lisp, and so loses the harsh impact required for the scene to work. In the end the director is so flustered that he quits the take, leaving it to the editor to cast the unwanted piece of footage onto the editing room floor somewhere back in L.A. (as it never did make the final cut).

This same routine of arriving, waiting, filming and returning to the hotel went on each day. Then during one lunch break I got lucky. I was picked out with three other Extras and asked to man the machine gun at the open doorway to one of the helicopters as it performed a fly-by over the village. The four helicopters used in the movie have been seconded from the Sri Lankan Air Force by the movie company, no doubt for a substantial sum, and are piloted by soldiers who have recently been engaged in heavy combat up north. Needless to say, I couldn't wait to get my ass into the Huey and my finger on the trigger of that fifty-millimetre baby!

## GUNSHIPS

The next day, as we shelter from the sun, we hear the thumping of unseen airborne beasts. They hone around the distant bend in the river, menacingly performing an overhead fly-by. They appear as huge deafening birds of prey and have me thinking how terrifying it would be for anyone on the receiving end of one of these fiends of power.

*Kaboom!*
*Lie down you: You're dead.*
*This is no game – this is for real!*
*Because…Yes.*
*Those really are your entrails cooling beside you – and the saddening Catch is that you're only 22.*

The noise thumping from the four sets of whirring blades fill the whole valley as they land a mere five hundred metres away. We chosen four, the 'extra' Extras, are willingly drawn from the pack and are led over to each of our machines. As I get closer to my beast, the beat of the downdraft is threateningly powerful. I clamber into the rear of the helicopter, escaping the might of the violent tumult. The co-pilot leaves his seat and harnesses me in place, then fixes my headgear and inboard communication. His smile is warm and childlike and it is strange to think that both he and the pilot are about my age, and were, only last week, wreaking havoc from the skies in the northern part of the Island. Behind this baby-faced facade of my co-pilot there is most likely to be a raw and battle hardened killer, and the cold revelation of this sends a shiver down my spine.

It is we three now. The pilot, the co-pilot and the Cheshire Cat rookie with his hands firmly placed on the machine gun's handles. This 50 mm tempered steel baby is capable of firing 750 rounds per minute, however there isn't any firing of weapons today as that illusion is left to the work of the special effects team. Yet, as I sit behind my 'non-weapon of mass annihilation' I cannot help but notice that the rounds of ammunition flowing into the gun are, in point of fact, live. It is only the absence of the gun's firing pin which prevents me from administering total mayhem on those village fruit stalls below.

*Oh for a paper clip!*

I feel the rotor's rhythm increase as the bird lifts away from the soil. It teeters slightly forward, hanging only metres above the ground before racing for a fifty-metre stretch at what is break-neck speed. Looking out of the machine's side door I watch the dirt racing by at a rate of knots, then the pilot pulls the helicopter into a vertical ascent, veers it off to the left, significantly increasing the G-Force, thereby throwing me violently to the right. I would literally be falling out of the side door if it weren't for the harness about my shoulders. It is exhilarating and I let out a wild holler to mark the occasion.

Each of the four helicopters fly in lineal formation, and we are the second bird in the wing. This snaky plumage of gunships winds itself away from the village and follows the river upstream. We are still flying at a relatively low altitude, as the hilltops are pretty much at eye level, but not for long. Communication between the other three machines has us lifting steadily upwards and banking heavily out in a wide arc. As I look back I watch the other two machines following in perfect formation as if being towed on an invisible marlin line. It is a fairground thrill and before long we are again level with the hilltops and heading back toward the village. It is a thrilling moment however the irony of it does not escape me. Onward Christian soldiers!

The village comes into view as we race around the bend and I see some of the Singhalese actors, dressed in their all-black Vietcong uniforms, panicking and running in all directions. Others are manning machine guns and finger pointing up towards us. Men, women, children and oxen are fleeing for their lives. The whole place has turned hostile and there are plumes of smoke erupting from different parts of the village. I see the occasional exploding incendiary device sending parts of the mock village into oblivion, plus the imaginary bullets spitting up trails of hot sand. I watch the decimation of fruit stalls too, all adding to the desired effect of a village under siege. It is exhilarating, and yet again, as I swing my fifty millimetre cannon to and fro, finger on trigger, 'virtually' annihilating the enemy, all thoughts of compassion have leeched from my soul. I have become a killing machine. Someone who has depersonalised all life below. I kill, kill and kill and after landing I reflect on how easy it must have been for some men to have become messed-up 'gook-killing' soldiers during that ungodly war.

That was the first time I had ever flown in a helicopter and figured I'd had my airborne exhilaration quota for the next decade. However, the next day was to be a further induction into the fun packed skies above. The director informs us that we are to be involved in a full frontal ground assault on the village, and that we will be using the Hueys as transport. We learn that we will disembark our Huey on the outskirts of the village then engage in an en-masse infantry attack.

Each of the four helicopters holds six of us. In the first ship is the leading actor, and we are in the second with one of the supporting actors. He is the bad-ass ARVN Captain, who previously tortured the Vietcong in forty four gallons of tepid water.

Before entering the Hueys we are given the pep talk by 'Ed'.
Ed has more respect from us than anyone else on the ground.

Ed is the *Man*.

He is the Technical (Combat) Advisor and we soon learn that this guy has done all of this for real. He's friendly enough, slightly overweight, but still possesses a menacing presence when standing in close proximity. Ed has a killer's confidence and the technique to match. Before a hand-to-hand combat scene is shot we are privy to a display of Ed's choreography with willing participants. Ed is bulky, but fluid, and demonstrates how easily he can disarm a younger, fitter man of his knife or gun, finishing atop of him with deadly precision. If this war was real, and you found yourself shitting yourself in the paddy fields amongst all of your dead and your dying, then Ed would be the man you'd want next to you passing over the toilet roll.

Ed says this.
'Under no circumstances are you to lock and load your weapons when in the Hueys. Also, under no circumstances are you to release your harness until the Huey has landed. You are to wait until the lead man (he means the actor) is out first before you exit, and only then do you load your weapon. Do I make myself clear?'

'Yes Sir!' we all reply in unison.
We'd learnt to do this over the course of different pep talks given to us by Ed, because in our tiny minds we are all authentic tin soldiers.

Yes Sir!
No Sir!
Three dollops of arse affecting curry Sir!
Thank you for allowing me to die in this war for nothing. Sir!

We sit in the Huey with the rota spinning as we await the lift. The six of us are sitting in the rear, three to a metal bench. Rod is opposite me, looking fierce in anticipation and likewise I feel armed and dangerous. The rpm of the engine increases, powerfully vibrating through the floor and causing us to sit a little firmer in our seats. The pilot then takes our machine to the skies.

All four helicopters, once again move in formation up-river and once again I'm greeted by the wonder of the tropics. Below us the hillsides are steeped in row upon row of saturated paddy fields, fuelled by manmade irrigation systems using simplistic gravitational overflow. I take check of all those aboard. There's Rod with his hands firmly gripping his M16, 'where's the camera' Herby, who loves getting his face in frame at any opportunity, Julian, who gets hurt later in the story, a Swedish guy who is the spitting image of the chef from the Muppets and one of the main actors, the ARVN Captain. All five are staring out of the side door as the beauty of our location unfolds below us, but instead of displaying relaxed faces I see those of urgency and trepidation. I feel it too, as the adrenaline pumps around my system with pancreatic sureness.

After all, we are going to war.

I look at each of the five faces of these young men; friends, one like a brother, and I cannot help but feel concerned for their safety. Obviously an instinctive trait for soldiers going to war, I realise this, but there's one huge difference here. My five companions, all with dreams of the future, all with someone back home to love them, are actually happy to be here. They are enjoying themselves. They are content. No-one aboard is pissing down their legs or shitting in their khaki pants.
Because *this* is not war.
There *will* be no death.

No everlasting agony of losing a close friend.
No bullet ricocheting from your thigh up into your groin, so ending your genetic lineage.

Because this is *not* war.
This is not real.

This is one hundred and ten percent gun-fun theatrics, played out in paradise. And we Extras are absolutely loving it!

Again we bank hard against the sky, cutting a wide arc back towards the village. We're going in and the realisation of this delivers an adrenaline spike, causing my heart rate to rise and my mouth to become dry.

Yesterday the helicopters circled the village at close range, however this time we perform a direct run and make our descent about five hundred metres out from the village, landing in one of the rice paddies. The director has previously demanded how and where each pilot is to land their machine.

'Do it precisely,' he said. 'Land all Hueys at the same time. Allow the troops to disembark then pull out fast.'

These are his instructions to these young veteran combat pilots and as I feel the Huey descend to our landing spot I look across at Rod…and he's itching. And I know I'm itching too. It ain't fleas nor ticks, but an itch to lock and load our weapons. Our hormones are dying to pump that first round into the breach and cut out our own little piece of history.

*We're going to war Brother!*
*Lock and Load!*
*Lock…and fucking Load!*

I swear its telepathy because we simultaneously lift our guns and pull back the bolt catch, locking the first round into the breach. We just can't help it. Neither the director, nor Ed are here, right? so what the heck. We look at each other, eyes transfixed and grins wide.

The skids of the machines have touched the dirt so we hit our harness release catches, then look to take our cue from our leading man. We all remember Ed explicitly saying that we are not to leave the aircraft before the actor does, but when we look to him for our cue we see nothing but frustration on his face. His harness has jammed and he is having trouble releasing the catch. Rod and I look at each other as the seconds tick by and the bird is whirring and we are all hanging with explosive anticipation and our weapons are loaded, and our trigger fingers are itchy and there's a village out there to be shot the shit out of for fuck's sake!

*C'mon!*

It is a knowing look from me, a supporting look from Rod and with the decision made we are up and into it and heading towards the exit. As I squeeze past our main man I pinch his catch with both of my thumbs and his buckle falls away. He's still there…but we've flown the coup, having gone to fight our war.

---

That evening the three of us are at the hotel chilling out on the veranda with a few well-earned beers. And I want to ask them about Mel. We were all peas in the same pod once upon a time, but before I draw the courage to ask, Jan has looked into my eyes and has already read my thoughts.
'You're thinking about Mel aren't you Rhys?'
'Bloody hell Jan, you're good.'
Rod remains quiet.
'Well she and Rick were having problems the last time we spoke.'
My heart bounces and my ears prick up.
In the past the four of us were inseparable. We would spend most nights in each other's company, listening to Wild Man Fischer singing on about fish heads or some other obscure track from another obscure album that Rod had dug up from his outrageously obscure record collection.

All vinyl.
All pristine.
All night long.

Sometimes the four of us would listen to these weird and wonderful tracks all night, sometimes drunk and naked, behind locked doors in our own exclusive platonic nudist utopia.

'Yeah, well that doesn't surprise me really. Deep down he's a bit of a shit.'
'They are well matched then,' says Rod, sliding into the conversation.
'That's enough my love,' says Jan, checking Rod from further comment.
Rod had sided with me, as did Jan, when the dirty deed was uncovered, but it was Rod who gave Mel a verbal dressing down the next time he saw her. Jan however, has preserved the friendship of sorts, as women kindly do.
'But,' Jan continues, 'I don't think she was ever right for you anyway Rhys?'

A moment of silence.

In the past I had always listened to Jan's counselling. Everyone did, and still does. She is wise beyond her years as they say, however I'm at odds as to whether I should mention the letter or not.

But I do.
I tell them.
About the Letter
The anger.
The hatred.
The forgiveness.
The confusion.
I go ahead and tell them all about *Pinkie*.
About Mel coming.
I go ahead and tell them everything, because I need to.
It has all come out in a bit of a rush, and now I stop because I am exhausted. I have only spoken for maybe a minute or so, but I feel emotionally drained.
Beaten.
Confused about the rest of my life.
And Jan is looking at me: Knowing.

Because she was there amongst it all.
Amongst all of the shit.
Amongst the betrayal between friends.

She was there the night they had to clean it up. His blood and mucus, soiling the floor of the carpark. It was Rod and Jan who took him to the hospital, took him there in all of his of blood and with his broken bones.

'You're a fool if you let this happen Rhys. You know I love Mel but she's no good for you. She'll only rip your heart out again,' says Jan.
'A leopard cannot change its spots,' Rod adds.
And Jan lets this one slide because she knows Rod is right.
I offer a plea.
'Maybe she's changed Rod? Maybe she's had some time to think now. It's been a while since I left. Maybe she's woken up to Rick and all of his bullshit?'
But I find no ally in Rod.
'Like Jan says, you're a bloody fool if you go on with this Rhys. We both love you mate but deep down you know we're right. But then it's your pyre. She's only going to mess you up all over again.'

And perhaps they're right, but the urge to give it one more try is too strong. I've already made the decision and my mind is set.

Because love will do that to a person.
Because love is a blind fool's nemesis.
And hope remains if there exists the tiniest of sparks.

---

Today the scenes being filmed are to take place in and around the village. We have been shooting for two weeks now and have reached the point in the movie where we are storming into village. We have been on set since seven thirty, without being used in any of the scenes, and it is now one in the afternoon. Rod and I are leaning up against one of the mud brick buildings and we're baking in our flak jackets and snake boots. The sweat is running off us and we continually swig back at our water bottles to prevent dehydration.

There are two other guys with us. Americans. And they're good lads. Julian, who was with us yesterday in the second helicopter, and his countryman Lance. Ed, the Military Adviser, comes over and asks us to join a handful of others in the next scene. Rod and I are as happy as a couple of sand-boys, not so much for the glory but just to get up off our arses and run around for a bit. Perhaps we'll even get to kill someone?

The scene involves us running from one mud walled building, across some open ground in the village, to another mud walled building. We are instructed to return heavy covering fire for our fellow combatants, who will be receiving sporadic fire from within the village. Rod and I move into position ready to let rip with our fully automatics.

Throughout the filming, the special effects boys have continually warned us where they have placed the incendiary devices, and we are heavily instructed not to get too close to them. After all, they are explosives and if they can send a market stall a couple of metres up into the air or insert a piece of wooden shrapnel six inches up your jacksy then you best not be too liberal with your navigation.

So we're told where they are.

And there are masses of them.

We are basically told to run snake-like through the set, fire our weapons, look realistic, don't look at the cameras and more importantly stay away from the explosives.

For this scene it is the first time the local fire brigade have been called in and we can see them waiting on standby on a nearby hill. It's a big moment.

And the whole scene pans out like this.

Rod, Julian, Lance and myself take off from around the corner of one building, heading for another. Canisters of green smoke, adding to the war effect, are bursting all around us, coinciding with the detonation of explosives. As we run amongst the mayhem it's hard to remember where all of the incendiary devices have been laid. On looking ahead I see Julian running straight towards one of these devices, he's dangerously close, so I shout out to him. But my holler is lost in the battle's noise and the bomb lets loose, tearing the M16 from his grip. It is blown from his hands as he falls to the ground. Lance is only a short way ahead of him but has avoided the full impact of the blast. Rod and myself are pretty well neck and neck, bringing up the rear. We're still firing for all our might, then break stride to take Julian by each arm. Rod also grabs Julian's weapon which results in searing pain. The gun had fallen onto hot ground and the heat from the incendiary device has also radiated into the gun's casing thereby burning Rod's hand. He drops the gun, but it's too late as the damage is done and by the time we make it to the second building he is in a fair amount of pain. A couple of the Special Effects lads take Julian from us, then Rod heads 'off set' to find the medical tent with Jan. Meanwhile, some of the embers from one of the other incendiary devices have blown onto one of the thatched roofs, causing it to burst into flames. The director is ecstatic, as an impromptu scene has just presented itself, free of charge. He comes over to Lance and myself saying that us he wants us to run back from where we have come, and to stop at the burning building, then take a few pot shots at the enemy. But I'm having no part of it. The building is now truly ablaze and so the Sri Lankan fire fighters burst into action. This however presents them with a physical dilemma. The truck is so far away from the fire that when these guys spill out the tonnage of hose it is too heavy for them to drag all the way to the source of the fire. It is as if I'm watching the Tropical Keystone Cops in full Technicolor from a ringside seat. A few of the crew and myself, on seeing their predicament, run to give them a welcomed hand. Before long the fire is under control so I leave the fire fighters to it and begin hunting around the extensive movie set for the medical tent.

I find it at the far end of the village, with its heavy off-white canvas flaps tied back to allow what little airflow can be channelled in this tropical heat. It is a tent from which you could imagine the Duke of Wellington exiting, and on entering I see the doctor tending to Rod's burnt hand. Julian is here too, lying on a makeshift bed, but he's asleep with half his face bandaged. The doctor is crouched down and has her back to me, which allows Rod to look over her shoulder and give me a 'she's-a-honey' mime. I acknowledge Jan's non-verbal retort of, 'he should be so lucky', and move around to take a better look at his hand.
I say,
'Don't' give him too much attention now Doc or else it'll go straight to his head and he'll think he's the leading actor.'
The doctor.
She turns quickly.
The tent is caught in a sudden gust and the flaps rap wildly in the hot blast. The Doctor and I make eye contact and call out simultaneously so that our words come together in a fusion of idyllic memories. The moment feels like forever, but in reality, it is over in one emotional

rush. Even so, enough time passes for the doctor and I to think a thousand words. Enough time passes for the doctor and I to swim in each other's delight. And enough time passes for the doctor and I to marvel at the hand of fate. When Aimee comes to me the warmth of her against me is a wash of pleasure. It rises up and over me, and showers down upon us like a first kiss. We hold each other for a moment more, forever, before we break away to laugh, childlike, in our newfound world. And it feels like a thousand smiles have lit up the tent. Aimee steps back and takes a good look at me in my flak jacket, my boots and battle dress.

'You make a pretty good looking soldier for a beach bum Rhys,' she says.

'And you make a pretty good looking doctor for a sand-angel,' I reply. We laugh. 'I had no idea you were coming up here to work. I thought you were going up north with Medicins sans Frontiers?'

'I was,' says Aimee. 'However I met with one of the actors at a restaurant and they offered me a good contract. They say their doctor became ill and had to fly home. I have already done much work with MSF but now I can save some money and have the opportunity to go to Thailand with the film crew for the next film. I am lucky, yes?'

And although it is great news for Aimee somehow I feel as if something has slipped from my grasp. Sure, I am excited for her, yet I cannot help but feel disappointed in some strange way to know that she is leaving again. I ask Aimee, with as much enthusiasm as I can muster, what the film is called and where in Thailand it is being filmed.'

'I cannot remember exactly what it is called,' she says. 'It is another war movie and is something to do with a morning in Vietnam, I think. But we are mostly filming in Phuket, this I know.'

Jan and Rod are understandably bewildered at this sudden turn of events and so Jan slides in between our conversation to ask with a smile,

'Are you going to introduce us properly then Rhys? To the good doctor here.'

'Hey, sorry you two. This is Aimee. We met back in Hikkaduwa a few months back. We're kinda' like...good friends.'

We both blush.

Rod, when I look over at him, greets me with a secretive look that translates between close friends as 'you lucky bastard'. I smile widely, then look over at Jan, who looks on with sisterly kindness.

Jan takes her cue.

'Are you able to join the three of us for dinner tonight Aimee? I'm sure Rhys would love that. Right Rhys?'

Aimee is visibly delighted and so the date is set. As I leave the tent, having checked on Julian, I steal a last glance back at Aimee who blows me a gentle kiss. I am so excited at the thought of seeing her tonight, and to have found her again, and to be able to spend more time with her. But thoughts of Mel now rush in. My Mel, who wrote me that letter, and who has decided to fly here to meet me. Mel, who has decided that we should start our lives over. Be lovers again. Be together again, forever. I feel as if I'm trapped between pillar and post. Stranded between two lovers, held fast by an invisible touch.

But tonight there is my Aimee.
My sweet Aimee.
My beer bubble blowing Aimee.
My Aimee who is fun.
My Aimee who is so beautiful, inside and out.
My Aimee who is joining me for dinner.
Tonight.

I meet Aimee in the lobby. I had showered slowly and prepared carefully. I went straight to my room after leaving the set and in a way I was thankful that Rod and Jan were on a different bus back to the hotel. My mind was whirring, jumping from one scenario to another and I really wasn't in the mood for conversation.

Aimee v Mel.
Mel v Aimee.
Long-time lover v Holiday romance.
Family dinners v Two days at a beach.
Betrayal v Honesty.
Commitment v Casual.
It's all such a bloody mishmash.

We head to the restaurant where we join Rod and Jan at a table for four. I sit between Jan and Aimee. As Jan and Aimee laugh together Aimee squeezes my leg under the table sharing the delight she is finding in Rod and Jan's humour. The four of us laugh freely as we dine and at times it feels strange seeing Aimee as part of *we four* instead of Mel...but it also feels right.

The night unwinds in that special way in which you feel the world is your stage and to add glitter to an already dazzling evening we are paid a visit by the director and lead actor. Julian, they tell us, is on his way to a hospital in Colombo with minor burns to his face and hands but that he is going to be ok. They have with them a bottle of scotch whisky which they duly hand over to Rod. He then asks them in no uncertain terms what it is like to be a bigknob in Tinseltown. They both laugh, staying for a pleasant hour or more, sharing their stories of L.A. and of other Hollywood antics.

Later, after having finished dessert, we head to our communal balcony with hands in hands and hearts closely knit. The refreshing breeze skims over the rice florets causing them to bow majestically, then it rises on up to our balcony to find the four of us reclining comfortably on two wicker chairs, with both girls sitting on our laps. It is all cuddles and kisses, friendly banter and moist warm moments.

And I am happy.

Happy, but still somewhat confused as I cannot help but feel this nagging loyalty towards Mel. I suspect it is born from my father and mother divorcing when I was only eight. That raw wound, that rough emotional scar, which has left me with the belief that relationships are vitally important. So imperative, that one should always fight to maintain them. To do your best to keep them alive.

'All in all pretty good blokes?' says Jan, referring to our dinnertime visitors and so breaking into my thoughts.

'Oui, they are really nice guys,' says Aimee. 'They mixed so easily with all of us.'

'A bit like their blended scotch then,' says Rod, holding up his glass to the moonlight.

'To the four of us then,' says I. 'To *The Splendid Blended!*'

With that we raise our glasses of honey coloured Chivas Regal, in a toast to our good fortune and to our everlasting friendship.

The following days are laced with joyous meetings between Aimee and myself. We try as often as we can to see each other during the day, but it proves difficult. I have to stay close to the shoot and Aimee has to be on duty at the medical tent at all times. On occasions we are able to meet up at the lunch tent but at the most this only pans out to a forty-minute tête à tête, if we're lucky. The evenings are different though as Aimee is able to come over every night. Our loving has become a regular thing but I know in my heart of hearts that sadly there is no permanency here as the nagging sense of commitment towards Mel is always present. And so there exists an inverse effect: The closer I get to Aimee the more I feel that I am betraying Mel. After all, it is Mel who is flying all the way to Sri Lanka to rekindle our lost love: However there is also this other nagging thought too…that Aimee feels like my soul mate.

It is a difficult and awkward conversation then, between Aimee and I tonight. We talk about Melanie and Aimee's manipulative ex-boyfriend. And we talk about Us. We talk about the way in which life has an unkind habit of throwing people together: Of those who perhaps should be together, but who are obligated to someone else, somewhere else, in another life. We talk about a sense of duty and about the importance of committing to relationships. We talk about her Dad and my Dad. We talk about loss. And we talk about loss a little more. And we cry. Then we cry a little more. We don't make love, we just lie together, close. And that was the last time I saw Aimee because the following day she went to Colombo to organise more medical supplies. The last kiss we shared together was neither that of a lover, nor that of a friend. It was something in between.

The following day, with bags packed, I say goodbye to Rod and Jan before they set off for the movie set, then wait for a taxi to pick me up to take me to the train station.

It is a mixed bag of tumultuous emotions as I exit the movie business, leaving Aimee and my closest friends behind before heading down the hills.

Back to the coast.
To the edge of another world.
To where Mel is soon to arrive.

# 1st April

## KANDY DANCERS

My throat is dry.
But not from the Bristol cigarettes I recollect lighting, then immediately stubbing out last night.
And my stomach aches.
But not from the consumption of several Three Coins beers: The empty brown bottles of which are now strewn around my room like fallen soldiers.
And my head is splitting.
But not from any axe wielding homicidal maniac.
And my heart is pumping frantically.
But it's no coronary attack.

And I have just woken up.
And it's six in the morning.
And I'm lying on my bed, swaddled in my lungi and last night's sleep.
And it is only four hours away.
The Touchdown.

The taxiing of an aircraft to a terminal.
The Arrival of Mel.

Now it is only three hours and fifty-seven minutes away and I feel like shit. I get up, cast off my linen and stand in the shower, inert. I just stand here, wait here, all the while being hammered by the force of the shower, hoping that the odorous water will somehow wash away my uncertainty.
But then I reason that Mel's coming *to me*.
She's flying a third of the way around the world to meet *me*.
It's not the other way around.
So with this in mind I settle somewhat and soap up.
 The arrivals area is busy enough but there's room to stand in a spot where I can see past the opening and closing of the sliding doors and into the customs area.

Looking for a glimpse.
A snapshot of my future.
An image of Mel.

My stomach is knotted. The cacophony of small talk mingles with the smell of sweat of those around me. There is a press of love and an eagerness about the place as the expectant sway from one leg to the other. I'm swaying too, however instead of bubbling excitement I taste only anticipation, causing a little bile to rise.

People begin coming through and I watch as brothers hug sisters, and sisters kiss, and brothers unite, and menfolk embrace, and women laugh with each other, and lovers love.

I look down at the bunch of flowers in my hand. They are an array of 'Kandy dancers', a delicate yellow orchid, resembling miniature chorus girls teasingly hilting up their skirts, before bursting into a sexy can-can. They are exquisitely wrapped in red cellophane and are finished with a bow of yellow ribbon around their midriff. As I was paying for them the flower seller asked,
'Is being for your *lover*? Yes?'
'Yes. They are being for my *lover*,' I had answered.
But looking at them now it is as if they are being held in someone else's hand. As if they are someone else's gesture of affection. The moment feels surreal. Sweat lines my back and my heart aches. I even question whether or not I should be here.
Then the automatic doors slide open once again and I see her...
a glimpse.
But she is not looking for me. Not looking to where her *lover* is waiting. Has been waiting for the past two hours, for days, months. Not looking for the *lover* who couldn't sleep last night and who had to douse himself in alcohol to extinguish the burning heartache felt beneath. Not looking for the *lover* who has been through so much shit that the least she could do was to seek me out, to comfort me with a look, to secure my doubts with a double overhead wave and a shriek of delight! Instead she is talking to a tall bronzed, blonde wavy haired guy, who has the appearance of a movie star in his fine linen and confidence, and whom I see making her laugh in a manner which is all too familiar. Then the doors close, shutting me out of their private world, and when the doors open again, allowing a passenger to emerge, to be hugged, kissed, and longingly embraced, Melanie is gone. I look, seek, crane for Mel, but she is no longer

visible. She is gone and with her disappearance I am enveloped within the cold shadow of paranoia, and again I have to steel myself to make sense of all this.

*She's only talking to someone else.*
*Someone else who just happens to be a guy - that's all.*
*For Christ's sake Rhys get a grip on yourself.*

My stomach is fluttering in spasms. I cannot even voice a silent reply. Instead I am just standing here: Waiting. In fact, what the hell am I really waiting for? For a moment I wish it were Aimee arriving and not Mel, for my past life feels a lifetime away. But it's not, its only seconds, because the doors glide apart and here she comes.

Mel is dressed in a pair of pale blue Indian pantaloons and a white linen top. Her smooth olive skin is partly hidden by a white pashmina, cast with flair and flamboyancy about her shoulders. Her shoes are of ballet style and are iridescent blue. She looks amazing.

In typical Mel style she adapts perfectly to her environment. To blend in, in her unique way, so all will notice her. Wherever she goes she offers a leading sense of style that others choose to mimic. She looks stunning, and on seeing me for the first time waves madly and blows me schoolgirl kisses. She drops her bags and comes running towards me, smiling, laughing, with arms out stretched, sending me all the way to Seventh Heaven.

When we're close enough Mel jumps into my arms, wrapping me with all four limbs and kisses the side of my neck. We come face to face and when our eyes meet it feels as if I've discovered a secret that everyone else in the world is still looking for. Our eyes smile as if we are one, then our lips burst forth with an energy all of their own. It is so powerful I feel both our bodies quaking in the aftermath of the embrace. Then I break from her: To look.

To see my Mel,
for the first time,
in what feels like Eternity,

Her jade green eyes are awash with tears and her small button nose is all screwed up. Strands of her strawberry blonde hair have loosened from their clips and have fallen across her face, fastened in salty tracks. I gently move her hair aside with my fingers and look again. Then in the heat of this moment Mel gasps between tears,

'Oh Rhys. My darling Rhys. I have missed you so much. It is so good to see you. I've missed you.… I've missed you.… I've missed you!'

She tightens her embrace and pulls herself into me. I feel each of her heartbeats pumping warmth into my soul. I smell the moment in her hair. I am trying to slow down time so that I may savour this part of my life, where all is good, and fair, and right, but the spell is broken by an unfamiliar American-Irish accent.

'I believe dis is yours Mel me darling.'

On turning my head I see the tall wavy blonde headed man that Mel was talking to earlier. I'm looking at the Greek God Thor, minus his hammer, holding onto what must be Mel's cabin baggage. Mel looks up and laughs and small flecks of spittle land on his forty-six inch chest. This guy is fucking huge.

'Oh hi Jeremy. Whoops! Sorry about that,' says Mel as she rubs the spittle off with her hand in an acquainted way.

'I believe des are yours?' And he holds out Mel's bags.

'God. Yes. Thanks. How silly of me. I became so mesmerised when I saw Rhys I just raced over here.'

'Well we are in de third world now me lovely and you should be a little more careful Girlfriend. Who's to say what little shit might run off with your precious possessions?'

Then this blonde, this six foot plus, wavy headed Thor looks down at me, and says, 'I always keep a firm grip on mine. How about you Rhys?'

I instantly relax. No karate chop to the neck required. No David and Goliath stony kick to the bollocks as there is a welcomed revelation that Jeremy's as gay as a bright summer's day! After a wink and laugh, Jeremy extends his right hand in open friendship and familiarity. And he's instantly likeable.

'Jeremy's the name, you fortunate bastard.'

We shake hands in a firm and friendly manner, then Mel and I wish Jeremy all the best as he leaves with his tour guide before we head out onto the street to catch a taxi to our hotel.

# PETALS AND THORNS

Mel is holding tightly onto my hand, fingers entwined, as we mingle within each other's space in the back of the taxi. We are not heading for the Ex-Serviceman's Hotel, but instead we are heading for the Supercontinental Hotel located on the outskirts of Colombo. I turn and look into her eyes, read it as a mixture of lust and desire and gently kiss her on the lips.

The Supercontinental hotel leaves the Ex-Servicemans in its wake. For a start, there is a doorman to open the taxi door, a bellboy to take Mel's luggage and a concierge to attend to your every whim. We don't bother with the elaborate front desk of walnut and marble, nor marvel at the water cascading over the dominant bust of Lord Buddha, resting magnificently in the ornate foyer. There are plush chairs on which to take high teas, all royale and cheese, but we bypass those also. There is the huge fishpond laden with Koi carp into which you may choose to throw coins to bring on a wish, but I have no need of this as I have my dream firmly resting on my arm.

It is us.
We two.
Mel and I.

We stand at the lift entrance, arm in arm, squeezing each other sensually, despite the sideway glances from our porter. Mel is bursting with contentment. She giggles at my touch, and I feel that I could literally walk on thin air. We enter the lift.

In my pocket I have the room key and twirl it excitedly as I have the most obvious of expectations. When I was here earlier, dropping off my luggage, I scented the room with frangipani flowers and I have even strewn burgundy rose petals on the bed in anticipation of this moment. I just want it all to be ok, but God, despite my excitement, I feel unnaturally nervous.

Mel squeezes my hand.

'You ok Rhys? You look a little edgy.'

'Yeah. I'm good thanks Beautiful. Everything's perfect.'

Then the doors to the lift open releasing us onto the fourth floor. My heart is pounding as we are lead to the room and we let ourselves in. The bellboy is handsomely tipped and with a vibrant wiggle he moves off leaving us in peace. What happens next is a torrid of emotion, a burst from the past. It's all tears, regrets and revelation. Mel cries as we make love. We both cry. We hold each other tight. Just the two of us…together.

---

We only spend the one night at the Hotel, but before we checkout we decide to take breakfast, which is a far cry from the egg hoppers and rotis sizzling down at the train station. Here you can eat anything and not concern yourself with any gastric consequences – it's probably a fair bet that even the water used to rinse the vegetables is bottled, therefore devoid of any E.coli bacteria concealed within a seemingly safe garden salad. And the clear water that sits in my glass tumbler is exactly what it appears to be: refreshing and safe.

I steal a glance across at Mel and watch as she deftly wipes away a smidgeon of butter from the corner of her mouth. Even this simple movement is executed with eloquent grace. She is a pleasure to watch. Then, once done, she carefully replaces the starched napkin back in her lap and continues her breakfast.

It is good to be with Mel.
My Mel.
Her company.
Her laughter.

Suddenly an all-consuming memory surfaces: A recollection of home, and of all of those sad and sorry nights of self-pity and soft-mindedness. Those nights spent alone. All of those nights where I'd find myself a third of the way through a bottle of hard liquor, dulling my senses, allowing me to slip into something as unnatural as alcohol induced sleep. At times it was like living between the lines of a Bukowski poem; living a dank and slow moving existence.
Mel looks up at me and smiles.

'What?' she says.

'Oh nothing, I was just…looking…thinking how beautiful you are and how much I love you.'

Mel's eyes display apologetic warmth. She reaches across the table and gently squeezes my hand. 'I love you too Rhys and I am truly sorry for all that happened with Rick. I feel so terrible about it all. It was stupid.'

The mention of his name sends a jolt through my body as if I've just been defibrillated. Christ, how can just one word have such an impact? How can one name change a situation so intensely? How can four letters crawl beneath my skin and cause an itch I can't reach? It takes all of my strength to focus on giving her an answer with as much sincerity as I can muster.

'I know Sweetheart. It's a silly thing to say, and you don't have to; really.'

Then her retort comes back at the speed of light and catches me completely off guard. She has regressed into one of her manic episodes with the tendency to boil any unsuspecting rabbit that happens to wander too closely by.

'So what are you saying then? And she glares. 'That I'm silly? That I'm stupid? You're calling me an idiot for apologising to you? Jesus Christ Rhys I was only trying to be honest! You can't even give me one tiny break can you, for one tiny mistake in the past?'

'No. I didn't mean that *you* were an idiot for fuck's sake Mel. I meant about you loving me, not about what happened before.' And as I hurl my reply at her my Adam's apple feels as if it has swollen to the size of a golf ball and is wedged in my throat.

Wack!
Wack!
Wack!

FORE!

Back into the rough!

Chip.
Chip.
Chip.
Chipping away at my sanity.

142

Then this volatile moment is coated with one sweet feminine laugh and a few softly spoken words. 'Oh, I'm sorry Rhys. I see what you mean now. Silly me.'

The waiter is at the table asking for our plates.

'Yes, I believe we're all finished here,' Mel says. 'It was just sufficient, thank you.' Then she takes out her purse and insists on paying for our meal.

As we leave the hotel I'm all over the place. My mind keeps replaying our last conversation. Over and over. Mel's insensitive words have opened another raw wound atop of the last mental scar. My self-esteem is somewhere between my throat and my tightened gut: And once again my thoughts turn to my friend, Aimee.

# BANG

On the street the carbon monoxide fuses with the dust. It is lifted from the street and blown in swirls about our feet. I decide that after the restaurant debacle I need a smoke to help settle my nerves.

'I need a fag Mel.'

'Yeah, sounds great darling. I've been meaning to give them up but this is a celebration, us being together and all, so I don't suppose one little puff will hurt, do you? And I'm so sorry for my outburst before. I really am.' She smiles up into my eyes.

'No. I don't suppose one little one would hurt,' I reply casually.

'Where do we get one? You must know the ropes around here so I'm putting myself in your capable hands. I feel so safe when you take charge.'

*Jesus! Talk about flitting from one world to the next.*

We cross the street, avoiding a flurry of taxis and curb crawling street vendors. Mel is fascinated that one of these vendors sells glass tumblers of clean drinking water from an aluminium cold storage box, set atop two bicycle wheels. It is a small, but lucrative business on a hot city day, and that's every day in Colombo. Bypassing an ice cream vendor, who has a similar contraption as the aqua-man, we stop at a cigarette vendor's cart. I buy a single Bristol cigarette for Mel, tailor-made, and a bidi for myself. Then I grab the smouldering rope from the side of the cart and light Mel's cigarette.

'Cool,' she says, and is as impressed as I first was when I discovered the end of the cart ember-bender.

I light up my bidi.

'What the hell is that?' she laughs.

'I dunno really? Some kind of leaf I think. It's a bit weird, but it tastes ok. It's a bugger to smoke though as it has a tendency to go out. No saltpetre I guess. Wanna try?'

'Uh, no thanks: Too weird for me.'

We both laugh.

Then something terrifying happens. I have never been anywhere near an earthquake. I've heard about them, seen the devastating aftermath on the television. The razed buildings. The trapped bodies. The death. But I have never been in an earthquake, and neither am I in one today…because what we felt wasn't a quake. Sure the ground moved. We all felt the tremor vibrate up our legs and into the pits of our stomach. But it wasn't a quake. It was far too loud for that. Far too explosive. Because an earthquake doesn't sound like that…but a bomb does.

I remember being in a friend's house once. He had recently bought a set of Bose speakers and I was lying on the floor between them, a mere metre and a half apart. He put on a track entitled, 'Hells Bells', by an Australian band named *AC/DC*. All five minutes and twelve seconds of it, and it almost deafened me for life. But that doesn't come anywhere close to describing the intensity of what just happened. Because, when a bomb blast surrounds you, it engulfs the very world you're standing in, and with it's thunderous intrusion come the deadly consequences for those at the epicentre. It's no ear-splitting three hundred and twelve second rock song. It is the sound of death.

Instinctively I want to run toward the blast. Run with all of the others who now run past us. All running straight into the epicentre, and I want to run there too. All running to help, and I want to help too.

Mel had practically jumped into my arms.

'Oh my God Rhys. What was that? '

'It was a bomb Mel. God, don't tell me the Tamil Tigers have finally moved into the city?'

I think back, remembering the night the Tigers rolled down to our mud huts at Arugam Bay, sticking gun barrels into people's mouths and causing some of us to piss ourselves.

'C'mon let's go and see what's happened. See if we can help?'

She grabs my hand and begins to take off but I don't move and she is jerked to a halt, held firmly in my grasp. She turns around with a wild look on her face, and screams at me.

'For Christ's sake Rhys. C'mon! There could be people down there who need our help!'

In an instant I admire her charitable qualities and altruism. I remember those charities she upholds, her work with Oxfam, her sponsorship of two small children in poverty stricken Africa, her time given up at the soup kitchen during Christmas.

All of these qualities are beautiful.
She can be beautiful.
But she can be wrong too.

'We're not going anywhere,' I say. 'We're not going down there Mel. It's too dangerous.'
'What do you mean, too dangerous? For God's sake Rhys there could be people down there who are hurt. Women. Children. What the hell is wrong with you?'
Our eyes lock, and I say.
'Because it could be a ruse.'
'A what?'
'A trick, Mel. We all race down there, right into the epicentre, then who knows? Kaboom! What if there is a second bomb? Another one set to kill even more people. And we're there, right in the middle of it. Imagine what that would do to our families. Sure I want to go down there and help, but it's too dangerous. We have to stay here. In fact we're going straight back to the hotel to get our stuff, then we're catching the next train down to Hikkaduwa.'

By the time we get back to the hotel it is close to midday. We pack and wait outside for a taxi to take us to the train station and before long are in a souped up Morris Thousand, with its smell of finely polished red leather, and its dashboard draped in soulful garb and colourful paper garlands. At the helm is a cheery driver, calculating how much he can scam off us, and he is fortunate, as I am not in the mood for hard bartering. We agree then, on a price well above what I wanted to pay, and a little below his first offer. As we motor through the streets we talk about the explosion.
I say,
'My friend will you be knowing what is being with the big noise happening earlier? Was it being a bomb?'
Our driver is practically jumping out of his seat to tell us that it was indeed a bomb.
'I am practically jumping out of my seat to be telling you two good peoples that is was indeed a bomb that was bombing up all of the Central Telegraph Office and it will be killing many persons. The Tamil Tigers very bad mens, now coming into the city to be making

bombings and scaring too many mens and womens.'

Mel looks at me sideways and I can see that her eyes have watered at the driver's account of something that has instantly ripped apart a dozen or so families, because in Sri Lanka everyone is someone's uncle or aunt.

As it turns out there *was* only one bomb, and not two, but there is certainly no, 'I told you so', from Mel, in fact she is quite shaken and is more than happy to be heading to the train station and out of this infected city.

## THE LAST SURF

The early afternoon train from Colombo arrives in Hikkaduwa train station with just enough time for me to race back to Sunny's house, grab my board and head off for a few waves before it gets too dark to surf. Even though we are loaded up with Mel's extra luggage we can still make it if we step lively.

We arrive at the train station and we wait.
And wait.
And as the minutes pass so does the prospect of catching the last few sets of the day. It's that finite, and I feel myself becoming more and more pissed off as the idea of getting in the water is ebbing with each passing moment. I really need this surf.

'Bollocks. That's it,' I rant. 'There goes my evening surf. Poxy bloody Sri Lankan poxy railway service. There's more organisation skills in a nest full of frigging ants!'

By now I'm pacing up and down a section of the platform and am attracting some quizzical looks from the local commuters. I have taken on the persona of a ranting, spoilt child. I know it, but I don't care, as it is helping to vent the frustration from past and present events.

Mel chimes in, 'For Christ's sake Rhys. Calm down will you. You can always go surfing tomorrow.'

As I wander up and down the platform, back and forth, quietly steaming, I come to the realisation that I haven't lost my temper once since leaving home. Yet, not two full days have passed with Mel being here and we have already argued twice. This sudden awareness doesn't sit well with me: It doesn't sit well with me at all, and so I really need this surf to numb the sting of the Dragon's tail.

The train is now an hour overdue and I've had enough.
'C'mon Mel, we're going to catch a bus. At least that way we're still moving and not stuck here sweltering beside these frigging train tracks.'

I grab most of the luggage and we head outside to catch one of the minibuses.

'Hey! Hey! Flip-flops! Flip-flops!'

It's Rocky D'Silva, the boy I first met on arriving at the airport. He's running over to us, fighting fit, as he shadow boxes his way through the teeming lines of traffic.

Then he's with us.

'Hey Rocky, you sure get to many places my friend.'

'No, I am not being Rocky,' the boy says. 'Rocky is being my twin brother. My name is Leonard. Sweet Sugar Ray.' He winks at Mel, displays a lollypop smile, then breaks into fits of laughter.'

'Ah, Mr Rhys. I am to be having a joking time with you Sir. It is really me,' and he taps his chest. 'Rocky Balboa.'

Rocky looks to Mel.

'Good afternoon most beautiful Miss. How rude of me not to be introducing my good person to you. My name is Diva D'Silva but you can be calling me, 'Handsome Rocky'.

He then bursts into another fit of infectious laughter whilst dancing around us in some weird Sri Lankan jig. And you can't help but admire this kid who has more front than a seaside promenade. Mel is enjoying Rocky's performance and my melancholy demeanour has dissipated as quickly as Rocky's humour has surfaced to save us.

'Where are you to be going now Mr Rhys?'

I explain to Rocky that we have been waiting for the train to Hikkaduwa, but that it didn't turn up. What Rocky says next has both Mel and myself frozen to the spot. He begins to tell us that the train wasn't late at all, but that it had become derailed (as Sri Lankan trains can sometimes do, due to the warping of the metal train tracks in the unforgiving heat) and was still squatting a few kilometres up the track. This news is bad enough as often men, women and children are hurt during such an accident, but what he tells us next literally chills us to the bone.

The train is now wreckage. In one of the carriages, a time bomb was planted that was set to explode as the train pulled into the station. It was timed to explode as Mel and I were waiting together for that same train. The very train that is now a strudel of hot twisted metal further up the track, but thankfully the bomber couldn't possibly predict this phenomena, this unpredicted derailment, and so this act of terrorism never took place as planned.

So we are still intact.
Our limbs are still attached.
No blood.

No gore.
No disembowelment.

Mel's lips are still where God placed them and both my testicles are obeying the laws of gravity. For others who aren't so fortunate they will be dead. Or lying with wounds too costly to cure, wounds that will fester into ensuing anguish and debilitating pain. Mel and I find out later that if Rocky was privy to more information than the beat of a jungle drum, he could have told us that twenty two soldiers and ten civilians lives were destroyed on that train. It is apparent then that the tendrils of Sri Lanka's civil war have reached this far. The war is no longer contained in the North but is now spreading its fear and destruction along the south-western part of the island, where both locals and tourists alike are at its indiscriminate mercy.

Rocky sees us to an awaiting minibus and I slip him a few extra rupees for old times sake. Thankfully the bus is only half full and we don't have to wait too long before it is packed to the hilt and racing us south, back to the sanctity of Hikkaduwa. Mel grips my arm tightly as we swerve to avoid oncoming traffic and overtaking equally manic vehicles on precarious bends.
'For Christ's sake Rhys don't these guys ever slow down. We nearly hit that poor man back there. He only just managed to get out of the way.'
And it's true that the occasional pedestrian is hit, spun, and killed along this stretch of road. I attempt to make light of it, hoping to ease Mel's discomfort, and say with a half-laugh, 'It's always like this Mel. I call it precision driving. It's perfected down to the last few centimetres. It's just that some drivers are better at it than others.'
But she's not happy.
'Oh that's all well and good for you to say but what if that guy had been hit and has a young family at home who depend on him?'
So I say, 'Well then, I guess the kids would be without a dad and their mum would have to look to the immediate family or village for help. There is an amazing support system out there. It's just the way it is Mel. Life here is cheap.'

I knew as soon as I said these words they sounded callous and out of character. But it's too late, they've been said, and have fouled the air between us.

Mel turns to me with those piercing eyes and with that sneer she wears when she thinks she's so bloody right. Suddenly I'm sitting next to a version of The Godfather with tits. A moment ago I'm comfortably savouring chicken soup for the soul, basking in the warmth, feeling the love, because my girlfriend is clinging onto my arm in desperation and fear. Then, within that very same nano-second my brains feel like they are being mashed all over the dinner table with a forty-two inch psychological baseball bat. Because Mel says,

'I can't believe you just said that. What're you Rhys? A moron? I can't believe you think it's ok for these dickheads to career around the place, smashing into people and then treating the situation as if it's *fucking normal*. You think that that poor man is simply another statistic, do you? And that's all ok as it justifies his family's loss?' For fuck's sake Rhys has this place messed your mind up that much?
It's a rhetorical question, 'coz I'm in the shit regardless of any reply.
Mel's voice then rises a couple more octaves as she moves into her reptilian fight mode. I've witnessed it all before, seen it, experienced it, and let me share with you, it's not a pretty sight. And so she licks her lips and continues to hiss.
'And another thing. You bring me to an island where people are killing each other and where there are bombs in the city and bombs on the trains. For Christ's sake Rhys what were you thinking?'
She has now thrown herself into the pit of absolute denial, so it's useless to even point out that it was her decision to come to Sri Lanka in the first place. Whichever way it pans out she's both the jury and hanging judge of this kangaroo court, and I'm the condemned man no matter how absolute my defence is presented. And she continues: She practically shrills. 'If you'd have told me it was going to be like this I never would have come!'
Her words pierce me as if someone has ice picked me in the forehead and I just shrug my shoulders as there is no point in replying to her rant. It's not that I cannot think of anything to say. I'm absolutely fuming. I have within me a barrage of ungodly words. Words of revulsion and loathing. I have within me black, sinister words, screaming to get out. But that's not who I am, or who I choose to be. So I remain silent and let the shit slide right off me.

Mel turns away and looks out the window. She has removed her hand from my arm. I look down the isle at the driver knowing it's not his fault. It's his life: and if he ever did hit, maim or kill someone, he would always include that person in his prayers and live the remainder of his life harbouring a painful and tainted past. The inhabitants on the island are a wonderful people, a joy, a smile upon the world. As those on the bus stare at us I feel their resolve and I share in their shame. Most of them would understand enough of the English language to have worked out the gist of what Mel has said. Understand the language, yes: but not the ranting of a beautiful white girl, who appears to have the world at her feet, yet is raining shit down on their homeland and its ways. It is an injustice, as it is an injustice to blame the driver whose boss expects speed: demands it even. He demands as large a profit as possible and so his driver has no option but to squeeze in as many precarious journeys up and down this steamy stretch of road.

Because it's expected.
Demanded.
And everyone's expendable.

Because there is always another driver in line who, like our driver, has mouths at home to feed. And after all, the driver didn't hit him, he had instinctively swerved with precision. He missed him. He is gone, but we are still madly racing south.

Another burning revelation is reached then. So cold, so icy, so finite, that I ache from the sheer chill of it.
And it's that Mel will never fit in here.
She'll never get it.
She'll never get *me*.
My heart feels so heavy because I feel as if I've really messed up and now there's no going back. Now I wish that I'd never read that pink letter, all perfumed with its scent of empty promises. God how I wish I could rewind the clock. How I wish I'd never allowed my heart to become exposed again, to have allowed a further part of it to be tainted by this woman sitting next to me. I have a deep sense of foreboding, a real sense of dread weighing heavily about my heart.
And I have to question myself.

*What have I done?*

## BOILED SWEETS

It is well past sunset when our minibus leaves us standing at the roadside in Hikkaduwa. The full moon is climbing into the warm sky, throwing blurred shadows about us.

I had such delight in telling Sunny that I was bringing Mel to stay at the house, but now I'm dreading it. I have a feeling that it is all going to go so horribly wrong. The house is pretty basic and on second thoughts perhaps I should have found more fitting accommodation for us. A hotel perhaps? But then I reflect that this is Sunny's home we're staying at, and that I've been accepted as one of the family, so why should I let this person dissolve away their virtuous ways and their homely hospitality? I figure if she doesn't like it, she can just fuck off and stay somewhere else!

Mel breaks into my thoughts as she speaks light-heartedly to me.
'So where is Sunny's house then? Is it far?'
'No. Just over there, over the railway tracks,' I say blandly, pointing toward the jungle track. 'It's only a short walk. Less than a couple of minutes.'
Mel picks up her rucksack with steadfast purpose, puts it on her back, slips her hand into mine and lets out one of her infectious giggles.
'Well c'mon then Spunky. What are we waiting for?'

*Jesus wept!*

Sunny and his family have been waiting patiently for us. They are at the front door as we arrive and he beams one of his casino smiles.
'So you are being Misses Mel.'
He steps forward, bends slightly at the waist and shakes Mel's hand.
'You are being my most welcomed guest. My house is being your house. My family is being your family, like it is being for Rhys.'
Sunny beams even wider, as proud a man as anyone I've ever met.
'Hello Sunny and Mrs Sunny,' says Mel warmly.

'Shanika,' I interject, gesturing with an open hand and smiling at Sunny's wife, trying to be as upbeat as I can, and believe me it's difficult. 'And these two scallywags are Nashanta and Lasanti.'
'Hello you two. Now wait a minute, I think I may have something for you?'
Mel puts down her rucksack and ferrets through an inside pocket. She straightens up and in her hand she has two large packets of boiled sweets, which she holds out to the two beaming kids.
After receiving an, 'ok nod' from their father, they giggle wildly then run around to the back of the house.
Mel looks warmly at Sunny's wife.
'Kids and sweets, Shanika. Such a good match, don't you think?'
Then Mel laughs warmly and embraces Shanika as if she is a life-long friend.
'What a beautiful garden you have,' she says on breaking the embrace. 'How I would love to have such beauty around my home. It is like a magical moonlit garden from a fairy story.'
And Shanika smiles the smile of a winning horticulturalist.

> *Christ, are we still on the same planet? What just happened to the female-fiend from hell? Did I somehow miss a 'suck-the-bitch-out-of-here-vortex', leaving this sweet sweet girl behind?*

Mel continues with her kindness.
'Please take us into your beautiful home Shanika,' as she motions toward the door, expecting Shanika to go on in, except that protocol cannot be usurped with such soft gestures and kind remarks, and it is Sunny who steps past his wife to lead us in, with Shanika comfortably following behind.
'Wow! You can really tell we are living in the jungle,' says Mel, and as if on cue there is a loud breaking of branches next door. Through one of the windows we can see the resident elephant next door playing with some fallen debris.
Mel rushes over to the window.
'My God Rhys. Look it's a real elephant! Quick, come over here and have a look!'
Mel's delight is infectious and she bounces up and down on the spot with childlike glee. I move alongside her and she wraps herself around me using both arms. One of her legs is practically at my waist.

'Look Darling, a real elephant.'

'Yes, she's awesome isn't she? Her name is Aliya, which I think means 'to go up'. Right Sunny?'

Sunny nods.

'And she actually works for her living, either hauling logs in the jungle or carrying tourists along the beach. I can organise a ride for you if you'd like?'

'Oh that would be fantastic Darling. How exciting! A ride on a real elephant. Could you do that for me? Could you? Would you?'

And she looks at me, smiles, and kisses me, being more of a snog than a kiss.

Mel whispers in my ear, 'Sorry about before Sweetheart. It's been such a big day and I guess I'm feeling a bit tired what with all of the travelling and everything. I'll make it up to you later, I promise.' And she winks!

Shanika has already moved through the house and is now out the back with her sweet-sucking children and her minimalist kitchen. It is life per-se for her, but for Mel and I, perhaps it is a new beginning?

I show Mel into our bedroom, half expecting her to balk at the coconut mattress and limited furniture. But in no time at all she has unpacked, asked Sunny if she may commandeer a small table from the main room, which she then covers with a colourful sarong of hers and on which she sets up her 'lady-likes' of perfumes, balms, moisturisers, face cleansers, and other female necessities. She has even put up a picture of us taken in Bishopston Valley on one of our many countryside rambles with her ridgeback, Cai. Now with an array of feminine clothing strung from a string line reaching from one side of the room to the other, the bedroom has been instantly transformed into a place having a soothing effect and a sense of completeness. This is a welcomed contrast to the previous abode of flung shirts, discarded boardies and a dishevelled bed. Even that has been transformed into a piece of furniture, in which you can imagine yourself making love instead of performing a quick jig and reel.

Mel undresses and wraps herself in a towel.

'I need to take a shower Darling. Where is it?'

'Uh, it's out the back,' I say. 'And you may want to prepare yourself; it's a little bit unorthodox.'

'Ha!' she laughs with stage-like passion, 'I'd expect no less from this weird and wonderful place. Can you show me?'

Mel follows me through the house, out into the back garden and past the tiny kitchen where Shanika is there peeling vegetables. They both give each other a friendly wave.

'There's only cold water,' I say. 'It comes from a tank up there.' I point.

'Just be prepared as some of the algae may come down through the pipes from time to time. It's harmless, but it does have a habit of catching you unawares. It actually saves you having to moisturise if you decide to leave it on and give it a bit of a rub in. Or if you let it dry it's great for exfoliation.'

Mel starts momentarily, gives me a quizzical look, then laughs,

'You're such a giggle Rhys! That's one of the things I love about you. You always find the fun in life.'

Mel leans over and gives me a sweet kiss on the cheek, then steps into the shower.

As I'm walking back into the house I'm half expecting to hear a high pitched scream coupled with a few choice words, but neither come, and ten minutes later Mel glides back through the house positively glistening.

It was good sleeping next to Mel, even though I woke up several times during the night due to two hot bodies in the same bed. She however, slept like a kitten and awoke me as the sun was rising with a pleasing encounter. I come to, from within the confines of my REM sleep with Mel making fine music down below. Then beyond these moments of pleasure and with fellatio finito, Mel moves up the bed and snuggles in under my arm.

She looks up.

'So what are we going to do today.... Piccolo?'

'Ooooo! That's it you little teaser. Now you're for it!'

She struggles in a forgiving way and before long we are embracing, engaging, laughing and moving toward further gratification before heading off to the slime room where we soap each other up, wash each other's hair and rinse each other down. Then with a quick towel-off we say goodbye to Sunny and head out of the house to check out the surf.

Mel hops onto the crossbar of the bike and we're off! It's all a bit of a balancing act as I have one hand on the handlebars and the other precariously holding onto my surfboard. Mel is squealing like a banshee as we navigate the pothole riddled jungle track toward the main road, and she's loving it. Once on the tarmac of Galle Road the bike is easier to control and now it's only a matter of avoiding being rammed up the jacksy by a Toyota roller Coaster. We make it, and pull into the Rasta Hut, one of the restaurants located directly opposite Hikkaduwa's main surf break.

The Rasta Hut is a classic place to hang out. It's theme is Rastafarian, and Victor, the owner, teases his fingers through greasy dreadlocks as he bangs out reggae music from dawn until dawn if you're keen enough to party that hard. There are no rules at the Rasta Hut, as anything having rhythm goes.

The wind at the beach has dropped off, almost to a dead calm. If anything, when it does muster up a wisp it gently blows offshore into the faces of the new swell. The waves are well over-head and breaking consistently, however because the ocean is unruly it demands some healthy respect. The point of 'take-off', where the wave is caught, is constantly moving, so the session is going to be a healthy paddling workout, having to be in the right place at the right time.

'Hail up Rhys man. Sun is shining. 'Ow you digging man?'

'Good Victor. Good. How's yourself?'

'Mi Irie Man. Tanks.'

Victor is dressed from head to foot in a Rasta coloured kaftan, he is a fluid swirls of reds, greens and yellows, and being a big man looks like a clone of Demis Roussos on acid. Victor's Jamaican accent is a constant source of entertainment borne from the grooves of every *Bob Marley* album that was ever pressed onto vinyl. There isn't a lyric that Victor hasn't chewed up and regurgitated, Sri Lankan style, and there are posters of The Legend all over the walls.

'You going out man. Irie waves man. Lively up yourself though. Old man Huey he is mighty fiery today ya know.'

With his surf report concluded he turns his attention to Mel.

'This ya empress man? Having this woman you no cry for sure man. Nice man. Nice.'

He smiles widely, laughs deeply, then moves in for Victor's customary double-cheeked European kiss. Victor is smooth with the ladies, and they must love him for it as he always has a cortège of

pretty ones in tow. With one grand sweep of an arm toward the ocean, then a more subtle approach toward Mel, he says,
'You go surf man and I'll fix ya empress one of my wicked true brew cocktails. She'll be irie man. You can trust old Victor you know.'
And he gives me a cheeky wink.
'Mel, you watch this slippery old Rastafarian. He's got more tricks up his sleeve than the Egyptian magician.'
'I'm sure I'll be fine,' says Mel. 'You forget I'm a brown belt in karate.' And with that she playacts a few moves from a kata ending it with her foot, unwavering, about two inches from Victor's face.
'Ey man this girl's got some Punch and Judy, ya know. Don't you go spending too much time in the water Rhys man. I'm feeling a little uneasy here with Boobs Lee ya know.'
With that he bursts into laughter, grabs a bottle from behind the bar and begins to make one of his notorious cocktails. I grin at Victor's antics, kiss Mel, then grab my board and head out into the beckoning surf.

# THE 9 - WORDED THREAT

The surf, as predicted, is wild and woolly. It is a challenging two hours of fun, has the heart pumping and at times a few of the larger ones test my experience.

Back on shore I meander back to Victor's only to find that Mel has taken herself off for a walk. Victor tells me that she has headed southward towards Narigamma beach, the place at which I had the near drowning bodysurfing experience.

'Fed 'er with a few of Victor's favourites man. Got her juices flowing ya know. All Pinky and Perky she was. Said she needed to walk it off. She' a wild one that girlie is ya know. Even showed me her tattoo way down south man. You've got a soul rebel there man.'

'Yeah thanks for the Mills and Boon synopsis Victor but keep your thoughts to yourself ok.'

My tone is both unfair and unjust. Victor, after all, is only the messenger, and it wasn't him displaying the *rosy peach*.

'Whoa! What's with the fussing and fighting Rhys man? You don't need to go shooting no sheriff man. Never seen you like this before brother.'

'Yeah well you've never seen me with a bitch on heat before Victor. Sorry man, I know it's not your fault or anything. I'll catch you later ok.'

'Irie man. Catch ya later.'

I leave my board with Victor, don my t-shirt and sunnies and head off to find Mel. You can imagine the shit that is racing through my mind now. Half drunk beauty wandering the streets of a tropical isle with a tattoo way down south, and on show to whoever is willing to buy her two pints of lager and a packet of crisps. All *Splongenessabounds*. And some may think this amusing, but it isn't.

I feel my pace quickening, and my heart rate rising as I pedal hard towards the southern beaches. Perhaps my emotional pangs are totally misplaced and unwarranted here, and that they have simply been dredged up from the sands and sins of times past.

Yes?
Possibly?
So why then is my stomach tight and the bile from it rising at each rotation of the bike's wheels.
You see, I've been here before.
But in a different country.
A rhetorical question runs through my mind and that is, 'Should I have ever opened Mel's letter, or should I have cast it aside with the contempt it deserved?'
And the other question on my lips is…'Where the fuck is Mel?'

I can't see Mel anywhere on the main drag or on the stretch of beach at Narigamma so I have pulled into four beachside restaurants within the past fifteen minutes, but still she is nowhere to be found. After a couple more restaurants I'm about to give up as I figure maybe Victor's got it wrong and instead Mel has headed back to Sunny's house to sleep off her cocktail indulgence. That is, until I hear her unique laugh punching through a *UB40* work of art. It sounds more of an exploding giggle than a laugh. One that evokes the turn of heads in a pub, and one that invites people to share in its excitement and frivolity.
And it is coming from over there.
From that restaurant.
From behind that two metre bamboo wall, each sturdy piece tightly bound, thereby shielding its patrons from the omnipotent traffic that races down Galle Road. Each piece hiding a secret garden in which laughter abounds and where the chatter is brazen.

In that garden is my girlfriend.
In that garden is the reason why my heart is palpitating and my muscles flexing, and my brain throbbing against the confines of my skull.
In that garden is my supposed future.
In that garden are my dreams and aspirations.
In that garden is the rest of my life.

Into that garden is where I need to go then, so I cast my bicycle to the ground like an aggravated schoolboy and go in.
What greets me is not unkind to the eye.

Pleasant enough if it were you.
Pleasant enough if it were me.
Pleasant enough if you were sitting back comfortably in a padded seat in some tarty nightclub watching your own private show unfold before you. And certainly pleasant enough if you are the lucky bastard who is smack bang under your girlfriend's sprawled demeanour, lapping it all up. And there is practically no reaction from Mel as I make my stage-side entry.

No dropping of the bottom lip.
No element of surprise.
No look of embarrassment.
No quivering of bared flesh.

It takes me about a millisecond to engage in the lewd situation and now I'm in full flight with teeth bared.
I raise my voice to the point of verbal abuse.
Disgusting decibels.
Using filthy foul-mouthed obscenities the football terraces would applaud.
Language befitting the walls of a sewer.
All guttural and ugly.
And I ask you, were you expecting a shriek from Mel? Her hand to her mouth perhaps, miming heart-felt humiliation? A flood of tears and a covering up of white flesh perhaps? And maybe you were, and in fact so was I, but then perhaps a reminder is in order here: that this is Mel we're talking about: a woman who thrives on excitement and daring. A woman who adores sex, and who rides on the heels of exhilaration.
My Ex, come regurgitated girlfriend.
The Dragonbitch: Remember?

Instead, she simply looks over in my direction, and I see that her eyes are blood-red, their wateriness blind to my ranting.
'Hey Rhys. Chill out darling. We are only having a bit of fun.'
(Present tense I may add.)

And she says this while straddled across this local's legs, sarong hitched up in her hands, still swaying gently to the slow rhythmic beat as her newfound friend peers around her, at me, within his air of comfortable amusement.
I can see that Mel is completely out of her mind, and she says,
'C'mon Rhys-ee baby. Come and meet my friend Scoobie.'
She gestures affectionately.
I am close now.
I have moved in.
'Meet your friend Scooby is it, you stupid little tart? Get the fuck off him.' And with that I grab her by the arm and yank her across his legs and into *my* space.

And this Scooby offers no resistance.
Not a skerrick.
I glare into her eyes with toxic hatred.
'We're leaving. Now! And as for you, you low life piece of shit...'
This Scooby hasn't even flexed, even though I am standing over him, practically foaming at the mouth, 'You come anywhere near my girlfriend again and I'll stick your head so far up your arse you'll be wearing your balls as a necklace. Comprende fuck-head?'

And he is one cool dickhead, this Scooby. He hasn't moved a muscle. Not even a twitch. He's reactionless. If you read his body language you would say it to be brimming with confidence. There is a sureness about his manner. He simply goes on to counter the event before him with a knowing smile, and says this,
(His tone, and detail I shall recall days later. His composure, the cold weight these words represent, and the chilling consequence of my brazen stupidity I will remember verbatim.)
He says nine simple words, does this Fuck.

*'You don't know who I am do you Tourist?'*

I shall also remember, and recall in detail the gold chains hanging about his neck, of which I am unaware in my current state of hatred. For I am a dammed fool who has unwittingly rushed in to this cobra's nest. I'm oblivious to the simple fact that while most of the locals have to walk everywhere, because they cannot even afford a bicycle, let alone exhibit jewellery, this lounger, this unperturbed perpetrator, this predatory snake, is laden with gold.

Fury is such a blind commodity. It is man-to-man, eye-to-eye, centre of the ring stuff. My blood is boiling over and I figure if he stood up now I would knock the fucker into next week. And so my response is quite natural given present circumstances, (and the fact that I have no idea who I am really dealing with.)
So I reply,
'I don't give a fuck who you are you slippery piece of shit. And as I said keep the fuck away from my girl or I'll fucking do you!'
And with a firm grip I begin to march my stupid nymphomaniac of a girlfriend towards the gate.

But it's not over yet…as there is more to come.

Again there are nine words spoken - though not by me. But these nine, small, and individually inconsequential words carry with them the razor-edged sword of Damocles. And they are these…

*In two days you will know who I am.*

Nine more words.

But I don't give a shit and I dismiss these words, and him, for the wanker I believe him to be and pull Mel out onto the road.
 If you can actually throw someone onto a pushbike then that's exactly what I did. The stupid bitch is still giggling as if we had recently left front row seats at the comedy gala. I, on the other hand, am tamping, and it is taking all of my self-discipline not to flip the stupid cow off the crossbar and into the oncoming traffic.
 When we arrive back at Sunny's, the door is wide open as usual but there is no one about. I march Mel into the bedroom were she flings herself onto the bed. She lets loose her sarong from around her waist and removes her tight clinging t-shirt, allowing her breasts to bounce free. All the while she is doing this she is looking me straight in the eyes. Then she upends herself on the bed lifting both legs in the air so she can slide off her bikini bottoms, which she does, enticingly. As mad as I am I am not immune to the appreciation of beauty, sex on a plate, and a delectable body. However appreciation is one thing but acceptance, tolerance and sheer hatred is another.
'You can't help yourself can you Mel? Even now when I have had to practically drag you off another man's cock you can't help but turn it

all into one big game. You really are some piece of work, you know that? You make me sick just looking at you!'

She lies naked, there on the bed, resting on one elbow with one leg straight and the other with knee bent. She looks at me seductively as she slides her hand between her legs, caressing herself, from bent knee to navel. At another time it would be intoxicating but under the present circumstances I want to puke all over her.

When she opens her mouth the tail of the devil rides out.

'You really could do with smartening up Rhys. I was only doing it for us you know. Don't you see, the more jealous you are the more I love you? My god Rhys if your IQ was any lower I'd have to water you. Oh, and if you're not going to enjoy me, could you please close the door on your way out, there's a good boy, as I'm in desperate need of a little privacy.'

With that the psychotic bitch discards her sarong, closes her eyes and begins to masturbate: Me, I slam the bedroom door as I leave, shutting out her repugnant world.

## TIME OUT

I pack my bags whilst Mel is in the slime room showering with the rest of her genetic siblings. There is no way I am spending another moment with the black-hearted bitch so I have decided to leave and have told her that on my return she is to have left the house. Sunny, although upset that I need to get away understands completely: After all we are now as close as brothers, and a strong family will always stand by you through thick and thin.

I have left my board with Sarat and Harry at the Dewa Siri restaurant and as I await the bus I sense an atmosphere of knowing on the street. The jungle drums have been beating whilst we've slept, and when I think back to the unusually long looks I received from atop of sewing machines, and from behind roti stands on my way to the bus stop, it is obvious that the street is fully aware of our social history. In Hikkaduwa, like any small community, news moves faster than small boys can scramble and dart to tell it. Faster than women can call it over bamboo fences.

I have decided to take one of the local red buses the seventeen kilometres south to the port of Galle. Here I can gather my thoughts and try to work out what to do next. I figure I need a complete break from all that is familiar; to clear my mind of recent events.

The day is hot, blue and depressing. And I am struggling with the fact that I have allowed my bastion to come crashing down, leaving a pile of emotional rubble at my feet. To catch the bus I have to pass Thora, the wrecked fishing boat, who quietly shared my trepidation and delight when I opened Mel's letter those many weeks ago. I gaze over at her now, to the place where I sat, and am instantly transported back in time; remembering her hard bow against my back and the smell of her dank hull about my person. Now, instead of my haven, a friend who shared a private moment, she appears as she is, a broken down vessel, empty of all that was useful, and never to be restored to what she once was.

On continuing up the road I see a crowd of onlookers gathered around an open patch of ground from where there is a wisp of smoke rising into the blue. I head over to be greeted by another one of Asia's unexpected distractions. The vertically challenged crowd allows me a clear view of the performance on show. There, in the middle of a patch of sun-drenched grass stands a wiry little man whose age is indistinguishable. His leathery jowls lagging from his cheeks and his spindly bowed legs poking from beneath his richcoloured lungi, could easily belong to that of an eighty year old man, or even someone half that age, it's hard to tell.

He stands bare chested, bare footed and with a large ball of string laying on the ground in front of him, the other end of which is firmly up one nostril. Then he snorts violently with the gusto of a cocaine addict in a nightclub cubicle. The ball of string on the ground twitches and unfurls slightly, as the other end proceeds to meander its way up through the man's nasal passages. With another violent sniff the show continues, the ball twitches once again, and the crowd lean forward in further appreciation of this incredulous spectacle. Further snorting and sniffing allows us to witness this ragged little man reaching into the back of his mouth, and on locating the snotty end of the string, proceed to pull it back into the world of sunshine and applause. What we further witness then, is the largest nasal flossing action known to man. He pulls the string, like coloured handkerchiefs from a magician's sleeve, at an alarming rate of knots out through his mouth, while the ball of string dances wildly on the ground.

Finally the theatrics are over leaving a mass of regurgitated, if we can call it that, pile of string on the ground in front of him. With a bow and toothless grin to his audience, he then begins to pick up the small amounts of change thrown at his feet.

But the show's not over yet. There is more to come, and this part of the act involves a series of watermelons arranged in rows before him. The little guy kneels down in prayer fashion and appears to call on help from those beyond we mere mortals. Once done, he brings his head down so that his forehead rests on one of the fruity footballs. To and fro, up and down he moves. He has become a human Texan oil well then in one final motion brings his head crashing down onto the melon, breaking it cleanly in half. He moves forward on his knees to the next melon, passing over broken pieces of fruit as he goes. There is no toing and froing this time as it's straight down to business...and smash! Another melon bites the dust.

And he keeps going.

Three, smash!
Four, smash!
Five, smash!
Six melons smashed, destroyed, crushed by this local nutter, who again smiles, bows, and collects his hard earned dosh.

However the pièce de résistance is yet to come. The trail of smoke I had seen earlier is the result of a small fire that has been burning quietly, and has now become the focus of our attention. The fire isn't smoking anymore but has instead become a rectangular length of coals about a metre wide and three metres long. And it's hot. Red-hot. Our little magician moves over to the edge of it, places his feet only centimetres from the sizzling embers, closes his eyes and once again becomes trance-like. I had heard stories of the 'fire-walkers' before. People who could traverse hot coals and yet feel nothing. However I had taken these stories with a pinch of salt, but now I was about to witness some desperate fool getting the best part of his soles burnt away. The crowd and I wait in anticipation, then the man's eyes open in readiness, milky-white in appearance. He doesn't run. There is no race to the finish line, no breaking of the winner's tape. Instead he simply walks. Walks, I say. I am witnessing what I had thought to be an impossible feat. Yet as I watch this grizzly little man walk this furnace, with the souls of his feet crunching the fiery coals beneath them, our little man appears to be oblivious to the fact that he is traversing a dragon's bed.

The magic concludes with applause from all, and again there is his gratitude. Again this little man bows, and again there is the collecting of his dinner money. The crowd now recall their daily chores and so disperse quickly, leaving this wondrous little man and myself alone. I watch as the little wizened wizard collects the last of the thrown rupee coins, putting them carefully into a small drawstring bag. I move up beside him.

When he turns his head toward me I see that his milky-white eyes also possess a dull bluish haze. This string snorter, this citrullus smasher, this fire-walker, is even more amazing than I first thought, because our wizened little friend cannot see. He is totally blind.

I am dumbfounded and bewildered by this revelation, as each of his movements during the act appeared to be visibly fluid. I have in my hand a one hundred rupee note, a monetary fortune to a blind wizard, which I place into one of his calloused palms. Now whether each note has an individual feel or a distinct smell to a blind man I cannot say, but he holds me firmly, this wizard does, by my gifting hand, and speaks to me in a voice hushed by the moment; and in perfect English,

'One hundred,' he says. 'The Gods have truly smiled on me today and may the Gods bless you in your time of trial within your heart Majan.'

They are unnerving words coming from a complete stranger, and later on the bus I reflect on the differences between us. I am fit, young, and relatively wealthy, whereas he is none of these. Yet, as I gave him this small fortune it felt nothing more than the soiled piece of printed paper it was, compared to this magician's aura.

*In my time of trial, within my heart for Christ's sake.*
*How the hell could he have known my troubled mind?*

# SANDY AND SPIRITS

The Galle Road we travel on runs parallel to the sea for the entire journey south, passing through small villages, whose individual aromas are puffed about by the gentle offshore breeze. As our wagon races through the villages I savour in the visual delight of children playing, of colourful vegetable stalls and of slumbering fishing boats nestled safely between small groynes after their oceanic hunt for shrimp and small fish. We race past coves and beaches that twist and curve alongside us, spilling their soft sand into the crystal clear Indian Ocean. If there exists an edge to Heaven then we are surely travelling along it.

At one point the bus pulls up to take on even more passengers and on the opposite side of the road I see a hierarchy of women sitting on ascending stones steps outside their house. A little girl sits at the base of a set of steps, her elder sister a step above her, their mother on the next step up and finally the grandmother above them all, each nit-picking away at the head below them. I watch them laugh and joke as they search out and thumb-squeeze the small biting animals that are a constant nuisance amid the family's fine locks.

Further on we cross a small estuary bridge where I see young men casting out circular throw nets with the ease of a discus athlete. The sand, the sea, the blue, the mud coloured water of the river as it glides towards the ocean, the dugout canoes, the white crested waves unfurling against smooth granite boulders in the distance, all seem so at odds with my current situation. The whole world appears so alive, so vibrant, and all I want to do is get out there and be a part of it. All I want is to savour its delights and to live a good life.

The bus pulls into Galle and I am greeted by the wonder of the natural harbour, with its infamous lighthouse and living fort, reputably the best example of a fortified city found in south-east Asia. The fort, I remember, was built by the Portuguese sometime in the fifteen hundreds, then extensively fortified by the Dutch in the seventeenth century. The streets, therefore, are set out in a rectangular grid pattern, with rows of low houses, having gables and verandas built in Dutch colonial style.

The bus meanders through these historic streets, sporting fabulous names such as Old-Rope Walk Street, aptly named for the manufacture of the old coir rope, and Chando Street where the small arak distilleries were once found, and Lace Street where silversmiths sold silver (called *Galle lace*) to visiting aristocrats. The entire place oozes culture and historical wealth.

The bus then makes its way through the Main Gate, on the northern side of the fort, no longer having its heavily fortified portcullis or drawbridge that long ago spanned over the purpose-built moat in which it was even rumoured the British once had crocodiles to dissuade the enemy from swimming across. Today though it is filled in, with not a crocodile in sight.

Whilst in Galle I have decided to splurge somewhat and treat myself to a stay at the island's oldest surviving foreign establishment, The New Orient Hotel. This exotic haven sits high atop the eastern ramparts of the fort, overlooking Galle's inner harbour. My thoughts of Mel seep in and leech out, niggling at tender nerve endings. My heart is heavy and I am hoping the lightness and historical beauty of this infamous hotel will at least quell some of my residual disappointment and grief.

The New Orient Hotel stands high and strikingly white in the day's sun. As I approach the building I marvel at the garlands of red hibiscus trailing its walls, adding vibrant colour and a sense of warmth to its romantic past. However, behind this façade of magnificence the New Orient Hotel possesses a mysterious and spiritual secret, laying deep within its bosom.

I walk into the cool Dutch interior and come to rest at a beautiful span of English oak, crafted into what is now the formidable front desk. On the walls are old paintings depicting numerous sailing vessels and steamships at anchor in the inner harbour, waiting to be laden with coffee or coal. There are also mail-boats and men-of-war, heavily weighted with cannon, there to support the land based, and Queen's own, 50$^{th}$ Regiment, the Ceylon Rifles. And since Ceylon, as it was know then, had superseded Egypt as the resort of choice for the more affluent Europeans wanting to escape their winters, there are also pictures of the fort streets showing the venerable emporium of foreign trade. They depict teems of Europeans in white morning dress, buying Madras cotton, Gale lace, and other such wares from the local Chetties or traders.

The man at the desk is none other than K.C. K.C. had joined the nearby Galle Face Hotel as a bellboy, come waiter, in 1942 and is currently 'on loan' whilst the hotel is undergoing maintenance. K.C. is infamous for having served Arthur C Clarke, Roger Moore, Richard Nixon, Indira Ghandi, Don Bradman and Yuri Gagarin. Perhaps they even passed a little time with him, and I can easily understand why they might, as he is finely eloquent, and emanates charismatic charm.

K.C's syllabic soothing tone is that of a smoky single malt, and his appearance is as much a part of history as the old colonial building itself. His eyes are a smooth hazel, harbouring a soft and gentle wit. His smart khaki safari suit is pressed to the crease and he smiles as naturally as I draw breath. Once he has me sign in the elaborate leather bound register he passes me the key to my room. The key is exactly as one would expect in such a fine establishment, large, weighty and made from cast iron. It has chunky old-fashioned teeth, and on it is stamped the number 25. KC has, for reasons unbeknown to me, chosen to place in my hand a key that opens the door to an infamous room in the hotel: A room in which a ghost is believed to reside.

I enjoy several quiet days at the fort, wandering the streets and savouring the cultural wealth that Galle has on offer. Some time later I am making my way out toward the fort's ramparts, passing the old Commandant's residence, gun house and arsenal. I have in one hand a bottle of tequila, procured from the bar, and in my other hand is a girl named Sandy.

K.C. told me that the best place from which to watch the sunset is Trion bastion, one of the fourteen bastions located around the fort. On our way there we stroll past the eighteen metre high lighthouse and on towards Flag Rock, from where muskets were once fired to warn the approaching ships of the hazardous rocky stretches below, before the lighthouse was built.

Sandy is nice. She has nice brown hair, nice white teeth, and a nice smile. Her body has experienced a little over indulgence, but in a nice way. And her ample breasts bounce in a friendly manner as she walks, which I also find nice. Sandy is nice to me and I am nice to Sandy. It is a nice walk and we are both a little drunk.

I met Sandy in the billiard room. She appeared sometime between a red ball and a coloured. 'Do you have anyone to play with?' she asked as the pink ball disappears into a middle pocket.

'No I don't actually,' says I. 'Are you on offer?'
Sandy giggles in a nice way and says that she is. So we play…and she plays well. She hits the red balls in lineal fashion and polishes the pocketed colours with her dress before re-setting them on the table. Sandy, in her nice way, is beating me in more ways than one. She is wearing a loosely fitting, thinly strapped white floral summer dress on which are printed small blue daisies. The translucent nature of the cotton allows her body form beneath to become silhouetted from time to time when she passes through the javelins of light streaming through the elongated windows. It is rewarding when I admire the curve of her breasts and the 'v' between her shapely legs. Sandy is refreshingly picturesque and as she prepares to take her next shot she straddles herself across the table. There's a pulse from below and I am hoping Sandy doesn't realise that I'm looking on in sexual appreciation, instead of good old-fashioned sportsmanship. Outstretched and poised, with one leg off the ground, (tightly tucked against the table I might add), she slides the cue back and forth between thumb and forefinger, delicately and in what appears to me to be a rather deliberate manner. Then with cue in hand and bent over in such fine fashion she looks up and catches me red handed, looking, what I can only fairly describe as, intently.
'Ahh! Forgive me Sandy. It's just that you look so…beautiful.'
Then she replies, with kindness, and in a nice way,
'You don't have to apologise to me Rhys. You're really nice…and it's kind of exciting having you watch me so . . . excitedly.' She giggles. 'I like it.'
Sandy smiles, then quick as you like, she looks to the white ball and doubles the black into the corner pocket with a solid and meaningful thwack! It is game, set, and a well met match. Sandy and I set up the balls, as is customary, then head off to the pool to enjoy a couple of quiet cocktails before walking out on our early evening stroll.

We pass Flag Rock bastion, hand in hand, and she giggles as I amuse her with some Welsh humour. I shower Sandy with easy affection because it helps fill the void, and because I like Sandy, and Sandy likes me. We stop at the Trion bastion, where a windmill once drew water from the sea to sprinkle the dusty streets of Galle. Far below us the Indian Ocean flattens out to the horizon, whilst behind us the grassy tiers carpet the fort's one hundred and thirty acres in patches of softened green.

As the sun begins to set I pour out a couple of shots of tequila, ring the brim of the glasses with some salt, and squeeze in a few drops of lime juice. I hand one over to Sandy.
'Uno ,dos, tres. Salud!' I say.
And we drink.
Only I don't swallow mine, instead I hold it in my mouth, lean over to Sandy and kiss her fully on the lips, passing the liquor into her mouth. Her eyes batter widely as she swallows my surprise.
She laughs, 'Oh Rhys that was brilliant! No-one has ever done that to me before.'
'Lets have another then so you can pay back the compliment.'
So we do. We compliment each other by taking it in turns to prime one another, and with each kiss we become more aroused as our intoxicated lips share one another's delight.

The sun has now relinquished itself to the onset of dusk so that a luminous curtain patterns the sky in rufous gold. I kiss Sandy once again and slide my hand in between her legs whilst massaging her spine with the other. I lean in and inhale the scent of her hair and feel her breathing change. It becomes shallow as I trail feather-light kisses across her shoulder and feel her legs part slightly, allowing me to delve a little further.
'C'mon Sandy, let's find somewhere a little more comfortable.'
Before she has answered I have her by the hand and am leading her across the lawns to a concealed dip, where the grass is soft and inviting. We lie together and kiss passionately, and we sex each other under the blanket of a tropical night.

*Christ I needed that.*

When I awake the hours are small and the drowsiness deep. I am dehydrated and reach across to the bedside table for my water bottle. As I do I catch something moving across the room, something amiss. It is the shape of man who then disappears into an Anglo-Indian wardrobe, which stands against the far wall. I think no more of it than it being my imagination and the evening's alcohol playing illusionary tricks on my tired mind.

That is…until the morning.

A friend of mine has a gift. She sees entities: spirits and ghosts. Spirits, she says, are souls continuing to progress on their spiritual journey. They are aware of their surroundings but given the right circumstances are able to interact with the living. Ghosts she believes to be those souls who have yet to cross over to the higher realms and therefore have become trapped in the lower astral plane. These unfortunate souls are often unaware they are dead, or perhaps are too frightened to progress on their spiritual journey.

I awake in my room, alone, as Sandy had to catch the midnight bus to Colombo, and this suits me, as I need a clear mind to think things through before embarking on my trip back to Hikkaduwa.

Before leaving the hotel I jokingly mention to K.C. that I saw a ghost in my room last night. His reaction, however, is not one I am expecting. Instead of finding humour in my story, dismissing it for the folly it is, K.C. recalls previous stories of similar sightings in Room 25 at the New Orient Hotel.

'That would be one Albert Richard Ephraums,' he says. 'The original owner of the New Orient Hotel.'

I feel the hairs at the back of my neck rise as K.C. goes on to corroborate this fact with the story of Mr Ephraums' granddaughter, Ms Nesta.

'One night, many years ago,' he says, 'the staff called Ms Nesta Ephraums to room 25, the room in which she was born. They had heard strange noises coming from within. When at Room 25 Ms Nesta looked on as one of the servants tried in vain to turn the door handle of the unlocked door, but could not. They witnessed that from under the door a light could be seen and that the sound of someone pacing to and fro across the floorboards could also be heard. Then when the pacing stopped and the door opened there was no one to be seen inside.'

K.C. continues,

'There is also another occasion, when Ms Nesta saw her grandfather cross her bedroom and disappear into the very same wardrobe you talk about. When the young Ms Nesta related her story to the family the following morning she was told that there was once a secret doorway where the wardrobe now stands.'

What I cannot explain is that, instead of being unnerved by these spiritual stories and my possible visitation, I feel strangely empowered by the whole incident. Could it be possible that spirits do walk amongst us and that there is more to this world than meets the eye, and that perhaps entities do disappear into ancient wardrobes in the middle of the night in a Sri Lankan hotel? And wasn't it the influential psychotherapist Carl Gustav Jung who once said, 'I shall not commit the fashionable stupidity of regarding everything I cannot explain as a fraud?' Yep, good old Gustav.

I bid K.C. farewell, but before I leave his company K.C. leans across the desk to share these words with me...

'Mr Rhys, may I be saying something to you?' And he does. He says this. 'The shadows in one's life are caused by someone standing in your sunshine. You must walk out of the dark and into the sunlight my young friend and leave the shadows behind. A man must live his life by a code Mr Rhys: An ethos. It is his shoreline. It is what guides a man forward. And you, Mr Rhys, you have a good code. You are a good man. I know this.'

K.C.'s words further empower me and as I leave the New Orient Hotel I am determined to cast the sordid memories of Melanie aside and to move on with my life.

# RAT

I get off the bus at the Dewa Siri Restaurant, as I figure there should be waves judging from the swell I saw crashing along the southern beaches. Sarat fetches my board from a back closet and I wax up. I need to surf before confronting Melanie back at Sunny's house, as in all likelihood she will still be deposited there.

The water is so warm in Sri Lanka that it cannot be described as refreshing, but spiritually purifying, and as I push the board through the oncoming white water and feel it rolling over my body it delivers a cool sensation of inner cleansing.

The waves are challenging, and there are plenty of them. And as in many sports involving physical exertion, with the release of endorphins and adrenaline, the body reaches a state of elevation. And so it is for me, but now it is time to leave the water, to dry off under the blazing sun, to leave my surfboard with Sarat and to engage in a probable face-off with Mel.

As I walk from the restaurant, along the sandy path towards the main road, past where Aimee and I loved, my mind is racing, calculating what I am going to say. Internalising it, editing it, aiming to have it perfect in its delivery. I am internalising words of hatred and deceit, betrayal and loss, and the future against the past. All of it an emotional onslaught of epic proportion. I am so engrossed within this inner turmoil, that in allowing another pedestrian to pass me beachside, I have wandered a little too far into the road and am nearly collected by a speeding vehicle. The close shave has shaken me up so I decide to plant myself on a seat at one of the roadside roti stands to recover.

It is then that I see Siri, my good friend and bicycle owner, or rather that he sees me. Siri has been seeking me out and is now cycling madly across from the other side of the road.
'Where do you go now majan? You cannot be going home. There are too many policemens there. They are looking for you. They are coming down the jungle track and are now being at your house!'

Siri is breathless, scared even, and his furtiveness aids in scaring me also. I attempt to ask him what is going on but he cuts me off.

'No time now majan. You must be coming with me. Quickly majan, be climbing onto my bicycle.'

I load myself onto the crossbar, allowing Siri to race off in the opposite direction to Sunny's house. My head is spinning with confusing thoughts. We head south and within minutes we are racing down a track and into the thickness of the jungle. Siri lays the bicycle against a nearby tree and explains.

Two police jeeps had cruised into Sunny's garden and are there now. They are looking for me Siri says. Hunting. This frightening news washes over me like a black wave, and has my heart racing and my temples pulsating as I try to make sense of it all. I turn. Spin. The weight of my predicament is suddenly as clear as the blue skies above. I figure that not only am I now trapped on the island, but I also have nowhere safe to hide. I am on the run. A fugitive.

Siri breaks into my thoughts, 'Majan, I will be going and checking to your house. You are to be waiting here and I will be coming back to you.'

I muster a reply and Siri leaves me alone, feeling totally exposed and acutely vulnerable.

Then the penny drops…The Sri Lankan guy at the beach. The one Mel was straddled over.

*What was it he said?*

'In two days you will know who I am'.

> *Christ, who was that guy and what if the police are driving around hunting for me right at this minute? What if they come down this track? What if they're on their way now? Sunny's house isn't that far. They could be here at any minute, any second. Christ, what a fucking mess!*

I think about running deep into the jungle but the last skerrick of rationalisation I have left prevents this. The police are in jeeps, and Siri said there are two vehicles. Jesus, they could even come from different directions. Outflank me, run me down like the outlaw I have become.

In my panic mode the only thing I can think to do is to climb into the dense vegetation alongside of the track and hide. And I do, I climb in, but it's not long before I begin to sink up to my knees in leg sucking swamp mud, and become stuck. I can't move. I'm trapped. The swamp has me in its grip so my only option is to crouch down to minimise my presence. My arse slops about in the water and I feel the fetid liquid move up my legs and into my shorts. My heart is rocking, tears are welling and I'm concerned that if I have a heart attack in here, in this oozing swamp-patch, I may never be found. Even Siri wouldn't be able to see me from the track.

*How long has he been gone now?*
*Ten minutes, twenty? I've even lost track of time.*
*Surely he can't be much longer. It isn't that far to Sunny's house.*

*The house.*
*Mel!*
*Mel is at the house!*

*She'll be mad as hell, fuming at my stupidity, blaming me as usual.*

But then my anger rides me out of this sense of responsibility.

*What the hell am I thinking? None of this would have happened if she had kept her fucking legs shut in the first place. If she hadn't have straddled, teased, leeched her suggestive manner in the company of that lowlife at the restaurant. If she'd had one ounce of decorum, had been virtuous in her ways, none of this mess would have happened and I wouldn't be stuck here in this stinking swamp, scared witless. If she wasn't such a worthless slut I could be sitting at a beachside restaurant, sucking on a smoothie, instead of squatting in this stinking hellhole sucking on fetid air.*

The realisation that this mess is really all her fault is making my blood boil. Then in the midst of this fury I hear Siri's voice.

'Here Siri! In here!'

By the time Siri helps me out using a long stick I am both waterlogged from the waist down and stinking like a sewer rat. But I don't care. It's unimportant. Inconsequential, compared to what Siri is about to tell me. He wears a strange mask. His customary smile is absent, replaced instead by a grave look of concern.

He has news.
Devastating news.
And it concerns Mel.

'They are to be taking Miss Mel,' he says.
'Taking her? What do you mean taking her?' My voice is angry, loaded with a poisonous undertone and I see Siri baulk a little. 'I'm sorry Siri! I didn't mean to sound so…it's just that…'
'No problem majan, I am understanding all,' he says graciously. Then continues, 'The police sergeant is a bad man, he is to be putting Miss Mel in his jeep and is to be taking her to the police station.'
I cannot believe what I am hearing. It's as if he is speaking in tongues.
'Jesus Christ Siri! Why the hell did they take Mel? You said it was me they were after.'
Then it dawns on me. There will be no game of cat and mouse. The police have the bait and I have no option but to surface like a beaten dog. No option but to go to the police station and exchange places with that stupid low-life. It is my code.
'Yes majan, it is you they were after but now they will be happy because they are to be having Miss Mel so they are to be doing a good job.'
'I know Siri. They will use her as bait, because now I have to go to the police station and give myself to them.'
'No, no, you are not to be understanding majan. The policemens, they are happy now,' Siri reiterates, 'because they are to be catching Miss Mel. You can be going back to the house with safety now majan. The policemens will not be coming for you anymore. They are already to be having their prize.'

I'm totally confused. None of what Siri has said makes any sense. Why are the police happy that they have Mel instead of me? It is me they were after, so what the hell has that to do with Mel, if she is not to be used as a lure?

Surely it'll pan out like this…
They have Mel.
I go to the police station.
They let Mel go, then they have me.
Case closed.
But this is not what Siri means.
I simply don't get it?

But the reason I'm confused is because not all of the facts are on the table. Because the hand being played has been drawn from a marked deck. I have been constructing a scenario with only part of the script, and with some of the most damning information missing. I have been conjuring up abstract fiction, without full knowledge of how this sinister plot is about to unfold. Siri has more to tell me, because he's yet to mention the most important detail of all, and it's a detail that is about to rock my world.

'You're saying I can go back to the house now Siri. You say it is safe. The police aren't looking for me anymore. How can this be Siri? What the hell is going on?'
I am practically pleading with Siri, willing him to explain more quickly. My arms are outstretched with my palms up, my knees bent, (before they buckle), and my eyes begging. Then he lets the bombshell drop, with another nine words.
Nine heavily laden words.
Different words.

Not - *In two days you will know who I am.*

Not those.
But another nine words: Having even greater impact.
Nine destructive words.
Nine words that will foul the air with poisonous consequences,
Nine words that slip from Siri's mouth,

Like this …

> *The police, majan.*
> *They are to be finding heroin.*

## BARS

The police station is located about halfway to the post office and it takes only a ten-minute bike ride to get there. It is a mediocre one-storeyed building, with a short yard out front, no more than six metres deep, serving as a sandy buffer to the main road. Surrounding this dusty yard is a low, carelessly built wall, which has been roughly plastered with light brown mud, which in turn has been layered with light brown paint. There is a short wooden gate set in the wall. It is open, and uncomfortably beckoning. There are two uniformed policemen on guard in the yard whose tunic buttons battle their podgy rice bellies. Their tarnished silver buckle and leather belts hold up their crudely fitting pants. They are customarily holding each other's index finger, whilst carelessly resting on the butt of their guns, with the rifle muzzles digging into the dirt. I choose not to acknowledge them as I walk past and up the three steps to the colonial wooden door.

Due to the poor amount of light filtering through the heavy cloth window blinds the interior of the police station is dusky and opaque. The dark wooden floorboards hinder what light is struggling to illuminate the dark corners and as I walk in my weight causes one of the heavy floorboards to creak loudly. The noise echoes down the long corridor, off which run several rooms, some with wooden doors, others only metal bars. These are obviously the holding cells, causing me to wonder in which one Mel is incarcerated.

Venturing further into the gloom I stop at the first room's entrance and am greeted by its sparseness. A metal filing cabinet, a ceiling fan, which appears to have been wanting to stop for decades, one bookcase and, hanging on the wall, a water damaged picture of the President. The room is dominated by a huge ornate wooden desk with fine brass inlay and a recessed rectangle of British racing green leather, on which lie papers, a fine fountain pen in a silver penholder, a military styled hat and a steaming cup of tea. Behind this decorative desk sits a burly man who smokes a cigarette, the curls of which become entangled in his thick well-groomed moustache, before escaping into the heavy air that engulfs us both.

The Moustache looks up.

'I believe you have my girlfriend here, Sir?' I say with as much conviction as I can muster, considering I am positively shitting myself.

'You will sit,' says the Moustache.

So I sit in the unoccupied chair opposite him. His black hair, clean and well cut, falls thickly onto his wide forehead. His large bulbous nose divides his beady black-eyed peas, which themselves are set in sinister fashion, having being genetically created far too close together.

Once I have sat the Moustache continues,

'So you are Mr Rhys Evans. I have been looking hard for you Mr Rhys Evans. And look, now you are here.'

His shoulders are wide and his arms finish in stocky forearms and powerful meat hams. Even his fingers look cruel, despite the existence of a wedding ring on his heavily bruised left hand. His words are not so much said with malice but with the confidence of a player who knows he owns the game. All the rules are his, the deck his, the dice his. His words burrow into me like a mango worm, leaving only one thought.

*Trap.*

'Yes, I have your girlfriend here Mr Rhys Evans,' says the smoke tinged Moustache. He is speaking slowly, forming each syllable carefully for maximum effect, ensuring that there can be no misconception as to the predicament we are in. I feel that the person facing me is more like the evil prison commandant bastard from the movie 'Midnight Express', than your friendly neighbourhood pavement pacing plod. When he speaks it is with a voice befitting his demeanour, dark and ominous, and even his mysterious English accent does nothing to allay my fear of possible restraint.

'She is in deep trouble Mr Rhys Evans, this you must know? You see heroin is a very serious offence here in Sri Lanka. It carries a penalty of thirty years and the prisons here are unlike those in your country. They can be rather unpleasant, especially for a pretty young white girl, if you follow my meaning.'

The mention of the words 'pretty young white girl' conjures up a visual burst of unpleasant and graphic images and the mention of thirty years…

…*Thirty fucking years!*

His words have stripped me of what little self-confidence I had to begin with. My voice is a whispering slurry of pain, distress and pleading.
'There must be some mistake Sir. We do not take drugs. My girlfriend has never taken heroin. It must belong to someone else?'
Then below the moustache a smile appears, displaying teeth well cared for, some even having gold-filled cavities. He appears pleased with himself. The Fucker. There is a huge sense of satisfaction pouring out from across his desk and his next card in the game is an obvious one, but my mind isn't up to speed. There has been too much to take in, so when he next speaks the impact of his words deliver another unforseen trick.
'So what you are implying then Mr Rhys Evans, is that the heroin belongs to you. Is this correct?'
I laugh, all instinct and survival. The bared teeth, and nervousness of a penned beast awaiting its slaughter.
'My heroin? No! No! Not my heroin. My girlfriend and I have never taken heroin! It is a very bad drug! Very bad for the mind and body! Very bad karma. Heroin is shit!'
My voice is an emotional plea, but it falls on deaf ears. Moustache continues as if I have said nothing.
'But it must be *someone's* heroin Mr Rhys Evans and it was found in *your* room under *your* mattress. You were not there but your girlfriend was, and so, fortunately for you she is here in my police station, instead of yourself. If you say it is not yours, then it can only be hers. This heroin business is a very big problem for your girlfriend Mr Rhys Evans. A very big problem indeed.'

His words cement the enormity of the predicament we are in and now all I am concerned about is where Mel is being held, and how she is coping with this terrifying mess.
So I ask in desperation,
'May I please see my girlfriend Sir?'
I see that Mel has been crying. Her eyes are blood-red and her cheeks are saline stained. She looks so helpless sitting on the rusty

steel spring bed, staring off into nothingness. She hasn't heard us coming but on calling out she races to the bars, clinging to them in the hope that they will fade away, but they don't. Instead it takes a large key to unlock the heavily barred door, allowing me to enter.

Mel rushes straight into my arms and she holds me closely as if, were she to let go, something terrible would happen. But I break away from her, hold her in front of me and look into her swollen eyes.

'Rhys they found heroin and they think it's mine! They kept asking where you were, over and over and over. Then they went into our room and began searching.'

Mel babbles all of this, syllables overrunning syllables, and I ask her, 'Did you go in the room with them?'

'No,' she tells me. 'They told me to wait outside and then they called me in. One of the policemen was lifting up the mattress while another was pointing to a plastic bag stuffed in the corner. Where did that bag come from Rhys? I mean, where the fuck did the drugs come from?' Mel continues, her voice breaking up in between fits and sobs, 'Then the one pointing picks it up, opens it, licks his fingers, dips it into the bag and tastes the powder. *Brown sugar* he says to the others in the room and then they all laugh. They all laugh Rhys. And I don't know what's going on. I'm really scared Rhys. Really, really, scared.'

Mel buckles, collapsing onto the hard bed and so I sit with her, putting my arm around her, trying to comfort the inconsolable.

'Why am I in here?' she sobs. She is finding it difficult to draw breath.

'I have done nothing wrong Rhys,' she wheezes. 'Nothing.'

I whisper for fear of being overheard.

'It's the guy from the beach Mel. Remember what he said?'

*In two days you will know who I am.*

Nine words.
Inconsequential on their own, but when strung together they have interwoven to form a noose.

'The reason the Police found heroin in the room is because the Police put it there. All this has been orchestrated by that guy at the beach. We've been set-up Mel.'

At this point Moustache returns telling me that I have to leave. He says I can come back in the morning with some food for my girlfriend, but now it is time for me to go. Mel is still sobbing uncontrollably and buries into me. I look up to plead with her captor.

'We can get money. Her father is a very rich man. Then we can pay for all your troubles Sir and make this terrible mistake go away.'

I see a reaction, a quick flicker of light behind the officer's eyes, nevertheless my words fall on fallow ground as he replies with calculated menace,

'You must go now Mr Rhys Evan. While you still can.'

The words are spoken in a deliberate tone, for maximum effect, and it works, causing me to reflect on how different this scenario would be if it had been me at the house and not Mel. The smell of wrongdoing fills the air with the stench of injustice. However, an invisible cloak of relief shrouds my emotional outpour. I wish with all my heart that it is not Mel sitting in this musty hellhole, but at the same time I am thankful that it is not me either. Even though I know it is not my fault Mel is locked away, I cannot help feeling that I am hanging from a Judas tree, swinging in the wind of self-preservation, with thirty pieces of silver rattling around in my inside pocket.

I turn to Mel who is sucking in air as if it is her last breath.

'I will be back first thing in the morning Mel.'

And I say, 'Hang in there.'

And I say, 'Don't worry.'

And I say that, 'Everything will be all right.'

And I promise.

But in my heart of hearts I don't believe a word of it. In my heart of hearts I think that she's totally screwed! But my sense of duty must outweigh my doubts. We are entrenched in this stinking horror together, and I feel it my responsibility to get Melanie out of this godforsaken mess and safely home:

*But how?*

# GLIMMER

Back at the Lucky Sun Inn I am greeted by Sunny and Siri. We sit down. Sunny hands me a soda from the fridge.

'It will all be O.K. majan,' says Siri. 'I am to be having an uncle in the police forces and he is being a very important man. He is a good man and he will be fixing all of this. He is being away in Colombo and is to be coming home in two days. We will be going and to be talking to him. Don't worry majan we will be fixing all of the troubles for Miss Mel.'

Siri's words comfort me, as I'm willing to grasp at any dangling straw. At least this will give me something positive to tell Mel when I see her tomorrow. Now we just have to sit tight and wait it out for two days until Siri's uncle returns. However we didn't have two days, because within the next twenty four hours the playing field was changed, and all of the rules along with it.

During the night I had one of those running nightmares when, no matter how far you run or how hard you try to get away you make no ground. We are running, Mel and I, when we see our parents calling us to safety from across a gentle river. But our feet are shackled to long chains so we are pulling and tugging on them, fighting to reach the river's edge. We are both crying as we claw toward the bank, with our nails stripped and our bodies shredded from running through the barbed jungle foliage. Our limbs bleed in streaks and our tears run red. Then the chains about our feet are wrenched violently and we are dragged backwards, in bloodied shackles towards a dark pit. I see claw marks on its muddy walls and coagulated blood over its rim, lying thick in slick blackened pools. In the pit are foaming rabid dogs and they bark expectantly at our edible bones. I feel the stickiness of wet blood seep into my clothes as I slide through the muck, then fall backwards into the abyss. Mel has disappeared now; now it is only me, tumbling downwards like some discarded ragdoll. On hitting the rocky bottom I awake with a sharp start to find myself drenched in the cold residual sweat of a night terror and I instantly think of Mel: Mel who will spend thirty years in a foreign gaol, whose lifeblood will leach away within the dank dark shadows of a living hell, and I race outside to throw up.

When the shards of first light strike into the darkness, the relief from my terror is overwhelming. I get up and make my way to the slime room where the freshness of an awakening jungle is welcome and the sound of its staccato existence helps to lend a little solace to my over burdened mind. I wash myself intensely, as if the scrubbing will help rid me of my despair, and once dressed I alight my bicycle and begin my journey back to the police station. If I hurry I could be there sooner than later. But I don't hurry. I take my time. I take my time because I have begun my journey too soon, without prior thought, and without a plan. Despite what Siri said about his uncle I feel that I can't truly rely on anyone and so I amble, pushing down on my pedals with just enough pressure to keep moving. At times I have to brake as I have gained too much momentum. I need to wait for my train of though to catch up. I am oblivious to everything around me and it is no small wonder why I am not knocked from my bike by the menace of Galle Road. I am capitulating question after question, trying to find an answer to this dilemma, trying to muster up a faint glimmer of hope.

As I pedal I think.

*What?*
*What?*
*What?*
*What am I going to do?*

I answer myself with these three possible scenarios:

> *Do I don the 'white-suit' and blaze in there like colonial gentry? Demand that this is a violation of our civil rights and how dare they bestow their corrupt and seedy existence upon a white person, and a woman at that? The British Embassy will hear of this, of that you can be assured!*
> *Or do I try the forlorn approach, a broken down man, who is to marry this girl, a girl who has promised to bear me fine children.*
> *Or do I talk money again?*

My mind is awash with love, hatred, fear, confusion, betrayal, honour: Heroes and villains. The Innocent and rightful justice. I should have ridden past the police station, gathered my thoughts, and formulated a real plan. Then I should have doubled back, but instead I have allowed my mind to become so preoccupied that I have already abandoned my bike, passed through the small wooden gate, acknowledged the guards this time around, and am now halfway up the police station steps.

I have even forgotten to stop and get food for Mel.

The morning light bouncing wildly off the tarmac behind me barely reaches into the doom and gloom of the police station. And it is with trepidation that I move further into this dark place, for I feel I am entering a spider's lair.

He'll be waiting there. Sitting there within his web of deceit, with his officious globular nose, heavy moustache, sweat patted brow and greasy palms. The fan will still be battling against the thick humid air and the smoky odour will still be clinging to the walls. And Mel will still be in there too, behind bars, behind lock and key, hungry, unwashed and expectant.

And sure, as I turn into the sergeant's office, the same layers of dust, the same pungent smell, and the same dull brown uniform confront me. However, unlike before, this uniform is not that of a Sergeant Second Class, but is one of a more senior officer, a Sergeant First Class, the three wider silver stripes on his epaulettes denoting this fact. Sitting before me then is a different police officer. The buttons to this man's tunic bulge more than the last but instead of the beady eyes of a ferocious ferret, I am greeted by the brown-eyed warmth of a favourite uncle. He strikes the pose of a 'distinguished gentlemen', and his shock of silver hair belays his eminent vintage. And so it is not the Moustache who sits before me, but Siri's uncle, having the same fine boned nose as my friend, the same jawline, the same warm smile. My delight and enthusiasm is uncontainable. I introduce myself and stretch across the ornate table to shake our saviour's hand with robust vigour.

'My name is Police Sergeant Malani and I am Sirinatha's uncle,' he says. 'His mother is being my sister.'

*Halle- bloody-lujah! My prayers have been answered. God is great! God is great!*

'Please be taking a seat Mr Rhys,' Siri's uncle says pleasantly.
'Thank you, Sir. Thank you.'
And I sit. And I begin my spiel in my best pidjin English.
'Sir, there is having to be a terrible mistake going on here. My girlfriend who is being brought here is an honest person and people are saying that the drugs they are finding are belonging to her, and that they are finding them in her room but I tell you now good Sir, I can see that you are being an honest man and that it is all being a terrible mistake and the evil drugs must have been there before. You must surely see that they are belonging to another man who is staying before in the house during last season.'

I am rabbiting on, sure. And I know this, but it is controlled and precise. My mind has sharpened, and as the imminent threat has passed I am delivering each word of this conversation carefully, because the next thirty years of Mel's life depends on them. Also, I am being extremely careful not to imply that it was the police who had planted the drugs in the first place. After all, although the man sitting before me is Siri's uncle, he is still an acting member of the local constabulary.
'Yes Mr Rhys, I am knowing who you are and all that is happening. I am coming back from Colombo early and am visiting my sister's house late last night. Sirinatha was there and he is to be telling me all the big problems you are having.'
'Yes. Siri,' I say, and wobble my head in effective readiness before I emit my next calculated delivery. 'He is being a very good friend with me. We are becoming like brothers. He is truly like a family person to me.'
And on quiet reflection, as I sit here in front of one of Siri's close family members, I realise that there is truth in my statement. Siri and I have become like brothers. Surfing together, partying together, and as with Sunny, sharing common aspirations, hopes and dreams together. I decide to edge a little closer to the precipice of kinship and so go on to say,

'Siri, he is telling me that you a good man, who is kind to his family and understands that life is sacred and is given to us by our God. That life is a precious thing and not to be wasted by the people of a young age.'

Siri's uncle smiles in acknowledgement, and nods in the affirmative.

'So I am asking Sir, and Siri is to be telling me that his uncle, who is a very important person, can be helping me and my girlfriend with this terrible misunderstanding. One day we will taking great joy in having many children and one day I wish to become a father like your good self. To love my family and to be a good person with all of the world.'

Siri's uncle smiles, voicing a reply that is both kind and understanding. He says,

'Oh yes, being an uncle and a good father is all such the most important job. I can be seeing that you will be making a good father Mr Rhys.'

He laughs, but although his words are warm, I detect a subtle cold change in the air, his facial expression changing slightly, and I question whether I momentarily witnessed a fleeting wave of sadness sweep across an uncle's brow.

But I dismiss this thought, putting it down to the emotional weight of the situation, to the extreme pressure. To the fact that Mel's life is in jeopardy and is resting precariously in my sweat lined hands. One slip up and the ball is lost, grounded by the other team, who'll go on to win thirty years to nil.

Siri's uncle's voice floats around the small room, pulling all things in close,

'And I could be helping you and your good lady with all of this.'

My heart flutters.

> *Did he just say what I thought he said? Didn't he just say that he could help us, make this all go away? Allow Mel to walk free, to come home with me now, to be safe? Isn't that what he just said?*

'Oh yes I could be helping yourselves because this is being my village and this is also being my police station.'

I am overwhelmed with joy, and the air of relief must be transparent. However because of this, because of my obvious delight, because of my look of triumph, Sergeant Malani feels the expedient need to clarify the situation at hand, before I succumb to further bouts of exaltation. And so the cold chisel of reality strikes its destructive blow. The wrecking ball swings from rusting chains, to smash a cruel path through my hopes, destroying my God given Faith, which only moments ago had warmed my soul like the words from a powerful sermon. But the words Siri's uncle utters are from no sermon. They are plain, simple words that sour the air like a regretful remark.

He speaks now, does Sergeant Malani, Siri's uncle, and he says this, 'But unfortunately now Mr Rhys I am not having any powerfulness in this matter. My hands, they are being tied by the wheelings of justice. It is a sad thing that I have to be saying this to you Mr Rhys, but I cannot be helping you in this matter with your girlfriend.'

My head feels like it is being squeezed in a vice.

Twist!
Twist!
Twist!

My heart has become so laden with cold stone it could well be stopped. My stomach is now so tight that it jerks into fits of nauseous convulsion. I rise quickly from the chair, leave the room and race outside into the front yard: To puke.

The two guards look on as I retch violently into the dust below, splattering my feet with the sickness I feel. I heave again, the fourth or fifth retch, I know not which, for I have lost all clarity now. I am devoid of further fluid for all I have left to regurgitate is the emptiness of longing, and there is no substance to that. One of the policemen on guard comes over and offers me some water from his bottle. An act that is a testament to the kindness of the Sri Lankan people and I gratefully accept it, tipping the tepid water into my mouth before heading back into the police station.

Siri's uncle is standing, smiling and wobbling his head as if these actions, in some way, will alleviate my immediate malaise. He is a likeable man and yet I am annoyed that he is unable to help. Surely there is something he is able to do? After all, he is a senior officer and the man in charge. After all, this is *his* police station, and as he said, this is also *his* village, which is probably the most important factor of all? I decide to pitch one last desperate shot.

'You are saying that there is nothing you can do Uncle. Perhaps I can be giving some money to someone for all of this trouble to go away?'

But as these words spill from my mouth, the distaste of acknowledging corruption with a man who has shown me nothing but courtesy and compassion since I arrived, bites like a wild Arugam Bay dog.

But his reply is by no means a rebuttal. There is no trace of resentment in his voice, quite the contrary, because he agrees that with the passing of money this could indeed be possible. Now I am completely confused by his words, as they make no sense.

'So you are saying Sir, that it *is* possible to be paying some money and to making this trouble to go away?'

Again Siri's Uncle wobbles his head, only this time it is in agreement, and again my body convulses in anticipation that there is still a chance that Mel can be set free.

'Oh yes. It would all have been most possible,' he continues, 'if your good lady was still being here in my police station.'

Bang!
Bang!
Bang!

'I do not understand Sir. What do you mean, 'not still being here'?'
So Siri's uncle clarifies,

'She is being taken away last night to Colombo. The desk sergeant is to be having a phone call from the Commissioner. He is to be making fast tracking for your girlfriend because she is being a foreigner and that possessing heroin it a very most serious charge in these times. The sergeant you are meeting before, he is being told that she is having to be taken to Colombo most immediately. Then he says this…(And listen carefully my friend for at first I too thought I had misheard.)

'And so they are taking your girlfriend away. They are to be taking her to *Slave Island*.

I check.
Rewind.
Re-run the last few sentences for interpretation, as surely I missed something, his broken English and village accent rounding off too many syllables.

'Excuse me Sir. Where are you saying my girlfriend has been taken?'

192

I turn my head ever so slightly so that I may catch each and every word. (And believe me there's no mistaking the words a second time around.)

'To *Slave Island*,' he reiterates. 'They are to be taking your girlfriend to *Slave Island*.'

I'm spinning around, on the spot, as if this will help to alleviate the panic. I'm twisting, turning, opening and closing my fists, gasping for breath and stamping my feet as if this will dispel the dark truth that Mel has disappeared, that she is no longer here: That she has gone.

*Jesus Christ!*
*Slave Island!*
*What in hell's name is Slave Island?*
*And furthermore…where the fuck is it?*

## LOST

To arrive at Slave Island you don't need a boat. It is an arsehole of a place up the proverbial shit creek, true, but all that is required is a cardboard train ticket and a red bus. For Slave Island isn't an island at all, but an outer suburb of Colombo.

The suburb is located in the southern part of Colombo, and was given the name Slave Island during the period of British occupation when the African slaves were held there. Now it is a multicultural mix of Singhalese and Sri Lankan Moors living a life that teems with day-to-day chores of those struggling to make ends meet. I see a man half-naked, who has been given the task of painting all of the street lampposts along the road in metallic silver, and has as much paint on himself as there is on each post. Elsewhere there are dilapidated wooden carts to which skanky horses are hitched and in which their fibrous limbed owners are asleep. The life of the undernourished and unemployed is depicted on every corner. Yet, as if to balance these tiers of birth-right, I watch as three ladies stroll by with their expensive saris flowing in pastel shades of wealth. All three are embraced in an air of self-importance, having tilted their noses ever so slightly, as if this will negate the stench about their feet.

I traverse this suburb, this Slave Island, with its mixed aromas and diverse culture, eventually reaching my destination. I am now standing face to face with the infamous Welikada Prison and it squats before me like a glandular toad. As my eyes scale the walls of Sri Lanka's largest maximum-security prison a blind man smells out my existence. I search my pockets for a two-rupee note, and as I do I feel we have much in common, this beggar and I, for we are both rummaging around these dirty streets seeking a little hope.

The face of the prison portrays the same finality of all such habitations built to thieve ones liberty. There is the customary archway, in which a double set of gun-metal grey studded steel doors are set, breaching its grimy off-white facia. These ashen steel doors reach to a height of perhaps six metres and in the left panel is a

194

smaller door through which visitors may come and go. In smaller archways on either side of the main doors are other entrances, and standing in each of these secondary doorways are male prison officers looking on in brutish deliberation. My timing is fortunate (some luck at least), as I have become part of the milling throng of expectant visitors, awaiting their once-a-month visit. I walk with the others, in single file, and have my bag checked (as do all) revealing its contents of biscuits, vitamin tablets, bags of assorted sweets and some fruit, which are left untouched by the guards, whereas other unfortunate visitors have some of their possessions picked out, likely destined for the warder's lunch-room.

After my body search I pass through the deep archway and into the largest incarceration facility on the Island, all forty-eight acres of it. The area in which I stand has three dusty roads running off in different compass directions and it is along one of these roads we hordes begin to trek. Everyone else appears to know where they are going, so I bleat quietly and follow closely. As we walk along the road one of the interesting oddities I notice, as if grasping at some thread of normality, are the well-kept gardens that run along either side of us. Their ludicrous lushness is a stark contrast to the multitude of small dilapidated buildings we pass, with their rusted corrugated roofs barely appearing waterproof. Laying out the front of these buildings I see a horde of empty plastic bottles, torn wicker baskets, and broken clay pots, strewn about, as if shipwrecked on a hopeless beach. Amid these shacks looms a three-tiered building in the shape of a cross, forming the bulk of the prison, in which the inmates are housed. I learn from one of my fellow walkers that the female cells are designed for seventy-five people, but with the overcrowding now sleep one hundred and fifty. And running around the perimeter of each cell is an open drain, infested with rabid rats whose bite is an immediate trip to a third world hospital. Within the cells there lies an absence of beds, mats or pillows and the squalor is devoid of fans despite the humid thirty-degree heat. There are only two bathrooms in which seventy five women perform their ablutions, and to make matters even more unbearable, the women are locked in their cells at five-thirty every night and are not allowed to use the lavatories until five the following morning. Therefore they are subsequently forced to sleep with piss and shit buckets alongside of them in case of a mid-night necessity. And there are kids in here too, having to deal with the violation of basic sanitary rights, in a gaol which runs on the rails of the prison ordinance, drawn up in the 1800s. And to add pressure to pain, most of the inmates are in here for non-payment of minimal fines, however, as far as the warders are concerned they bear no discrimination between these non-payers and the sex offenders or even the mass murderers: Everyone in Welikada prison is given the same shit-bucket deal.

It is a place where men and women bathe, sleep, and wake, to begin it all over again. It is a place where men and women waste away like forgotten cattle. And it is a place in which Mel is concealed, somewhere amid all of this squalor and filth.

The fortress, that is Welikada Prison, has an air about it of the downtrodden and abused. And it is a place that sweats.

The people sweat.
The beds sweat.
Even the fucking walls sweat.

Its decaying off-white shantytown existence is like being entangled within the lungs of a chain smoker, where each small cell is a carcinogenic pocket of incarcerated pus. We visitors are ushered into a room about the size of two squash courts which is divided in half by a wooden counter that stretches from one side of the room to the other. Rising up from this counter is a squared wire mesh that runs to the ceiling. At the far end of the room, beyond the mesh, is a wall of bars and a door and behind this runs a parallel corridor along which the prisoners will come. I am among mothers, fathers, brothers, sisters and children, all jostling for what little standing room exists near the mesh. Fortunately, being taller and more robust than most, I manage to secure a place up against the dividing mesh. I wait. I am nervous. Christ, how I am nervous. At any moment Mel will be coming along that corridor. I breathe deeply, and breathe deeply once again, willing my body to calm, not only for my sake, but for Mel's too. The last thing she needs to see as she looks into our room is the only person with whom she has any outside contact looking distressed.

The tension within the room heightens as the white prison-uniformed inmates begin to appear in the corridor then enter though the door. Even though everyone is dressed alike, I look for Mel and am surprised that I haven't spotted her already, being a white woman in a room full of tanned Sri Lankan faces. I scan all the faces again, but still can't find her. I look harder for how can I possibly miss her height or white face? But again: Nothing. Panic begins to surface. Fear rises. My muscles tighten and I feel as if I am choking in this smoker's lung of a prison, as if there are hands about my throat. It's been one emotional disaster followed by another. Disappointment piled upon disappointment. Heartache after heartache. The exponential effect finally kicks in, and it kicks in hard. I begin to tremble. I feel sick. My vision becomes tunnel-like and so I stumble through the crowd bumping against people until I can go no further. I hit a wall then slide down its length to the solitude of the floor. I'm detached from my surroundings. Detached from myself. I huddle inside my own small world: Inside my cocoon. There is pressure building within my head, adding to the gut-wrenching truth that Mel isn't here.

And if she isn't here…

Then where the fuck is she?

# M.F.B.

A male prison guard comes over to me and drags me up from the floor. He shakes me, to get a response, then escorts me out of the room.

Outside stands a female guard. I am handed over to her and she sits me down on a chair in the corridor. She gives me a bottle of water and I drink deeply. When enough time has passed, when I have sufficiently recovered, she offers up an explanation. The female guard explains that Mel isn't here because I have wandered into the wrong part of the prison. Mel is being held in the Detention Sector, located in another wing. My young guard is civil enough, with her newly pressed mud brown uniform, her long freshly washed brown hair, and her youthful good looks. She introduces herself as Miss Emily, then leads me along the corridor and out into a small yard where a group of prisoners are performing the ritual exercise of 'walking in meditation'. On seeing my confused look my guard explains that they perform this exercise to spiritually escape the boredom and daily confinement that comes with prison life at Welikada. As I look up and over the walls to a clear blue sky I think that if this is all the escapism they have I hope to God it bears them some relief. My guard, Miss Emily, then leads me out of the yard and into another building, via a heavily barred gate. We go down a five metre wide corridor with small, but decent sized cells to the right and left of us, some of which are open but devoid of inhabitants. I look into one as I pass and am surprised at the order in which they are kept. There is a small table with a pile of reading material on it, two blanketed and pillowed beds, and a small window to the outside. Compared to the three-tiered rat-hole I had walked past earlier, this place is palatial. Who is held here I have no idea and before I have time to think on it I am instructed to follow more closely.

At the end of this corridor is another heavily barred metal door, in which lies another cumbersome lock. My guide chooses the appropriate key from a large iron ring and ushers me through. We arrive at another door, though this door is wooden and on which my guide knocks with official decorum. I hear footsteps approaching from the other side, then witness the brass handle on our side twisting a half turn. The door is initially held ajar so that we may be scrutinised from within, and on establishing our identities the door is fully opened and I enter alone. The female guard accepts a curt command from a male voice within and closes the door firmly behind me.

The large room is a clean, cream painted office and in complete contrast to anything else I have seen in the prison. The bookcase, which is to the right of me, is of beautifully crafted Dutch teak, and is lined with books, all gold edged and masterfully bound in green and burgundy leather. Alongside the bookcase is a large three-panelled wooden framed window, also made from teak, from which a private and well-kept garden can be viewed. The two metre long English oak desk has been so exquisitely oiled over time that the handsome depth of grain has been smoothed to the point where its contoured lines read like a fingerprint. There is a curved Rococo chair, crafted from the same English oak, with the uppermost part of its embracing arms finished in the same tone of burgundy as the leather bound books. Behind and above the chair is the customary portrait of the President, but unlike the soiled photograph hanging in Hikkaduwa Police Station, this is a commissioned oil. Either side of this painting are staffs, on which hang the Sri Lankan flags, and further to the left of these is a huge antique globe, about a metre in diameter, depicting the cartography of old sea-trading routes, which, when split in two, becomes a spherical drinks cabinet.

I cannot see the entirety of this alcoholic orb as it is partially blocked by a man. This man sports a large handle bar moustache, grown to further enhance the seriousness of his face. He stands in the same mud-coloured uniform as the prison staff, only his uniform is decorated at the left breast with a flurry of colourfully embroidered bars of cotton, signifying length of service. He has the stature and presence of a man whose orders are obeyed. He looks to be a man of power, purpose and stealth. However he is nothing compared to the overbearing presence of the man sitting behind the desk. Compared to this man, the man standing could be described as almost bland and insignificant.

There is an ornate plaque sitting on the desk that reads 'Commissioner Sanjayan', but the man behind the desk is no prison employee, of this, or any other prison in Sri Lanka. He is not even part of the prison fraternity. I know this because the uniform he wears is in stark contrast to that of the Commissioner's. I know this because the uniform he wears denotes that of the significantly more powerful Sri Lankan Military Police.

On each shoulder of his immaculate cream coloured uniform are epaulettes, on which are sewn petal-shaped insignias. A golden braided lanyard runs from his left epaulette past a commotion of embroidered 'colours' sewn above his breast pocket. On the right breast of his tunic is a black leather name tag sewn on with silver braid which is further complimented by the silver tailor-made buttons leading up to the man's powerful neck. His black and silver peaked hat sits on the desk, alongside a tightly bound black leather baton and a pair of expensive black leather gloves. His presence breathes of wealth and power.

The lustre of this man directly contrasts to the way I am feeling: All blackness and ice. I swear my legs are about to buckle from the sheer weight of despondency. And when I look past this man's finery, I see that his heavily oiled hair is combed stylishly over his skull and is buzz shaved closely around his ears. His black moustache is pencil thin, finishing in twisted curls, whilst above his square set jaw are eyes that look to conceal a menace beneath.

Before me then is,

The Main Man.
The Alpha Male.
The Top Dog.

Sitting before me then, is undoubtedly, *Mister Fucking Big* himself.

## STRIKE

*M*ister *Fucking Big* (MFB) leans back in his chair and gestures that I am to sit in one of the two chairs opposite. I sit in the one that is vacant, because someone else has already occupied the other: Mel.

She has neither moved nor said anything since I entered the room, and she looks terrible. It has only been two days since the fateful arrest but the grind of reality has obviously taken its toll. Thirty years is a bitter pill to swallow when you can't even muster up one ounce of spit. Her hair is unkempt as if she has slept on the floor and her nails are full of prison filth. As I sit next to her I notice an odour of disinfectant and realise that the unpleasant smell is from her hosing down on entry to the prison.

I place my hand onto her knee to comfort her, but she flinches at my touch.
'Are you ok?' Which is the most idiotic question I could ask. It is obvious that Mel is not ok. She is on the brink, teetering at the precipice.

*Jesus, what a fucking mess.*

My thoughts are interrupted by MFB, who in his clipped British accent says this,
'I shall get straight to the point Mr Evans. It *is* Mr Evans isn't it?'
Before I can answer his retrospective question, MFB continues.
'What we have here is a grave problem Mr Evans. Miss Young has been found in possession of heroin, which in Sri Lanka carries a mandatory sentence of thirty years.'

The pressure is too much for Mel and her fear spills. Black and thick. She drops her head to her hands and begins to sob uncontrollably. I get out of my seat to comfort her, encircling my arms around her shoulders and draw her head into my chest. She buries in deeply and now her sobbing is interspersed with violent gasps for air.
'Ssshhh. Ssshh Baby. Ssshh.'

I wish I could say more, be more convincing. I wish I could let her know that everything will be ok, but I can't, because I don't even believe it myself. Then she cracks, breaks, and verbalises her terror.
'Rhys I'm so scared. This place is so terrible. I don't belong in here Rhys. It's an evil place. An evil, evil place.'…and although she continues speaking her words have become only bubbles and spit.

MFB has little time for theatrics and so interjects with cool intent, 'Sit back in your chair Mr Evans as we have much to discuss.'
The words are no request. They are a command to be promptly complied with. So I sit. I am a dog waiting for a bone to be thrown. Any titbit. Any morsel: Anything to alleviate the desperation I feel.
'I shall get straight to the point Mr Evans. Miss Young has found herself in quite a predicament, but fortunately for Miss Young, my colleague and I are here to offer you both a solution; a way out if you wish?'
MFB waits for his words to take effect, then continues in his deliberate and methodical manner,
'Today we have been presented with covert information which confirms that many prison staff will be exercising a walk-off strike related to a pay dispute and that a State of Emergency will be declared. Therefore my men, the Military Police, will be summoned to take up these vacant posts. During this change-over the stations will be unmanned for a short period of time and at this time there will exist a great deal of confusion in certain quarters, especially in the Detention Sector in which Miss Young is currently being held.

MFB delivers his words in a slow and measured manner and I hang on to each one, because he says this,

*So at this time Miss Young may leave the prison undetected.*

My eyes narrow like a hawk on the wing, fixing intensely on the man across the table. My ears prick up so as not to miss even the faintest word. I am on edge, electrified by this news. Even Mel has stirred silently. But I am also confused. Surely he didn't just say that Melanie could leave? That she could escape? Did I just hear that there really is a way out of this terrible mess?
MFB continues, 'But as with all procedures, such as this, there is invariably an administrative cost attached to it.'
On hearing the mention of money the deal instantly assumes an air of credibility.

So I say,

'Yes Sir, I understand there is always a cost attached to these situations.'

There rests an unnatural silence, a calculated silence, heavy and expectant. The penny drops. It is my financial cue. I hear my own words spoken, as if some ventriloquist's dummy has taken the stage.

'And in your opinion Sir, how much do you think the paperwork will cost for this process to succeed?'

'Mr Evans,' MFB says, 'let me explain to you first the order of events that must take place. After this we can discuss the finances. Firstly, you will need to purchase a one way air ticket to England for Miss Young.'

I am leaning in now, listening intently for I must miss nothing of what is said. This is one scenario I do not want to screw up.

'Secondly, you must bring the ticket here in an envelope addressed to the Commissioner.' The Commissioner smiles on cue, for I bet he can already smell his dirty money.

MFB slides a business card across the table as he says,

'Thirdly, Mr Evans, you will deposit ten thousand American dollars into a bank account, the numbers of which are on the back of this card.'

He taps the card deliberately with his forefinger so that there can be no misunderstanding that this is Mel's one and only opportunity of escaping Welikada Prison.

'Once all of these actions have been undertaken Mr Evans, Miss Young will be escorted from the prison, then taken directly to the International Airport where she will be taken to the Departure Lounge and put on board a plane home.'

MFB rises from his chair and extends his hand.

'And so Mr Evans you may leave now as I'm sure you have some urgent business to attend to.'

With that the meeting is over. I shake his hand, and that of the Commissioner who has moved in from the periphery. Then I crouch down at Mel's side.

'See Babe, I told you it would all work out. You'll be home with your mum and dad before you know it.'

But she has regressed and can only muster up a series of rapid mute nods and a tight-lipped smile. I brush her tears away with the back of my fingers. 'You must be strong now Mel. Ok! I'll be back as soon as I can.'

There is sheepish fear written in droves across Mel's face. Despite everything that has happened within this room I can tell that Mel isn't in the moment. She just can't grasp what is taking place. She grips my arm tightly but says nothing. She appears hopelessly scared, and who in their right mind wouldn't be? What's worse is that I have to leave her in this state of mind, so I do my best to comfort her again. 'Don't worry sweetheart. It'll all be ok. I promise. I'll be back soon, ok. Hang in there babe and before you know it, all this will be over.'

However she has sunk into an abyss. I am witness to it. Melanie just can't function. Her thoughts of incarceration and the possibility of being buried beneath thirty years of filth has taken its toll. It is obvious that she is unable to grasp the fact that soon all of this will be over, but, for now, there is nothing more I can do for her.

*Nothing.*

So I leave her in that room, alone, scared and vulnerable. Alone with those two men. I leave her because I have no choice: Because I now have a life-saving phone call to make.

   A phone call home to Wales.
   A phone call to Mel's father.

## JIGSAW PIECES -
### THE HONEYMOON SUITE

Mel is ushered back to her cell, while I am being escorted out of the prison by the same female warder who had escorted me earlier. The route out of the prison labyrinth is practically a mirror image of the one I had taken to the Commissioner's office, but instead of passing under the main gate, I find myself exiting through one of the small arched doorways.

The first place I have to find is somewhere that has an international telephone facility so I can make the life-saving phone call to Mel's parents in Wales.

After having been launched over the first stumbling block by MFB; namely having the drug charges stalled, I now have to clamber over the second obstacle on my own, which is to reveal everything to Mel's parents.

*Christ what a mess!*

The taxi trip back to Colombo CBD is full of isolated thoughts and uneasiness. My mind is working overtime, deliberating on how to jigsaw together all the critical pieces so that Mel can be freed from that foul-smelling place and put safely on a plane home.

Normally I would head to the Central Telegraph Office in the centre of Colombo but the building is still under repair after the recent bombing, and only some of the more affluent business sectors of Sri Lanka have communications access to the outside world. Instead, I decide that my best bet is to go back to the Supercontinental Hotel where Mel and I spent our first night as I know they have telephones there. I only hope that they are still working.

The taxi drops me at the hotel and it is certainly uplifting being surrounded by people having clean-shaven faces, expensive perfume and smart luggage, and yet bizarre to think that, not long ago, Mel and I were here, full of beans and luxurious cocktails. It is also refreshing that I am greeted by the same sweet-smiling desk clerk, who, miraculously, even remembers my name.

'Good evening Mr Evans. How nice to be seeing you again. And where is your lovely wife?'

I'm not prepared for this and am taken by surprise.

'Uh. Oh Mrs Evans? She...she's out shopping. You know how it is with women. They love to shop, as I'm sure you do too?'

'Oh yes Mr Evans. It is a most pleasant past-time.' She smiles at the thought of shopping herself, perhaps?

'Will you and Mrs Evans be wanting a room?' she enquires in a soothing front-desk manner.

'Ah. No. Not at the moment. What I would like though is to use your telephone to make an overseas call.'

She pauses briefly so that she may take a moment to mentally delve into the archives of the hotel's manifesto.

Then she says,

'Oh I am so sorry Mr Evans, only hotel guests are allowed to use this facility at present because of the bombing of the telephone exchange.'

I can see the unwritten apology in her face, but even as I plead with her that I am in desperate need and that it is an emergency: A matter of life and death, she goes on to inform me, in her kind melodic sing-song tone, that she is so sorry, that it is company policy and that she is not at liberty to waver from this most important house rule. Her manager, she explains, has expressly said this.

'May I then speak with the manager please Jayan?'

(I have read her nametag).

'I am sorry Mr Evans but the Manager is off-duty.'

'Well could I speak to the Deputy Manager then, please?'

'I am sorry *Sir*, (she has become officious now), the Deputy Manger is in a meeting with the Concierge.'

'Is there anyone I could speak to, anyone at all, that I can ask about making a phone call?'

Jayan looks confused.

'But you have Sir. You have asked me. And I have regrettably informed you of our current policy. I am so sorry Sir, but as I have previously mentioned, only hotel guests may use this facility.'

I am now practically pulling my hair out and feel like throttling the girl. However deep down I know it is not her fault, but my blood is curdling at about one-ten degrees. Because I'm desperate. Because I

have run headlong into a third world, pedantic furnace, and no matter what I do or say this little desk-phoenix is not about to rise to my rescue.
Then I have a brainwave!

*Only hotel guests have the use of this facility!*

'Yes. On second thoughts Jayan, I *would* like to take a Standard Room please.'

*Bingo!*
*Winner!*
*Problem solved.*

Why didn't I think of it before? At least tonight I'll have a decent warm shower and get a comfortable night's sleep. However, Jayan, my sweet melodic princess of a desk clerk, instead of checking the hotel register, then drawing out a checking-in card and raising her pen in readiness, looks up from behind her rampart and delivers the following sentence.
'I am sorry Sir, but there are no Standard rooms available.'
'Right. Ok then, I'll take a Deluxe room.'

*Christ, anything to solve this fucking problem.*

But once again, Jayan, my sweet melodic princess clarifies that,
'I'm sorry Sir, but there are no Deluxe Rooms available either.'

Blood boiling.
Pulse pumping.
Head splitting.
Temper fraying.

I raise my voice, not for effect, but out of sheer bloody frustration.
'You're telling me that in the entire hotel there is neither a Standard nor a Deluxe room available! That is just impossible. Look at the size of this place for God's sake. It's like Buckingham fucking Palace!'
There is no jolt to her demeanour as Jayan has experienced it all before: the request for the late checkout, the lost luggage, a missed flight, the blocked sink, the obnoxious guest.
'I'm sorry Sir but since the recent bombings no one is choosing to stay in the centre of the city and at this time there is also an

international convention being held in Colombo. You will find all of the hotels in this area fully booked and with the same policy. We have been receiving people all afternoon who cannot find a room.'
'Jesus wept! So I have just been through all of this palaver,' I tell her, 'for absolutely nothing. Why didn't you tell me there weren't any of these rooms available in the first place?'
And her answer would astound many, but in truth it is just another anomaly when dealing with the third world.
'Because you did not ask me Sir?'
'But you asked me if I wanted a room when I first came in!'
'Yes Sir.'
'But you have no rooms.'
'Oh yes, we have rooms Sir. Both the honeymoon suites are available.'

*Honeymoon suite! Jesus Christ, can this get any more fucking ironic?*

'Right. Fine. How much are they?'
'Four hundred American dollars a night Sir, with a minimum stay of two nights, due to present circumstances.'
The eight hundred bucks is an impossible amount of money for me to come up with. I simply don't have the cash. My world, once again, crumbles about me. I thank Jayan for her time (as best as I can muster), and retreat to one of the lounge chairs in the foyer to think. The chair is so comfortable that I wish it's reassurance could, in some way, seep into my body and calm me down. Instead, I sit with my elbows on my knees and with my head in my hands.

*Think!*
*Think!*
*Think!*

The pressure pulsating inside my head is colossal, and I haven't any painkillers to dull the torment. As I sit here I can't help but think how absurd it is, that while Mel is stuck in that shit-hole of a place, I am sitting here in the lap of luxury, yet both of us are trussed by powers beyond our control.
I feel so helpless.
I promised Mel it would all be ok and I can't even make one simple phone call home. My self-preservation is flat-lining and I swear I can hear the solitary tone of an ECG machine humming in my ear.

Then a soft, velvet voice breaks into my isolation. It is one of the hotel staff and he is standing over me.

*Here to help perhaps?*

But No.

'I am sorry to be informing you Sir, but company policy states that the foyer chairs are for guests and the acquaintances of guests only, so I must regrettably ask you to leave.'

The staff member looks over at the front desk to where Jayan is acknowledging him with a curt nod and a practised smile. I don't even bother to argue with his ludicrous request. I simply get up and step out into the closeness of the night: into a tropical straightjacket. I am so tired. I have a time restraint pressing down on me, an international deadline in which to come up with ten thousand dollars, plus I have to somehow buy a plane ticket and deliver it back to the prison by tomorrow. And whilst doing all of this I have to remain sane.

So I ask myself

*How in God's name am I going to make all of this happen?*

## JIGSAW PIECES -
### KING GEORGE

There is nothing else I can do but go back to the Ex-Serviceman's Hotel, grab a room for the night and try to think of a way through this crisis. I get the taxi to drop me off a little way from the hotel so I can grab some air before locking myself away in my room.

My feet drag.

> *If only I hadn't acted so bloody angrily that day down at the beach restaurant, none of this would have happened. I could have dealt with Mel's misgivings differently: Couldn't I? Perhaps I should have laughed it off? Perhaps I should have simply left without saying a word? Yet, here I go again internalising my thoughts, blaming the one person who is truly not at fault. None of this was my doing. No-one can blame me for what happened. Surely my responsibility isn't for the culpability of others? (And part of me wishes I'd knocked the fucker into next week instead?)*

But as I walk back to the hotel, justifying everything, I become mad with myself, reasoning that all of this mess *is* my fault and that I should have played the whole beach thing out differently. Then the words spoken by KC, at the New Orient Hotel, come to mind. 'You have a good code Mr Evans. You are a good man'. And KC's right. My code is good. I *am* a good person and my ethos *is* strong. I feel a reserve of strength. None of what has happened *is* my fault. I'm actually the good guy here. Nevertheless, there is a fight to win and honourable promises to fulfil. I draw strength from words once spoken by my father. 'There are no problems in life Son: Only solutions'.

> *Now all I have to do is find them.*

I find myself back in Bristol Street standing outside the Ex-Servos, opposite of which is George's Travel Agency. The door to the small office is open, and located on the curb to the left of it is a tall drinks fridge from which you can select anything from a biro to a beer or a carton of coconut milk to a pot of red nail varnish. Quite an enigma; but then so is George, who is presently standing in the doorway smiling and waving for me to come over and join him. Every time I have met George, he is freshly dressed in the same short-sleeved blue shirt with a yellow band across the chest, long grey trousers and good old-fashioned rubber flip-flops. He probably has a 'clothing factory connection' as nothing would surprise me about Capable George. He strikes me as someone who has never let anyone down. Since first meeting George with Tyrone and Tony on the night of the Perahera festival, George and I have developed a warm friendship. When in Colombo it is always a pleasure to look him up and we have shared numerous beers on many a late night after the close of business.

'You look troubled my friend,' says George, as I step up onto the curb and grab two beers from the fridge.

'Yeah, big trouble George. Big trouble.'

George grabs a couple of wooden chairs from the office and we sit outside. I talk and drink, and talk some more. It feels so good to pour out my heart and to vent on the day's frustrations to a compassionate ear. Soon George is up to date with all that has happened since we last met. And George has sat in silence whilst I related the sad and sorry facts of my ordeal, and on coming to the end of my story I feel exhausted.

In life some of us have had doors that have been closed in our faces: the empty promise of promotion, or the blind date that never showed, or the deed of an unfaithful lover. Yet there are doors too, that when opened, let in a fresh breeze to cleanse a stifled mind. And God bless the King, because George has the key to one such door.

There is only one entrance to the office named George's Travel and Information Agency, however when it comes to the man, there are more attributes to him than a dodecahedron.

'A one-way ticket to London. No problem,' he offers. 'Aeroflot. They are to be departing tomorrow via Moscow and I can be issuing you an inexpensive ticket this evening.'

*One down - two to go!*

'And as for making the phone call Rhys, my good friend, you can be using mine.' And he smiles.

It is good of George to offer, for he is a kind man, but kindness alone cannot traverse the world's skies.

'That's very kind of you George but perhaps you didn't understand what I meant. It is not a local call I need to make, but an overseas one, to Mel's parents in Wales.'

George laughs in his all inclusive way. 'Yes. As I am saying to you my friend. You can be using my phone. It is the one being inside.'

'You mean you can make overseas calls from here, from your office? But I thought after the bombing only the big businesses could make phone calls to other countries?'

'Ah my friend,' and George, he laughs gently. 'You are to be thinking that to be a big business you must be having a big office, a car and many staff. My business is being big, because you see I have a big heart and many people are knowing this and are helping me in many ways. This is why I am helping you Rhys. My heart is being like your heart.' And he taps my chest. 'We are to be having a gift from the Gods you and I.'

And as George laughs at this I swear I can see his ears wiggle.

'Come on inside. I will be showing you how to be making it all possible.'

I don't ask George how he can be 'making it all possible', or how he has a phone to the outside world when most can't even ring around the corner. And at this point in time I don't particularly care, because all I need are solutions, not explanations.

George leads me into his small dark office in which he offers me his chair, set behind his simple desk. On the desk lay neatly arranged business cards for practically every activity available to a tourist, and a selection of well thumbed maps of how to get there. In a holder made from porcupine quills there are colourful brochures to elephant parks, bird sanctuaries, secluded beaches, hideaway hotels, places to dine, places to scuba dive, places to snorkel, and places where you can mine blue-haze moonstones, if you've fossicker genes running through your rich veins.

And there's a phone.
Right there on the table.
In front of me.

It is big.
Red.
Clumsy.
And old.

Its white-faced dial harks back to the early seventies, but George says it works and is a phone on which I can make a call home to Mel's parents.

Paul, Ann, and I, are very close. In his youth Mel's dad was a champion high diver, and an excellent tennis and darts player. Ann enjoys her painting, loves her ballet, her local amateur dramatics and was once a silver medal-winning gymnast at the Commonwealth Games. She laughs now that her knees have 'gone' and the best she can manage nowadays is to flip an omelette. And because I love them like parents, and that they treat me like a son, I'm dreading the thought of breaking the terrible news.

## JIGSAW PIECES -
### PARENTS

The inner workings of the phone vibrate, causing the ringing tone to begin. My heart is thumping like a jackhammer. In my mind I have gone over and over and over what I am going to say to Mel's parents but no sooner do I get to the end of my script I have forgotten what I was planning to say at the start.

And the phone is ringing.

My subconscious is wishing that Paul and Ann's phone would click over to the answering machine and that I could simply hang up, wait for a few hours, regroup, down a few more beers, and fuel up some Dutch courage.
But No.
No sooner has this thought materialised, the phone is answered and there is a sing-song Welsh accent at the other end.
'Hello. Who's speaking please?'
It is Ann.
She has answered the phone before Paul, as she usually does.
'Hello Ann, it's me, Rhys. In Sri Lanka.'
'Rhys! Well, well. Hello my good boy. How are you? And how is Mel? We miss you both very much you know, my lovely?'
'Oh she's . . . ok.'
I pause for longer than I care too, but I need time to build up the courage to continue, to tell her the truth…
'Actually Ann, she's not ok. She's not ok at all. Melanie's in jail.' As I say it, as the words tumble from my lips, I can hear their heart-wrenching impact hitting a world thousands of kilometres away.
'Jail! Oh my God Rhys. What's happened? Are you ok? Jail? What do you mean jail?'
As I am about to explain to Mel's mum that her daughter has been found in the possession of an A-class drug. That she has been charged with the possession of heroin, and is currently looking at a

thirty year jail sentence, she doesn't give me the chance as she is now frantically calling Paul to the phone.

'Paul! Paul! Quick Paul! Come to the phone. Something terrible has happened to our Melanie!'

Paul has dealt with many a crisis. His business demands it, be it time constraints, competitive quotes, management and staff issues, hungry creditors or lazy debtors. However, what I'm about to tell him is beyond the realms of daily business. There are no phone calls he can make to smooth this transaction, no favours he can call in to scratch his back. I am his 'unscratchable' itch. Me. On the end of a Sri Lankan telephone. Asking him for ten thousand American dollars so that I can send his only daughter back to him.

Back home.
Back to her family.

Paul comes to the phone…and I spill.
I lay all of the facts before him. I hold back on nothing. It's repugnant. Brutal. But now it's said, and once said it is as if a huge weight has been lifted from my shoulders…a problem shared… and all that.

Paul has all of the facts before him. His understanding that we didn't want to have the British Embassy involved, as the charge would carry over to the UK. His understanding that ten thousand American dollars must be transferred to a foreign bank, and his understanding that there is the necessity to make this all happen today, as Melanie's escape is dependant on the supposed Warder's Strike. The incident at the restaurant was only ever mentioned once.

Paul is a practical man, shrewd and pragmatic. He has conceded that it is only money after all, just numbers in a bank, if you have the authority to manipulate them, and he does. Paul can get ten thousand American dollars at the drop of a hat and so he says to me, as I am waiting in between fits of panic, a dry mouth and baited breath, 'I can get the money Rhys, this is not a problem. But what I need to know is that you are sure this will fix the problem and that these bastards won't come back for more.'

'Yes Paul, the money will fix everything. I am one hundred percent sure. I have met with all of the key players today and they are as keen as us to see this end.'

But, as I say these words, subconsciously I am thinking that I really have no right to make such a promise to Mel's parents. To the mother and father whose daughter is locked up in a Sri Lankan hell-hole. There is no absolute guarantee that there will be a prison guard walkout, or that the bribe being paid to Mister Fucking Big will orchestrate Mel being released from Welikada Prison and allowed to go home.

*Christ, I hadn't even considered this myself until now.*

It is a gamble. A huge risk. A game in which the cards are still stacked against us. But what can we do? We have no option but to play out the only hand we have with ten thousand paper-thin cards. I am worried, and Paul must hear the anxiety in my voice because he says, 'You must steel yourself Rhys. Be strong for Melanie's sake. Everything will be ok, I'm sure of it. Now give me the bank account details and I will go straight to the bank before they close today. I'll have the money transferred immediately. Call me back in three hours and I will give you the transfer lodgement and receipt numbers. Then you can go to the prison tomorrow and get Melanie out of this mess. Now do you understand all that I have said?'

I reiterate that I understand, and that I am to phone back in three hours to get the transfer details, and that I don't know how to thank him for what he is doing. And that…

'Let's keep the thanks until later, shall we? Stay calm. Do what you have to do and get Melanie out of that place and home to us. Ann and I are both counting on you Rhys. It's all up to you now son.'

I lay the heavy handset back in its cradle, sit back, and close my eyes.

## JIGSAW PIECES -
### THE PAYOFF

George and I had consumed several beers last night whilst we waited the agreed three-hour countdown. Good old George, what a Godsend of a friend he is, and I say this with hand on heart because he waited there with me, allowed me to use his phone once again and double-checked the bank transfer receipt details as I nervously sounded them out.

George's Travel is closed as I descend the wide stone steps of the Ex-Servicemen's Hotel the following day. Why open early this when the only people on the steamy streets are those who have no place to rest, those trailing home after a twelve-hour night shift, those who are off to market to haggle for a bargain, or those who are off to meet a big fat fucker?

These are my thoughts as I hunt down a taxi, but I feel no kinship to a cavalier or caballero, no claim to being of the same ilk as that of a knight in shining armour, riding off to defend the honour of a Lady stranded in an ivory tower. Who I am is someone who is heavily apprehensive and fearful about the impending events ahead. In other words, I'm really fearful that this could still go so horribly wrong.

I have in my pocket Mel's plane ticket and a slip of paper with two sets of numbers on it. The piece of paper is the only weapon I have, which I touch from time to time, just to make sure it's there. But even when I feel its existence between my fingers, I know that compared to the might of the Military Police, its worth could amount to no more than the flimsy scrap of paper it really is.

With its pungent whiff of care and neatness the interior of my taxi exudes the scent of an expensive lady's handbag. The multi-coloured glass beads that hang from the rear view mirror, the garlands of flowers across the peeling dashboard and the friendly smile of my driver, allow me, (at least for now), to rest back against the red polished leather seat and take a moment. I make an excuse to my driver that I am feeling unwell and that I would rather rest than talk. He is disappointed, and so turns up the radio a few notches and begins wobbling his head in rhythmic time to the static of a Sri Lankan pop song.

The taxi meanders its way through the busy streets of Slave Island and comes to a stop outside the hard metallic gates of Welikada Prison. I am back on edge. This time, unlike before, the ominous main gates are firmly bolted, as it is not 'visitors day'. One of the small archways to the right however, is open, and on seeing me alight from the taxi I am hailed by the warder, Miss Emily.

'Mr Rhys, I am told to be waiting for you and that you will be giving me an envelope. Is this correct?'

And as I hand over the envelope containing Mel's plane ticket it feels as if the opposing team are scoring points in a rigged cup match, and not only is my team losing but there isn't even anyone in the terraces cheering us on. I am alone, and there is nothing I can do about it. The die is cast, and having been allocated the status of a pawn in a Master's game, I can do nothing but comply. It is black and white, me against them, and it is sickening. I hate the fact that I am being manipulated by forces beyond my control, who at their whim, could take away someone's liberty at the turn of a key.

I ask about Mel.

'Can I see my girlfriend please?'

'Yes,' Miss Emily replies. 'I am told you can be making one quick visit to her. Come. Follow me.'

Again I follow Miss Emily, in her bleak brown prison uniform, her freshly washed brown hair and eyes that would be pleasant enough to share a joke with, if only the circumstances were different. This time I am led through an unfamiliar part of the prison, in and out of doors, past women who are hand-sewing garments, when perfectly good electric sewing machines lie idly by. We move further into the bowels of the prison, along more corridors and through barred doors, past crammed cells and the smell of filth, before finally arriving in an open courtyard.

The large, foot-trodden, yellow-sanded yard, the size of two tennis courts, is encroached by tall prison buildings that cast dark shadows before us. At the far end of the yard there is a small courtyard that is segregated by a tall wire fence. It's one huge chicken coup, in which is set a door through which prisoners enter the yard for their daily hour-long exercise, but there are no prisoners here today.

Except for Mel.

She is standing up against the wire fence with her face pressed against the ring-lock. Both her hands are extended above her head and her fingers are curled through the enclosure like a primate at a second rate zoo. And at this point in my story I could paint a picture of desperation. A picture of someone clinging to the last straw of hope. Someone who, in their fretful state, is crying out for freedom. Someone who is eager to see a loved one, if only for a brief moment. To hold them. To kiss them. To cherish a moment of closeness with someone dear to their heart. However, to paint such a scene would be false, because Melanie displays none of this.

Written on the face pressed against the wire is not anxiety, but calmness. Instead of curled white fingertips, desperately clinging to wire, there is an overhead stretching exercise being performed, and instead of tears, there is a smile, and instead of fear there is joy, and instead of despair, there is knowledge, because Mel already knows that the plan is in place.

Mel bounces off the wire as the warder and I approach.
She is positively ecstatic. A hot bath, mad with bubbles.
'I'm going home Rhys! I'm going home! You've done it my beautiful man. You've done it.

I love you!
I love you!
I love you!'

Mel is twirling and dancing on the other side of the wire. It is as if the prison has melted from around her, leaving her spirit to run free. She is fresh, bright and as vibrant as a new day.

Home!
Home!
Home! she cries.

Then in a serious tone, that bites into the moment, she says, 'Rhys, where's my plane ticket?'
I explain to Mel that the Commissioner has it and that she is flying home with Aeroflot on the earliest plane tomorrow.
'God. Aeroflot! That's Russian isn't it? Couldn't you have got me on British Airways or something? And look at my tan. If I'd have thought I would have told you to bring some suntan oil so I could

have at least gone back looking a bit browner. Look at me. I'm positively anaemic.'

It's all I can do from not blowing my stack completely and I visualise nutting the stupid cow right through the wire.

'For fuck's sake Mel. Aeroflot was the only ticket I could get!'

I rant now. My lips are curled and I'm baring teeth at the ungrateful bitch in the locked enclosure!

'And as for the fucking suntan oil! Would you listen to yourself for fuck's sake? It doesn't matter if you go back looking like a ghost so long as you are out of this shithole and back with your parents!'

Yet, even after I have stated the obvious, there is still a distinct lack of reasoning between the bimbo's ears. She just can't help herself. Her self-centred vanity is all too much and she even goes on to collaborate this by saying,

'God Rhys keep your hair on would you. I'm only saying that it would have been nice, that's all. Just to show off a little brown flesh down the pub. You just don't get me sometimes, do you?'

At this point I feel the necessity to jolt some sense into the stupid bitch. Who's to say that the ten thousand dollars will have simply been pissed down a Sri Lankan drain and that the whole idea of escape is a fictitious farce? I move closer to the wire so that we are only lips apart and I whisper to her for fear of being overheard.

'Have you forgotten that you can only escape from here during the Warder's strike? And if that never happens who knows when you'll get out: If ever. Now you fucking listen to me. Keep your mouth shut and don't make any waves: Got it? The ticket is here and when I leave her I'm meeting the Police Commissioner to finalise the money. They said you'll be taken to the airport tomorrow during the chaos. Then, and only then, when the wheels of that plane lift off the Sri Lankan tarmac, are you free.'

I spell it out for her, in cold syllables.

'You are not free *yet*!
You are *still* in prison.
Look around you.
You are locked up in a foreign country…comprende?
Behind this wire.
In a fucking chicken coop, for Christ's sake.'
She winces.

'Furthermore I am not allowed to go to the airport with you tomorrow so I won't even know if you've made it out of this place until you are home in Wales. Do you understand Mel? You are on your own as soon as I leave this prison. Don't say anything stupid and there shouldn't be any problems. Fucking suntan oil. Jesus!'
Finally the truth of her situation hits home, dissolving Mel into shock and tears.
'There won't be any problems Rhys, will there? Tell me there won't Rhys. Please tell me there won't! I need you Rhys. I really need you!'

I reassure her that there won't be any problems if she keeps her cockiness in check, and does as they say. Our time is up so the guard instructs me that I am to leave. I kiss her briefly through the mesh and on leaving I turn back to look at her, but true to her nature she has already turned away and is heading back into the prison without so much as a goodbye glance. I can't help but think about how engrossed she is in her own self-preservation, and of how little respect she has for me; especially after all I have done for her. Her narcissism eats away at me like a maggot. And so I question if I am truly in love with this person or is it only a sense of responsibility that has me continuing to placate our relationship? Is it all borne from a deep-seated sense of duty? Seeded from the time my father left us when I was aged eight? When, at such an impressionable age, I wished my family would hold together no matter what? But it didn't, it broke apart like an upended jigsaw. Broke into dysfunctional pieces. Perhaps then, my current sense of responsibility towards Mel is borne from that? From a sense of duty. And so, despite my nagging doubts about my love for Melanie, I therefore feel compelled to do what needs to be done to have her freed and on a plane back home: It's simply who I am.

I check the address that is scribbled on the back of a business card. An address where I am to hand over the bank transfer details, for ten thousand American dollars, to Mr Fucking Big.

My taxi is still waiting. I guess he knew that he'd pick up my fare if he waited long enough. It is a long ride, full of anguish and calculated thoughts. My mind is racing, jumping, flipping from one scenario to another. The beach restaurant. The swamp. The police station. The prison. And now the meeting with Mister Fucking Big.
The taxi pulls up.
As it turns out the address isn't that of the Military Police Headquarters as expected, but that of a two-story residence in one of

Colombo's more affluent suburbs. I pay the taxi driver a few scrunched up notes and wait outside a large metal security gate. A voice comes over the intercom panel. It's MFB.

The heavy metal gate slides automatically to one side and a jovial Mr Big walks out to greet me. He has miraculously transformed from prison ogre to favourite uncle. It is amazing what ten thousand dollars worth of plastic surgery can do to heighten some Hollywood star's self-esteem, or what the equivalent ten thousand American dollars can do to alter the facial expression of a corrupt Sri Lankan officer.

The smiling Mr Big escorts me into his house, then into his grand study, where the water is bottle filtered, the air purified by quiet machines and the room cooled by modern evaporative technology. Mr Big even offers me a drink, a soda, from a nearby fridge, and I accept gladly as I had neglected to buy any water when leaving the Ex-Serviceman's Hotel.

'I have the bank transfer details here Sir,' I say, and take out the piece of paper from my pocket, handing it over to Mr Big.

'Yes. Yes. You have done very well Mr Rhys Evans. I will check all the necessary details to ensure everything is in order. The Commissioner has this minute telephoned me to confirm that he has received the airline ticket, and that Miss Young's flight is departing tomorrow. This is good. This is very good news indeed.'

Then Mr Big finishes off his greed with pleasantries.

'Well it has been a pleasure knowing you Mr Rhys Evans and if you ever visit Sri Lanka again, as you will no doubt be leaving soon, please take more care with the people you meet.'

There is no menace in his voice, but there is certainly the underlying directive that it is best if I were to leave the island sooner than later. And I couldn't agree more.

## JIGSAW PIECES -
### THE PLAN

After my meeting with Mr Big I am in need of a bit of R and R and so I head off to find George to give him an update.

I find George, again in a fresh blue and yellow striped shirt, sitting at his desk in his small office, rummaging through some paperwork. He's pleased to see me and I hand him over one of the beers I grabbed from the fridge outside. We sit together, curb-side, and I relay all that is new.

'It is all sounding as if it is going very much to plan my friend.'

And I say to George. I say that none of this would have been possible without his help and that he has really saved my bacon.

'Bacon? What is being this bacon?'

I laugh and realise that for the first time in ages I am not uptight and drenched with concern.

'No, there's no bacon George, it's what foreigners sometimes say when they have been helped by a true friend. And that is you George, a true, and honest-to-goodness friend. I really cannot thank you enough for all the help you have given us. Without you George, I never could have got Melanie out of this mess.'

'It is nothing my friend. Truly. It is nothing.' And he upends his beer allowing the last of it to drain away. 'It is to be my shouting as you say in Old Blighty,' and George moves to get up.

'Whoa George! You'll be getting no beers tonight my friend. Tonight all of the beers are on me. It's the least I can do for the hero who has saved the day.'

Time passes. George and I are full of beer and cart vendor small-eats. Today's exhausting mission is finally behind me and I have relaxed, enjoying the company of my friend. Then, from left field, the reality of Melanie still being in jail resurfaces. The fact that this whole state of affairs still sits in someone else's lap has come back to haunt me. It has worked its way through the numbing alcohol, leaving in its sobering wake a dread that this could still go so very wrong: That Melanie could remain locked away on this island for another thirty years and my heart bleeds for Melanie's parents.

*But I've done all I can. There is simply no more I can do.*

And I have done all I can. There is no more I can do, but wait out this intolerable stage? And I must believe that everything will be ok, and that Mel will get home. I must believe that everything will be ok, else tonight I'll go positively mad. Yet, as I sit with a pleasant and merry George, as I watch him sup his warming beer, I think of Mel and what she must be going through back at the prison, and I think of what will happen if MFB's plan goes horribly wrong?

### The Plan – As told to me by Mr Big

**At sun-up tomorrow, during the warder's strike, Miss Young will be taken from her cell and escorted through the prison corridors by Military Police. There will be an awaiting vehicle in the prison grounds, in which is a hidden compartment. Miss Young will be concealed, then driven out of the prison grounds during the confusion to the airport. There she will be handed over to armed security who will escort her through the back channels of Immigration control and into the departure lounge. From here she will catch her plane.**

I visualise this scenario. The mayhem at Slave Island, the hasty exit along the prison corridors. The running. Mel being crammed into a hidden compartment. Stuck in some small hole, perhaps gasping for air. Then at the airport, having to do her best to tidy herself up. To make herself look presentable, before being smuggled through the arse-end of the airport, and into the departure lounge.

Travellers and tourists alike will look at the strange entourage accompanying this woman. They will wonder why she is amongst them. Why she is surrounded by men, with partially concealed weapons, and an air of immunity about them. They may think Mel a VIP, or an undercover agent, or perhaps a war correspondent in need of protection from those who wish to silence the truth. But the reality, and so the truth of it, will be that she will look to others as she presents: A haggard and apprehensive individual. One who is wary of the company she keeps, and when studied further, will be viewed as an enigma whose story they cannot fathom.

*But…*
*What if the Warder's Strike doesn't take place?*
*What if greed stands in the way of honour?*
*What if the ten thousand dollars was simply a con?*
*What if Mel never even makes it out of her cell?*

*What if…?*
*What if…?*
*What if…?*

## JIGSAW PIECES -
### THE WAITING

I start more than awake gently and am up and out of bed and looking out of the window into the vast Sri Lankan skies because today Mel is supposed to travel the eleven hour, eight and a half thousand kilometre journey to London, via Moscow. I check my watch, it is just past seven, and I look to the skies again. By my reckoning if Mel is sitting on the seven a.m. flight out of Colombo then I can make a phone call home to Wales in seventeen hours to find out if she is safe. This, however, rests on the proviso that she escapes the prison, is safely escorted through Immigration at Katunayake airport, makes a successful connection in Moscow and doesn't hit bad traffic on the M4.

Seventeen long hours – by my reckoning.

It is now seven thirty. I look to the skies again but can see nothing. Mel should be out there somewhere if all has gone to plan. She will know that she's safe, but for me, I have to wait until midnight.

I literally cannot bear this, to watch the hours, or even listen to the hollow seconds tick by, one empty click after another. Instead I have decided to visit the dark side of Colombo, to a place of winding alleyways and of whispery talk: To a world behind secret doorways, to where opium dens lie nestled amongst dense shadows.

But they don't exist, these opium dens, these figments of a vigorous imagination, because opium dens are illegal in Sri Lanka. Even if you did happen to stumble across a secluded doorway, down a wrong alley, on your way back to your hotel, it would never occur to you that beyond that peeling door is a world of make-believe, a world of soft cushioned sofas, and of opium filled pipes.
But I know.
I know because when you have frequented this capital city as many times as I have, you obtain knowledge by way of osmosis. You come to know where the whores loiter, though you want no action. You

come to know where the dealers meet, though you'd be foolish to score. You know where the black marketeers haggle, if you want a more profitable currency exchange, and you also know where the opium dens lie, because one of the old boys at the Ex-Serviceman's Hotel has told you.

My *boy* sets my cushions on a long chaise-lounge and packs the flanged bowl of a long opium pipe, fashioned from the bone of a cow. He strikes a match and lights the black putty-like substance. I lay back, pulling gently on the pipe as the burning opiate cackles like the spells of a witch. I share in the mysteries and mystical attributes that is opium, and in all its wondrous qualities fools find addictive. I am in sublime solitude where the only person that exists in this moment is *Me*.

*I am light. Now I fly. Now I see beneath myself. Now a god dances through me.*

I ride out the day in a state of euphoria, then sleep it all off until enough hours have passed. It is time now for me to leave this fantastical den of iniquity, to find George and his red Bat-phone, and make that impending phone call home to Wales.

---

As the taxi pulls into Bristol Street I sense a distinct air of quietness, and really this should come as no surprise as it is well past midnight. This part of Colombo has shut down for the night.
And George's Travel Agency is also shut.
The windows pasted with faraway posters are fastened.
And the door to George's office is locked.

*Did I mention that?*

That it is shut?
Bolted.
Barred.
And on reflection I think,

*What was I expecting - A fucking welcoming committee?*
*Jesus Christ, how the hell am I going to make the phone call now?*

The taxi has long gone and so I find myself standing in front of George's office contemplating breaking in.

*I mean, I could justify it, right? After all it's a matter of life and death? I mean to say this is my life we're talking about here. My future: With Mel. Surely that is reason enough to smash down the door to George's Travel and Information Office and use his phone. The door can't cost much surely? Look at it? It barely presents a barrier.*

I figure that a couple of good kicks would get me in, and then I could be on the phone to Mel. But as you would agree it is not in the nature of a friend to smash down the door of another. After all, it was George who had come to the rescue in what was a hopeless situation. I just can't do it.

I resign myself to sitting in the doorway to George's office for the moment, near the fridge, which I wish was unlocked so that I could at least drink myself to sleep. I am so wired up from anticipation that I stare longingly at the beer bottles behind the wire-meshed Perspex door, wishing that I could at least muster the resolve to break in. But no, the fridge is also George's, and so I can't. And honestly, even if it belonged to someone else I still couldn't do it. After all, these people live on such a tight shoestring budget you couldn't even tie a bow with it.

Then from above my head I hear a rattle, a slip of metal. It is the sound of a bolt being drawn back and a lock being unfastened. The door, on which I am leaning against, gives way, and I tumble backwards practically onto George's feet.

'Bloody hell George! What are you doing here?

'Waiting for you my friend. I have been sleeping inside knowing you would be needing to be coming back and to be using the phone to call Miss Mel.'

I am elated. So ecstatically happy that I jump up and give George a huge embrace.

He hugs me back.

Good old George…What a Legend!

## JIGSAW PIECES -
### THE PHONE CALL HOME

'Quickly, be coming in now Rhys and speaking to Miss Mel, she will be waiting for you to be calling.'

We both go into the office. I sit behind George's desk and pick up the phone. It feels heavy and cumbersome in my hand, a far cry from the light-heartedness I feel within. I place my index finger into the zero recess in the white plastic rotary dial and spin it one full revolution to begin the international dialling code. The phone whirs and the dial returns to its starting point. I dial the second zero.

I look up at George and note a look of concern. It lies there because he knows there is still the possibility that Mel may not have made it. That she is still within the confines of Welikada Prison. This moment of excitement has run away with me. It is true. Mel could still be at Slave Island. Set to boil bags of dirty washing and massage the heads and legs of the female warders for the next thirty years. George reads my anxious look and so places a friendly hand on my shoulder. And as I acknowledge George's kindness the Bat-phone sends an electrical pulse to run along two copper wires and out through an International Gateway Exchange. I hear the phone on the Welsh side finally ring and as I listen to the hollow sound of the echo I am cast back to the last conversation with Paul, about getting Mel out of Sri Lanka.

About Mel's freedom.
About her escape.
About the rest of Mel's life.

I hear the empty click of a lifeless connection before I hear the voice. It is an unexpected voice. Not Mel's, but that of her eight year old brother, Carwyn.
'Hi Carwyn. It's Rhys. Is your sister there?'
And it's just as well that I'm sitting down, as his reply is shattering, because he says this,
'No she's not here. I don't know where she is? It's just Nanny and me.'

229

I recoil.

Bang!
Bang!
Back to prison.
Back to the grime, the dirt and the squalor.

*Christ...Mel never made it then!*

I need to hear Carwyn reiterate this and so I ask again: To find out for sure. To make absolutely certain.
'Have you seen her though Carwyn? Recently? Has she come back from her holiday?'
There is a pause before he answers. A short pause. An empty moment that feels cold and hollow.
I wait.
'Yes I've seen her,' he says. 'She gave me a jumbo-jet plane as a present. It's so cool because it makes the real sounds of the engine when I whizz it along the floor.'
'But she's not at home now? Your sister is not in the house with you at the moment?'
I am finding the conversation confusing.
'No, it's just nanny and me. Mum and dad have gone out and so has my sister. Nanny is looking after me.'
I think,

*Why not? Why wouldn't she be out celebrating?*

But then she knew I was going to call. Mel would have known that I have been waiting an arduous seventeen hours. Waiting to know. Needing to find out if she'd made it home. Of course she couldn't have known that a friend had waited up late for me: That I was able to make a late night phone call from his office, and not have to wait until morning, but even so, she did know that I *was* going to phone as soon as I could. Mel could have at least waited in, just in case there was the remote possibility. Surely she could have gone out afterwards and celebrated then?

As I try to make sense of this moment it feels as if there's a piece of the jigsaw puzzle I simply cannot place.

## THE JIGSAW –
### THE FINAL PIECE

Carwyn, Mel's kid brother, is a great little lad. He plays rugby for his school and had just started surfing before I left home. The world he lives in is that of the innocent eight year old, but the next batch of poisonous sentences he speaks carry no known antidote. For between his spoken words lies brazen deceit, shameless treachery, and the indecency of someone who has so effortlessly cast away another's feelings: Like broken limbs to black ravens. He has no idea that his next batch of words will peel back my skin to bare the very core of my being. He has no idea that these words will leave me exposed to the filth of his sister's vile world, and no idea that his next few sentences will contribute to my unimagined fate. He knows none of this and how could he; he is only eight. Nevertheless these rancid words do escape from this excited young boy, from a fine lad who has been given a new toy plane by his loving sister,

Carwyn says this.

*'Her friend Rick was here and he went down on his knees. It was really funny. And he gave my sister a big diamond ring and when she saw it she cried like she was a baby and then they said they were going out to celebrate. I don't know why mum and dad got really upset but they have gone out somewhere too, so now it's just nanny and me and we're playing airports and .... .... .......... ...... ............ ............ .......... .......... ............,'*

The remainder of Carwyn's words have faded into a world of inaudible white noise. He is no doubt still talking about his imaginary aviation game but all I can hear are deadened sounds, as if my life has liquefied and that I am drowning within my own existence.
My world feels dead.
Is dead.
All of my future dreams crushed by the enormity of what just happened. My dreams have been spewed out onto the floor like a junkie's waste: Like the bile of the dragon. An emptying of all that is lost. Time stands still. It is frozen by this moment. I feel as if I have

lost everything. Lost Melanie. Lost my sense of direction. Lost faith. And once again I question the idleness of my God.
*He gave her a big diamond ring......celebrate........celebrate.........celebrate...*
My thoughts jump from one ugly scene to another. They explode inside my head.

Thumping!

Relentlessly.

They strip away at my worth.
They devour my world.
And now I see the two of them again:

NAKED.

FUCKING each other.

And I hear myself whispering behind all of this madness,

*You've been such a fool Rhys.*

But for a while I really thought I was winning. I really thought it would work out between us. Like when I first read Melanie's letter, *Pinkie*. Then when I read it again, for the third, fourth, and tenth time. When I read that it spoke of her desperation and how her superficial love for another was blind and misplaced. How she was full of regret. How the sorrow of losing me became such a desperate, desperate thing for her. And I thought I was winning when the fear of having lost Melanie drained away like dirty bathwater. When I was left cleansed with her presence. Her laughter. Her affection. But not her true love: Not that. Because somewhere during the re-kindling of our relationship I must have misconstrued so many of *our* moments. When, during our lovemaking, she would caress my body with delicate hands. When, after our lovemaking she would whisper the words, 'I love you so much Rhys.' When we joked how our daughters would look if they ended up with my nose? How our sons would be good looking, and grow up strong. When we talked about growing old together. When we laughed about visiting our children's homes for Sunday roast. And when all that mattered in the world was *Us*.

Yes. I must have misunderstood completely what I thought was her love for me. I must have completely missed the fact that I was simply a puppet within her world. A jester playing a cameo role in a light-hearted performance: A clown for her amusement. A fool then, to be disposed of in the Second Act, with just one flick from the tail of a cold and callous Dragon-Bitch.

---

George is still here. He has witnessed it all. Has heard it. Seen it. Shared in my heartache, and still has his hand on my shoulder. I turn and look up at George. And if I were him, in his thongs and in his blue and yellow striped shirt; if I were him, looking down at me with his kind eyes and gentle ways, I would see a broken man. A man disillusioned by his love for another. A man run through. A man whose beliefs have been flailed raw. Whose loyalty and devotion have caused him to bleed out: Black and empty.
And George, I know, he sees all this in my eyes and he speaks to me now…as gently as a prayer.
'We must not be holding onto sadness my young friend, because we cannot be undoing what is already done. Regrets, they are to be belonging in the past. But your life, it is only to be belonging in the future. True love, it is always winning. And one day you will find your true love. This is being your destiny. I know this because you are a good man Rhys Evans. I know this because I have lived through sorrow also. Your destiny will be true to you. Your karma is strong, I feel it. This moment in your life is your rebirth Rhys Evans: A new beginning, not a time to be buried in your sorrowfulness, but a time to be celebrating the gift of a new life.'

George's words wash down upon me. I taste the spiritual goodness in them. Their nourishment rekindles a dying spark and I feel that an enormous weight has lifted from around my neck, that a chain has been broken from around my heart.

I feel suddenly unburdened.
I feel free from the responsibility of another.
Free from Melanie.
Free from her infectious influence.
Free to finally move on…

On the wall behind George I see a poster for Thai Airways, and on the poster are the words:

'Let us fly you to the *destination* of your dreams'

… but in my mind I read it as saying *Destiny*.

I look to my good friend, George. I look to George with a smile and a request.
'George,' I say,
'I wish to buy a one-way ticket to Phuket.'
'Phuket?' says George. Then he beams one of his insightful smiles, because my friend understands.
'You are needing to be finding a lady doctor who is being perfect for you. That is being most correct, isn't it my friend?
'Yes George. That is being most perfectly correct.'
With that I smile again, for now I feel that my world has no endings, only moments leading to new beginnings.

And this is one…

If you enjoyed the book there are a selection of original pictures, plus some information linked to the events that took place in Sri Lanka during the book's timeline.
Simply go to
https://www.facebook.com/stingofthedragonstale

TO THOSE THAT HELPED IN GETTING THIS BOOK TO PRINT
MANY THANKS!

*Sharky* Mark Simpson
Chris *Chris* Morgan
*The lovely* Breda McCarren
Tracy *Smiling* Shaw
Ken *Agent K* Fraser
Andy *Kool-Kat* Marsh
Jj Stewart
Gus *Hot Cross Bun* Taylor
Suzanne *Jogger* Stewart
Ross *Cadillac* Morgan
Angharad *Parrot Whisperer* Thomas
Simone *You're Welcome* Banatee
Lee *I Was Actually There* Ewing
Steve *'Fire-Fighter'* Watson (R.I.P)

## ABOUT THE AUTHOR

Mark Probert grew up in the infamous Welsh surfing village of Mumbles on the Gower peninsula. Mark began surfing at the age of twelve and could then only dream of surfing waves like those splashed up on the makeshift screen during surf club movie nights. Then, during the eighties, having finished his studies, Mark decided to travel to Asia to discover these waves for himself. He spent much of this time in Sri Lanka and on the mystical islands of Indonesia. Mark now works as a teacher and lives with his family in the wine producing Swan Valley in Western Australia. Mark still surfs whenever he can.

Made in the USA
Middletown, DE
01 May 2017